CONVICTION OF A WITCH

THE SAVANNAH COVEN SERIES

SUZA KATES

ICASM PRESS
SAVANNAH

Published by Icasm Publishing LLC
5710 Ogechee Rd. Suite 200 #278, Savannah, GA 31405
www.icasmpress.com

Library of Congress Cataloging-in-Publication Data

Kates, Suza
Conviction of a Witch / Suza Kates
    p. cm.

ISBN-13:978-0-9845929-9-9
ISBN-13:978-0-9845929-8-2 (ebook)
I. Title

Printed and bound in the United States of America

10 9 8 7 6 5 4 3 2 1

To my sister, Donna,
for walking the walk

Anna St. Germaine
Hair: Long, straight, sable brown
Eyes: Sapphire blue
Color: Sapphire blue
Cat: "Ivy" gray female with lime green eyes

Anna sees visions of past, present, and future. She is the coven's head witch and is a descendent of the three women who originally banished the demon Bastraal three centuries ago. Her ancestral home is on an island off the coast of Savannah, Georgia and now serves as coven central.

Claudia Grant
Hair: Straight, long, flaming red
Eyes: River green
Color: Coral
Cat: "Rowan Von Ashbi" coloring of an American Wirehair with yellow eyes

Claudia is a history professor who only needs to touch an object to sense its past and previous surroundings.

Hayden Wells
Hair: Brownish red "caramel"
Eyes: Golden brown
Color: Pale pink
Cat: "Daisy" black tortoiseshell with yellow eyes

Hayden is a medium from San Francisco who sees and talks to spirits/ghosts.

Kylie Worthington

Hair: Long, wavy golden-blonde
Eyes: Hazel
Color: Yellow
Cat: Sassafras "Sassy" also a long-haired blonde but with bright yellow eyes

Kylie is a college student who's "on a break" to do her part for the coven and is able to control electricity in any form.

Lucia Ruiz

Hair: Long, wavy deep brown
Eyes: Brown
Color: Red
Cat: "Iris" black Persian with blue eyes

Lucia was born to privileged wealth in Spain and has the ability to find anything that is lost. She is an adventurer, world-traveler, and renowned relic-hunter.

Paige Reilley

Hair: Shoulder-length, white-blonde with ragged bangs
Eyes: Turquoise blue
Color: Turquoise
Cat: Tiger Lily "Tiger" brown and gray with white chest and belly, bright green eyes

Recently discharged from the military, Paige is a soldier in every way with the added abilities of super-strength and speed.

Shauni Miller
Hair: Long, straight, black
Eyes: Emerald green
Color: Green
Cat: "Cuileann" black short-hair with green eyes

Shauni is a nature-loving biologist from Colorado and communicates with animals telepathically.

Viv Sakurai
Hair: Shoulder-length, black, angled bangs
Eyes: Gray
Color: Purple
Cat: Kikoku "Kiko" orange tabby with yellow-green eyes and a grumpy disposition.

Relocated from Chicago, Viv is a physicist searching for an explanation for her own special power of telekinesis.

Willyn Brousseau
Hair: Wavy, shoulder-length, light blonde
Eyes: Pale blue
Color: White/cream
Cat: "Snowball" pure white with golden eyes

Willyn is a nurse, a mother, and a Christian. Raised in Alabama, she uses her healing powers to help those in need. She came to Savannah with an additional package, her young son, Tadd.

1

"Kill the witch! Kill the witch!" Contorted, angry faces pressed in from all sides, chanting the words over and over as the mob circled closer. A few in the crowd stepped forward to threaten or even slap her, taking advantage of her vulnerability. There was no way for her to protect herself with her hands tied to the wooden pole at her back.

Three older women stood on the perimeter with their hands clasped together and lips twisting as they prayed with the fervor of zealots. The others in the crowd pulsed and writhed in a furious rhythm with male and female alike participating in the torment. They jabbed fingers in her sides or screamed in her face, spittle flying from their demented and blood-thirsty mouths.

This was the same band of pioneers she'd traveled, laughed, and worked alongside for weeks. Even the man whose child she had nursed back to health was ranting and waving his arms. He came closer with a pair of scissors in his hand. He cursed in her ear and yanked her long blonde braid tight, sending bolts of pain through her head. The man whose child she had saved then roughly cut her hair off at the base of her scalp before waving it in the air like a prize.

She had no more friends here. There were none who would stand beside her, none who would risk being associated with her. And all it had taken was one word.

Witch.

"Please. You don't understand." She fought the tears struggling to break free. Pleading was bad enough, and she feared a further show of weakness would only encourage them. The mob had death in their eyes. Her death. Her punishment. She wanted to beg for her life and defend herself, but what could she tell them? The indian attack hadn't been her fault nor had the spoiled food, but she knew none of that really mattered. The peaceful and friendly people she had known before were now in a frenzy, because they believed her to be a witch.

The real problem was... they were right.

She would never do them harm, though. It wasn't her nature. She was a kind person, a faithful woman, but her previous good deeds had all been forgotten. Because of him.

The noise died down as the preacher spoke in a whisper. He didn't need to shout over the throng, since they heeded and praised his every word. Though the man had only recently joined the party traveling west, he represented authority, leadership, and salvation. He counseled and consoled those who were swiftly becoming his flock, and he brought the word of God to a weary and fearful group. But he was a lie.

There was no moon above to shed light on the horror the mob intended, and the expansive sky above was black, devoid of even a single star. She felt utterly betrayed by their absence. The only illumination came from torches in the hands of mad men, and the wafting smoke made her think of brimstone, though the only hell she would experience was the one that had found her here on earth.

The preacher crept through the crowd as it parted for him, each man or woman moving aside as if repelled by an unseen force. "We shall hear what the witch has to say," he said, thumping an old Bible against his palm. "Every soul that has forsaken the Lord shall be shown the way back." The preacher raised his voice now, not because he had to, but because he reveled in the power. "First, we must cleanse each and every sin from that soul before it is returned unto the Lord."

His watery, gray eyes stared into hers as he stepped closer, flames flickering on his face and morphing into shadows. He seemed to be changing right in front of her as evil roiled under his skin, his mask. That evil wanted out.

The true nature of the man before her became clear. His hands turned into claws that raked the side of her neck and down across her breast, leaving trails of blood as he tore her flesh. His lips peeled back to reveal sharp, brown teeth. "What say you, witch?" the preacher asked in a graveled voice just before he thrust at her with a snap of his ferocious jaws.

Lightning cracked and Willyn woke with a start. Her heart was pounding and her hands were clenched on the white satin bed sheets. She wasn't sure if fear had chased her from the dream or if the booming thunder outside had shaken her awake. Either way she was grateful. The tingling sensation along her neck and chest reminded her of the pain she'd felt in the nightmare. It had been so real, and her gut still churned as she thought of the horrible preacher and his teeth.

A gentle purring came from Willyn's left, bringing her attention to Snowball, her white cat who'd been sleeping beside her. The feline's gold eyes blinked slowly while she nuzzled Willyn's arm, offering what comfort she could. The nightmare, Willyn thought. Snowball must have sensed the intrusion of something dark. She rubbed the cat under her chin, grateful for the friendly presence.

Along with unique talents and the sudden urge to travel south, all of the women in the coven had another thing in common. They all had cats, as any good witch should, and for reasons no one could explain, they'd all named their cats after flowers or plants. When Snowball had arrived on her front porch one morning years before, Willyn had taken one look at the fluffy kitten and had immediately thought of the delicate white flowers that symbolized hope and purity. Her new "sisters" had teased her about Snowball's name, saying it was typical Willyn. Each woman's feline was a reflection of the witch that had claimed it, so she guessed she could see their point.

After a stroke along the soft, white hair and an appreciative smile for her pet, Willyn rolled over to grab her cell phone, swiping her thumb across the screen to check the time. It was only six-thirty in the evening, but a summer storm had covered up the sun and engulfed the island where she lived with her coven. Her room was dark and cool, thanks to the pounding rain and impenetrable clouds, but despite the chill, her T-shirt was damp with sweat. More evidence of the disturbing dream.

Willyn ran a hand through her blonde hair, untangling the waves that caressed her shoulders. She wanted to take a shower and change, but first things first. She needed to check on her boy.

With a soft sweep over the hardwood floors, she opened the door between her bedroom and the one adjoining it. The pale buttercream walls and creamy pastels she preferred transitioned to deep blues and reds, a palette more to Tadd's liking.

A small, Crimson Tide lamp, with an elephant trumpeting as the base, cast its light on the far corner and her son's bedside table. She could only see his tousled blonde hair, since he liked to sleep with his face covered, as he had for the last two years. Ever since his father had died.

Willyn swallowed the regret and focused on her child instead. As she watched the gentle rise and fall of Tadd's chest under the sheet, love swamped her and tightened her heart, just as it did at least ten times a day when she looked at the little miracle she'd helped create. She listened to the rain and watched her son sleep for another minute, appreciating the precious moment.

Assured of his well-being, Willyn backed out quietly and was heading for the shower when someone knocked on her door. "Willyn?" a voice said in a low tone before another soft knock.

The voice belonged to Hayden, who was obviously hoping to wake her as unobtrusively as possible. The sweet woman with caramel-colored hair was one of the more mellow witches in the coven, a pretty good trick considering she dealt with restless and needy ghosts on a regular basis.

Willyn sighed, deciding she could at least be thankful it wasn't Paige who'd come to rouse her. That warrior-woman probably would have pounded the door down and woken Tadd in the process. Mellow she was not.

Another tap came from the other side of the door. "Come in," Willyn called, despite being in her T-shirt and underwear. She was amazed how comfortable she was with women she'd known only a few months, but in a way, they'd all had a connection for a much longer time. Three centuries, in fact, and their mystical ties were part of the reason the eight women had forsaken their normal lives without question.

They had all relocated and now lived on an isolated island off the coast of Georgia. The ninth woman, Anna, owned the home and served as their hostess as well as witch educator extraordinaire. They all needed the help, too, since none of them had even known they were witches before they'd arrived. Unfortunately, that was one thing Anna hadn't *seen* coming.

The door cracked open then swung wide. "Good. You're awake," Hayden said with a smile. "Did you sleep well?"

Willyn decided to keep the dream to herself and put aside the disturbing images. She would swear she could still smell blood and smoking torches. "Nothing like a rainy day for sleeping. I just thought I'd lie down with a good book while Tadd napped, but somewhere along the way I joined him."

"I wanted to let you know we're having a meeting." Hayden

grinned and added in a stiff-English-butler tone. "Your presence is requested in the grand hall, Madam."

Playing along, Willyn curtsied. "I'll be right along. I just need to finish my toilette."

"By all means." Hayden jerked her head. "I'm on my way up to the third floor to pull the princess away from her iPod." She shook her head and rolled her eyes.

Willyn laughed along with her as the door closed. The princess in question was Kylie, the youngest of the coven and the most unlikely hero. At least at first glance.

Though the vivacious blonde was full of *laissez les bon temps roulez* and was a fiend for expensive clothes, she had turned out to be surprisingly thoughtful and reliable. Kylie was still young and impetuous but fierce when she needed to be and loyal like no other. Yeah, Willyn thought as she rubbed her neck, the kid had turned out to be a keeper.

With one last glance toward Tadd's room, Willyn dispensed of her clothes as she walked then cranked up the shower, letting the water get good and hot. Summer in Savannah never lacked for heat, but she felt the need for a nice, long soak. She was still chilled and a little bit shaky. Stepping under the stream, she squeezed out some tropical island body wash in an effort to take her mind to a more soothing place. She closed her eyes, trying to picture breezy palm trees and sweet, blue water.

It didn't work.

With a sigh Willyn let her head drop forward to the tile, so the shower could massage her tense shoulders. She didn't know what had happened in her sleep, but the shivers just wouldn't go away. Despite the creature comforts and presence of friends, her mind was still stuck in another time, another place.

She was trapped in the memory of her murder.

~

Downstairs the television blared, as was often the case with so many people residing in the home, or mansion-slash-castle, as Willyn liked to think of it. She stopped just outside of the grand hall, the epicenter of the home and unofficial coven hangout. Mahogany wainscoting covered the walls, broken up by various works of art, including a mammoth painting that slid to one side whenever someone wanted to watch the huge flat screen TV behind it.

The room always felt welcoming and warm, despite the slate flooring and ceiling that rose to the upper level. Classic yet comfortable seating areas filled several corners, providing plenty of places to lounge, read, or visit. Someone had lit candles on various tables, turning the air sweet with the scent of lemongrass.

"So what's up?" Paige asked in her straightforward way. The long-legged ex-soldier tossed popcorn in her mouth after directing the question to the redhead beside her on the green velvet couch.

"How should I know?" Claudia asked. "I've been here with you the whole time." She grabbed some popcorn for herself and glared at Paige. "Two hours of my life that I'll never get back, by the way."

"What? You didn't like the movie?" Paige blew ragged bangs off her forehead, a habit of hers. The white-blonde hair and turquoise eyes were a striking combination, but her beauty was deceiving. Paige was a lethal weapon all on her own, and she definitely knew how to use it. "I thought you were into history." She pointed a shaking finger at the plasma screen on the wall. "That was history."

"That was bloody," Claudia shot back. "And one Mayan temple does not constitute educational merit, especially when zombie pygmies come out of it at night to eat your intestines."

Paige continued chomping and lifted one shoulder. "I liked it."

"Watcha' watching?" This from Kylie as she bounded down the wooden staircase, iPod still in hand. Spying the screen she said, "Ooh. The Feeding. I loved that movie."

"See?" Paige said as if justified. "Not everyone likes dried-up documentaries twenty-four-seven, Teach."

Claudia huffed and raised a hand to Willyn, who was standing in the foyer, watching the antics. "Thank goodness. Willyn, save me from horror movies and blondes." She threw up her other hand. "Oops. Forgot you were blonde for a second, but that's probably because you don't act like it."

"Hey. Watch it, Carrot," Kylie said before squeezing between Paige and Claudia on the couch. She hugged the red-headed history professor, who she loved to tease. The banter was fine with Claudia, who also gave as good as she got.

"Is that the most imaginative name you can think of?" Claudia asked.

With a devilish smile, Kylie said, "Well, I was going to call you the ever-popular fire-crotc…"

"Thanks." Claudia held up a hand. "Carrot will do for now, and be grateful I'm not as temperamental as you are blonde."

A new voice entered the conversation in a clipped, moderate tone. "There is no scientific correlation between hair color and personality traits. At least not in hard science." Viv Sakurai glided into the room, a glass of white wine held carelessly in one hand. She dropped into a fancy chair and crossed her legs. She wasn't wearing her serious, black glasses at the moment, which meant she'd probably been working for hours on some quantum-physics theory and had worn her beautiful Asian eyes out. "So how do we account for you?" she asked, with a nod to Kylie.

"I'm going to choose to not be insulted by that, Doc," Kylie said. She eyed the popcorn in Paige's hands then stole it after a brief tug of war.

Claudia pushed up from the couch. "Where are the others,

and does anyone know what's going on?" The rest all shook their heads.

Moving farther into the room, Willyn remained standing, her arms wrapped around herself for warmth. She had a bad feeling. First the nightmare, now an impromptu gathering, and to top it all off, her belly was still churning. Maybe her gut was trying to warn her of something. No one had told her to wear her dress, though, so maybe it was a simple household meeting. The coven had several matching gowns made for rituals and ceremonial occasions, each woman with her own signature color. Willyn's was white.

She looked down at the amulet on her chest. The large stone in the middle was clear, like a diamond and was surrounded by an intricate, Celtic weave in silver. Eight stones of various hues decorated the edges, symbolic of the women in her coven and their union. Willyn had always been an only child, but this past spring she'd been blessed with eight sisters of the heart. Or of the craft, as it were.

After rubbing the necklace lovingly, her hand shifted higher to clasp the silver cross hanging from a separate chain. She was still a Christian, despite having learned she was also a natural-born witch, but no one in her new family begrudged her the additional jewelry. She was who she was, and they accepted that.

Willyn had, however, changed out her previous gold cross for silver, so it would match her amulet. She was still female after all, and such things mattered.

She looked up as three more of the pack arrived, laughing over something and clutching their stomachs. Hayden was in between Shauni and Lucia. She'd evidently rounded up the last of the witches. With her reddish-brown hair contrasting against the ebony locks of the other two, they looked like a caramel-centered-Oreo.

"Ah there's the mother of that bad girl," Lucia said in her

Spanish accent. She pointed at Paige. "Your Tiger Lily was really getting it to those boy cats."

"*Giving* it to them," Hayden corrected. "I hate to ask, Paige, but has Tiger Lily been spayed?"

Paige jumped to her feet. "What? Oh-no-they-don't!" She started off in a run, but Shauni intercepted her.

"Don't worry," Shauni said. "I don't think she's interested. She was giving it to them as in she was whipping their butts for sniffing too close."

"Oh." Paige deflated. "That's more like it."

"I would still consider getting her to Michael's office, though." Shauni leaned in closer to whisper. "She was thinking about losing."

Willyn grinned at the look on Paige's face. Shauni would be dead-on about what the cats were thinking, because she had a special gift that allowed her to communicate with animals and actually understand when they communicated back. Her boyfriend, Michael, was a veterinarian and a perfect match for the animal whisperer. Good thing too, since there were nine cats and one puppy running around the mansion-slash-castle.

As if on cue, Willyn heard the elevator open into the foyer before Anna rounded the corner with a wiggly puppy following close behind. "I can't understand why this dog likes to ride in the elevator so much," she said, watching the black and white bundle rush to Shauni, his rescuer and favorite human on earth. He came to an abrupt halt at her feet, sliding the last bit before crashing into her shins.

"Probably because it's close quarters, and he can control his momentum," Shauni said with a rub on her pet's neck. The aptly named Skid panted and smiled from the attention.

"So, Anna," Claudia said, putting her hands on her hips. "We all have a feeling something's up." Her straight red hair hung freely down her back, but as usual, the history professor was dressed in style. Her burnt-orange jumpsuit had a deep v-neck and a gold belt looping her tiny waist. Willyn always wondered what Claudia wore when she taught classes and would love to see the reactions of her male students when hot-for-teacher walked in for the first time.

Anna nodded. "It's time for the next to be chosen," she said, cutting straight to the heart of everyone's concern. The nine women had come together for a reason. Their coven was part of a three hundred-year-old prophecy, one that included an immortal witch who was determined to raise a demon. The witch, Ronja, surrounded herself with a pretty nasty crew, the Amara, who each had talents of their own. The Amara's sole purpose was to take out Anna and her coven, clearing the way for the demon they planned to raise.

Each of the witches had a role to play, a challenge of sorts, though none of them knew what their specific test would entail or in which order they would be called to perform. So it was no surprise when each of the women tensed at Anna's declaration and glanced at each other for support.

Even Shauni looked worried, but it was only out of concern for her sisters. She had been the first of them, thrown into a trial on the first night she'd arrived in Savannah. The other women had pulled together to help her as much as they could, but none of them had truly known what to expect. Even Anna, the seer, hadn't known which path to take, so she'd ultimately patted Shauni on the back and put the entire coven's faith and future in the animal whisperer's hands.

Shauni had come through successfully, with the added bonus of Michael and their newfound love, but the experience had been a gauntlet of emotional and physical beat-downs. It was no wonder the witches were all wondering the same big question. Who was next?

Anna gravitated toward the others as they all stood or walked forward, making a circle amidst the furniture. They moved in unison without realizing it, guided by instinct and forces from beyond.

"Can you feel that?" Kylie asked with a shiver. "I love it when that happens."

"Ding-dong. Magic calling," Paige added with a wry smile.

Willyn felt it, too. The warm tingle that suffused each of them when the nine came together. Tonight there was a stronger undercurrent, hotter, more insistent.

Though wearing faded jeans and a simple blue top, Anna stood with a natural grace and a regal presence. As a descendent of the three original witches who'd both defeated the demon in the past and foretold the prophecy of the coven, she was as comfortable in the cloak of magic as most were in their own skins.

"A nagging suspicion has been following me all day," Anna said. "I had a feeling it was almost time, so I pulled out my Tarot and asked." She met each of them eye to eye, still giving no indication of whether or not she knew who'd been picked. "I was sure after the first card."

"Don't keep us in suspense," Hayden said, her golden-brown eyes wide but steady.

"You know it's not for me to say," Anna responded. "Magic does the choosing. It just gives me a nudge when it's time for us to come together."

"Should we go get dressed?" Lucia asked. "I'm dying to wear that hot, red number." The Spanish vixen's color was red, the color of passion. Completely apropos.

"Something tells me that's not going to be necessary," Viv said. Her gaze remained fixed in one direction until the others all saw what she did.

The looks of distress and worry should have been Willyn's first clue, but she waited for clarification, hoping to delay confirmation of what her gut already knew.

That reprieve wouldn't be coming. Shauni smiled at her with a mixture of understanding and empathy before telling her in a gentle voice, "Willyn. Honey, you're glowing."

2

"Yes, they are both blue, but not the same color blue, so they don't match." Willyn ran through the same lecture on hues and proper attire that she had delivered every Sunday for the last few months. Tadd tended to grab anything from his drawers to dress himself and was satisfied with tops and bottoms that had at least some of the same color. Jungle-print shorts and a lime-green football jersey? It didn't matter, because in his stubborn five-year-old mind, green was green.

Now he had his lips clamped together as he studied his navy blue shorts and teal, clamp-on tie. He pointed to one then the other. "Blue and blue," he said as if his mother were the one who needed educating.

"Here, Tadd. Let's switch that tie for this one." An older, black woman came down the stairs and traded out the problematic accessory. Claire was a Godsend in Willyn's mind and offered the simple solution with the ease and grace she seemed to embody during times of calm and crisis alike. It wasn't the first outstretched hand she'd extended to Willyn.

Wife to Joe, the estate's caretaker, and mother to Joe. Jr., who was also in the family business of running interference for Anna and the coven, Claire had learned to handle just about any issue that arose either here on the island or at the house on the mainland. A willful child was no match for Claire as she smiled and clipped on the navy tie with no trouble at all. Of course, her cooking would rival any chef in the area, or on TV, and Tadd was probably thinking about the cookies she usually made after church.

Tossing his little hands into the air, Tadd blew blonde bangs off his forehead. "Okay, but I still don't get it."

Willyn patted his head. "You will, but until then, just trust us to steer you right." She winked at Claire and mouthed the words, "Thank you."

With a smile and a nod, Claire called for Tadd and took him outside to keep him occupied until Joe showed up to take them to the mainland.

Smoothing her hands over her simple cream dress, Willyn contemplated how quickly things were changing with her son. Small issues were now becoming more complicated, since Tadd expected a good reason for the things Willyn told him to do. Her little boy seemed to be a lawyer in the making and had a valid question for each of her directives. Bed time and grown-up movies were the latest items on his convince-Mom-she's-wrong list.

Willyn slung her purse onto her shoulder and was moving toward the front door when the elevator in the foyer opened to reveal Anna inside. She stepped out with a frown on her face before noticing Willyn. Quickly realigning her features into a mask of serenity, Anna took in Willyn's dress. "Off to church?"

"It is that time again." Willyn tried to make the comment sound light, but her own worries and Anna's troubled expression collided and were too heavy to ignore. "What's the matter? You look upset."

Anna shrugged. "Nothing for you to worry about. We're going to have a visitor. I'm just not sure who it is."

After tossing her way through a sleepless night, Willyn was hyper-alert and couldn't stop imagining possible scenarios. It was her turn to face a challenge, so she was sensitive to anything that affected her or the coven. She had to figure out what she was meant to do, so new developments or new faces were subject to intense scrutiny.

Plus, if Anna was concerned, Willyn was concerned.

"You can't see everything. You've told us that yourself." Willyn cast an eye toward the massive front doors then back to Anna. "What bothers you about this person?"

The doorbell chimed a pleasant tune, and Anna gestured to the ornate, wooden entrance. "Why don't we find out?"

Since the head witch stayed rooted to her place in front of the elevator, Willyn had no choice but to offer herself as welcoming committee. She walked forward with slow but steady steps, swinging the massive oak open before she had time to reconsider, but if it were a monster on the other side, Anna surely wouldn't have let her go alone.

Sun blasted into the room and into Willyn's eyes, causing her to blink rapidly and tilt her head to the side. The man standing with his face in shadow laughed deep in his throat before speaking. "You're not Anna, so you must be one of her girls." He moved closer, effectively blocking the sun and forcing her to take a step back.

Willyn's first impulse was to reject his classification of her as one of Anna's "girls." The way he'd said it made her feel like she worked at a brothel where Anna was madam, but once she got a good look at the visitor, her breath caught in her chest and left her mute. He had seemed tall before, but after moving inside, he actually towered over her. Since she still couldn't find her voice, she simply looked to Anna, hoping for an intervention.

"Dare," Anna said with some satisfaction. "I guess that explains why I couldn't see you."

Ignoring Willyn, the stranger offered both hands to Anna as he went to greet her. "No offense, but I wasn't sure you'd receive me, considering everything you've got going on these days." He spared a glance for Willyn as if remembering she was there. "Is she one of them?"

Laughing out an insulted breath, Willyn finally found her voice. "If you're referring to me, then yes. I am one of them. I'm one of Anna's girls." The heavy dose of sarcasm did not go unnoticed, causing the man to return his full attention to her.

"I apologize." He inclined his head.

Willyn tried not to notice how dark his hair was or the full, masculine lips that seemed to be on the verge of a smug smile. He had an air about him that bothered her, and she couldn't say if her defensiveness was justified or if her nerves were just too frazzled to be reliable.

Despite his soulful, blue eyes, everything about the man pulsed with an overwhelming sense of ... desire. That was the only way she could describe it. His eyes were hungry, and he seemed to be looking for something. Considering his sudden arrival on the island, whatever he wanted had to be here.

Willyn tore her eyes away from his and pretended to adjust the flap on her purse. All she had to do was make nice then mind her own business. She was literally heading to church, and here she was being rude to a friend of Anna's. It didn't matter what she felt. This was still Anna's home, and Willyn was a guest. Plastering on a fake smile, she looked at the man. "Sorry. I'm a little tense this morning."

"Willyn, this is Dare," Anna said.

"Dare?" Willyn asked. "That's certainly different."

He continued to assess Willyn, making her feel like a newly discovered bug. She imagined he was thinking up a new name for her species. *Witchus cautionarius*?

"It's short for Darius, my given name," he told her, letting a black bag slide off his shoulder and onto the floor. "It never really suited me."

Hoping to smooth things over with small talk, Willyn said, "Darius. It's from the Bible, isn't it? The man who threw the prophet Daniel in with the lions?" Realizing that didn't sound like a compliment, she added, "It means protector."

With a frown he said, "It also means 'one who upholds good.'" He thrust his hands in the pockets of his black pants. "But like I said, the name never really fit."

"Then Dare it is," Willyn said. Having moved closer while they'd spoken, she offered him her hand. "I'm Willyn."

Dare lifted his hand to shake but froze in mid-motion, brows crashing together and lip curling back in a snarl. He pointed to the base of her throat, holding his finger inches away from her skin. "What the hell are you wearing?" he demanded. The previously mysterious blue eyes were now alive with undisguised malice.

Willyn jumped away from him just as Anna put her hand on Dare's arm. She spoke to both of them in a voice that was quiet but rigid. "I think we've had enough of a meet and greet for now. Dare, we can talk in the study. It's through that door." Anna gave him a gentle push.

With a glare for Willyn, Dare hefted his bag and strode toward the study.

Clutching the cross around her neck, Willyn held her breath until his footsteps receded and the study door closed with a resounding thud. She was still shaking. The aftershocks rocked her. It was like she'd almost been attacked by a growling dog.

"I'm so sorry, Willyn." Anna placed her hands on her upper arms. "I promise he's all bark, though I'm sure that's not very comforting right now."

Anna had surely read her thoughts. Snarl. Dog. Bark. Somehow Willyn didn't believe her and fully expected the angry man to come complete with bite. "I think I should get to church. I need it more than ever." She cleared her throat and met Anna's gaze. "Is he going to be staying?"

Hesitating, Anna bit her lip and nodded. "I believe so. Don't worry. I'll talk to him." She put her finger on Willyn's hand where it still held the cross. "You just gave him a start, but don't judge him too harshly." Anna's eyes grew distant. "He has his reasons."

"You said you understood why you couldn't see him. Does he have power?" Willyn looked in the direction Dare had gone. "Because I felt something."

"Let's get into that later. I'll make sure the coven knows he's here, and if I know Dare, he'll be happy to answer any question you put to him. He's never been shy, for lack of a better word."

Willyn crossed her arms. "You don't say," she murmured, the dry tone evidence she was recovering her strength. Without another word she walked out to meet the others who were waiting for her.

~

Anna waved to Willyn as she climbed on the golf cart with Claire, Tadd, and Joe. They'd drive to the dock then take a boat to the mainland. It was quite a trip from the island to downtown Savannah, but Anna knew how important Sundays were to Willyn. They were a lifeline for a good soul adrift on a dangerous sea.

Closing the door, Anna firmed her lips and went to meet Dare. His being here couldn't be coincidence, and she intended to find out what he knew and what he wanted. She had strong feelings for her old friend but was well aware of his hidden talents, as well as his personal agenda.

Willyn had said that Dare had made her feel something, and knowing the man like she did, Anna wouldn't doubt that one bit.

He was waiting with his broad back to her, hands still in his pockets as he stared out the window. On the other side of the large, French-paned window, the day was golden with the special glow of a southern summer, but the man standing there carried his own personal rain cloud over his head. Darius Forster. What a sense of humor the fates had.

Deciding to make a point from the onset, Anna allowed herself a rare show of temper and slammed the door to announce her entry. She also wanted to keep the conversation private.

Dare turned with brows lifted in surprise. Then his face quickly dropped into a scowl when he saw Anna with hands on her hips and braced for battle. "Guess I'm in trouble now, right? What else is new?" he asked.

"Don't try to pull that with me, Dare. I've known you too long. That misunderstood rogue routine may work on most females, but I'm well aware that you're anything but." Anna tamped down on her anger as she remembered Willyn's fear and shock when Dare had turned on her. She didn't want to rage at him too much, but he also needed to understand what was expected. He was here for a reason, and why that made her stomach flutter...well, she'd think about that later.

Crossing his arms over his chest, Dare narrowed his eyes. "What kind of coven are you running here, Anna? Did I see what I think I did? Now that I look back on it all, was she dressed for church?" He shook his head like someone had just declared the earth flat once again.

"Her name is Willyn, and she has enough to worry about without you coming here and judging her. Let me rephrase, without you attacking her." Anna moved to a nearby desk and uncorked a decanter of brandy. It was early in the day, but turmoil seemed to be part of Dare's repertoire, whether he meant it to be or not. So she needed a drink.

After tossing back a glass, she nailed him with a look. "Her beliefs are her choice, and they have not affected her ability or desire to serve this coven and ensure the prophecy turns out the way we want it too. Considering she has more at stake than any of us, I hold her in high esteem. She deserves our respect."

Dare took his hands from his pockets and clenched them

into fists. "She's a damned Christian!"

Slamming her glass on the desk Anna met his stare with one of her own. "She is one of the nine, and you would do well to remember that."

Dare drew a deep breath. Then another. "Fine. Of course. It's not my place to question." He moved to a burgundy leather chair and dropped to it. "I apologize, but I hope you understand my reaction."

"I do," Anna said, her heart and countenance softening as she looked at her old friend. "Of course I do, but you cannot let your reasoning affect Willyn." Anna paused, unsure how long Dare would be involved or to what extent. As usual, magic enjoyed keeping some secrets, preferring to let destiny reveal itself in time. For the powers that be, the world truly was a stage.

She poured herself another glass and one for Dare, taking it to him as a peace offering and additional fortitude. "Willyn has been chosen. She is being tested."

Serious brows clashed together, as they often did on Dare's serious face. "Since when?"

"Last night." Anna saw his comprehension and wondered again what had prompted his visit to her home.

"Hmph," was all he uttered before tossing back the brandy.

Leaving him to his own thoughts, Anna stepped to the same window Dare had just vacated. The tarot reading she'd performed just before last night's ceremony was bothering her, begging for clarification.

She'd only told the others she expected another witch to be chosen, but there was more. The card she'd pulled in the one card spread had been The Empress in an upright position. It stood for Mother, abundance, and healing. Absolutely no question who that referred to. Willyn was a mother and a nurse and tended to nurture everyone around her.

Anna had been curious after that and had decided to do a

three card spread, just to see what else she might discover. The first card she'd chosen had been Strength, upright, indicating a moral force. Definitely Willyn again. The next card had been a little more disconcerting, though it had also been upright. The magician, master of special knowledge and focused energy.

Anna glanced at Dare, afraid she now understood the second card. She knew he wasn't an overtly cruel man, but he did have his demons. Pain and fury held him on his course with a single-minded goal. Anna just didn't know how he planned to go about it.

And that was why the third card was now even more troubling than it had been when she'd pulled it. Willyn was going to her trial. Dare had suddenly entered the picture. And the third card had been the Ten of Swords. There were different ways to interpret the card in its upright position, but certain words pounded at Anna until she wished she'd never even looked into the possibilities. Failure. Defeat. The end of a cycle. And of course there was the one she'd rather not consider, the more literal meaning she hoped wouldn't apply.

She glanced again at her moody friend as he stared into his drink, then she imagined sweet, trusting Willyn. Anna took a fortifying breath. The Ten of Swords could also imply that someone would suffer a letdown or a betrayal.

That they would be stabbed in the back.

3

Hot. That was always the first word that came to mind when Willyn was asked what she thought of Savannah. The spring had only been a prelude to the heat that poured down on the city in June, turning cars into convection ovens. She couldn't bear to think about August. Not just yet.

Of course, there was more to be said for the city than its weather patterns. Much more. Savannah's history was steeped in triumph and tradition, with its fair share of tragedy thrown in for flavor. Still, the second word that came to Willyn's mind when asked about her new home was...breathtaking. There were times when her lungs seemed to function on amazement alone, as one enchanting block of old townhomes rolled into another. Huge, live oaks stood as sentries all around, providing perfect settings for tourist pictures as well as shelter from the brutal southern sun.

As Willyn rode in the back of the car, she looked up to see twin spires jutting into the sky. They sat atop one of the oldest churches in the area and one of the few structures grand enough to hover above the tree line. The gray and gold peaks marked the spot where she and Tadd were headed now, to attend mass with Claire and Joe. Willyn had been raised among Baptists but had eagerly accepted Claire's invitation to attend the Catholic services. She trusted Claire and Joe and felt more comfortable entering a new environment with the older couple at her side.

They had tight and well-tested ties to Anna, her family, and now the coven, so Willyn knew she could trust them. Most importantly, she could trust them with her son. Claire and Joe adored Tadd and had done so much to make his transition easier. They knew just about everything there was to know about Willyn and her late husband, because Tadd loved the older couple as much as they did him. And when Tadd trusted, he talked.

"Look. Look. Look," Tadd said from beside her. His small finger tapped at the window and pointed toward a horse pulling a carriage. "He's so big! And look. He just pooped!" His smile filled his little face. "It's really big, too!"

Willyn nodded and laughed. "It sure is."

The carriage pulled out in front of their car, forcing them to a crawl until they rounded Calhoun Square. Patterns of light and shade decorated sidewalks, a lovely carpet for both tourists and locals. The city as a whole seemed to take one long, deep breath before exhaling in relaxation. A Sunday in Savannah.

Pulling to a stop in front of the church that would be better described as a cathedral, Joe let Claire, Willyn, and Tadd get out then drove off to park. The face of the church was elegant, artistic in the way of historic architecture, with a creamy stone structure and gold trim. Arched, wooden doors welcomed them into opulence, and Willyn felt worlds away from the small brick church she'd attended in Alabama. She glanced at Tadd, who was still holding her hand, and felt a wash of peace as he waved to another small boy.

Catholic, luxurious, and Georgia. All things different for her and her son, yet they remained the same in the way that mattered most. These were good people who had allowed her into their family, even if she didn't quite fit the papal mold.

After escorting Tadd to the room for his age group, Willyn rejoined Claire in their regular seats. Mass would be starting soon, and Willyn took a moment to squeeze Claire's hand. "I want to thank you again, for all you've done for me and Tadd."

"Child, you've thanked me enough. Besides, Joe and I are happy to have someone along, now that Joe Jr. has decided Saturday night suits him better." Claire dug in her purse and turned her cell phone to vibrate. "Can't have Proud Mary breakin' into the Lord's Prayer."

Willyn smiled at the reminder. She'd nearly jumped out of the pew last Sunday when Tina Turner's voice had burst from Claire's phone.

As the lights dimmed, Willyn let her mind wander to Tadd, who was probably soaking in the day's lesson. He was such a quick learner and as observant as a miniature detective. She knew he had questions about their new life swimming around inside his bright little brain, but so far he'd only given her a few quizzical looks. Unfortunately, each of those looks had come after someone had slipped and mentioned coven business where he could hear.

Willyn had been preparing her answers since the night she'd learned she was a witch, because as hard as it was for her to accept, she couldn't begin to imagine what Tadd would do with such information. And she wouldn't lie to him, though she knew some parents would if they felt they were protecting their child.

Willyn and Tadd had grieved together when his father had been killed in a car accident. They'd been forced into a mourning that no one should have to endure, and while one part of their life had been carved away, a new bond had formed between mother and son. He was wiser than a five-year-old should be, and Willyn doubted she would be able to fool him for long. Regardless, she would be honest with him, because how could she preach it if she didn't live it?

Willyn knew the dreaded discussion about witches and magic would be coming soon, and now that she was about to face off against the Amara and their evil forces, she had to take care of business. She had no intention of departing this earth before her time, but she couldn't risk leaving Tadd behind with secrets that might grow into resentment. The thought alone almost broke her heart.

She just hoped her son could be discreet. After she revealed the truth about the coven and her own powers, there would be the risk of others finding out. A young boy didn't always understand the magnitude of adult matters, and she could just imagine a first grader who had a witch for a mom. She shuddered, envisioning the topic of his first show-and-tell.

A rustle of movement drew Willyn's attention across the aisle. A young woman with long brown hair in a braid slid into an end seat, staring straight ahead the whole time. Though she'd been attending the church for only four weeks, Willyn was sure she'd never seen the girl before. That alone wasn't all that intriguing, but the girl's way of moving was. She seemed nervous, eyes wide as she listened to the priest. The hands in her lap were wringing and twisting the entire time.

Willyn tapped Claire's thigh but kept her eyes on the girl. "Who's that?" she asked.

Shaking her head, Claire whispered, "No idea. I've never seen her before." She turned and spoke to Joe then whispered again to Willyn. "He doesn't know either. Is she alone?"

"I think so," Willyn said, facing forward and hoping she wasn't disturbing anyone by talking. "I'll introduce myself after mass."

"Why are you so curious? I can ask around."

"No. I'd rather talk to her myself." Willyn's inner witch was humming. "I can't say why, but she looks like she needs a friend." A vision and a riddle tapped into her memory. "She looks lost."

The remainder of the service seemed to drag, making Willyn feel guilty for not paying attention, but she couldn't stop checking on the girl. With her hands now braced on each side as if trying to stay upright, the young stranger seemed ready to bolt at the slightest movement. Why would she come to church then act as if she were awaiting her own verdict?

It was a good thing Willyn had discussed her plan with Claire, because as soon as the congregation was released, the girl shot up and scurried toward the doors. She actually pushed one side open before the attendant had a chance.

Willyn was staying close, hoping to catch up to her before she got too far ahead. Luckily, the girl slowed once she was halfway down the block, giving Willyn a chance to catch up. "Excuse me," she called. The girl kept walking. Either she hadn't heard Willyn, or she didn't want to acknowledge her. "Miss?"

The girl stopped, her shoulders heaving so greatly Willyn could see the sigh from behind. She turned, and for the first time, Willyn noticed her eyes. They were large, blue, and full of apprehension. What had the poor thing been through?

"I'm sorry." Willyn halted a few feet away and offered a smile of assurance. "I don't usually chase people down in the street. It's just that I noticed you in church and wanted to introduce myself."

The girl shook her head and started to back away, looking at Willyn as if she were offering to carve her up instead of making her acquaintance.

"My name's Willyn. I'm new at the church, too, and it can sometimes be overwhelming. All that quartz and stained glass." Willyn laughed. "Don't get me wrong. It's beautiful. I'm just used to simple wooden benches and banana pudding in the meeting hall after services. The singing we did was a little more upbeat, too. Not quite as somber."

Whether it was the bit about Baptist hymns or banana pudding, Willyn couldn't tell, but the girl lifted the corners of her lips as if testing to see if her smile still worked. Willyn waited, hoping silence would encourage a response.

"It is big," the girl said then fell mute again.

Willyn's turn. "The church? My little boy actually tested its echo ability when we first visited. Luckily, only tourists were around at the time, and they all looked as if they'd wanted to do the same thing." Willyn chanced a step closer. "I don't know about you, but I could stand a coffee and something sweet. I know a good café. It's a short walk, but I'd be willing to treat if you'd come along. I hate eating alone."

"Well, I..."

"Please. We could both stand to make a few new friends in town."

The girl frowned. "How do you know I'm new in town?"

"I could just tell." Willyn walked up close then eased past her. "You should taste their black bean burrito. And they have these little desserts, chocolate with a sweet cream in the middle. I'll have to pick one up for Tadd." With that Willyn kept moving, hoping the girl would follow.

She did.

"What's your name, or is that classified?" Willyn asked. This time the girl did smile.

"No. Not classified. I'm Beth."

Satisfied with the progress, Willyn decided not to push any further. Instead, she pointed out her favorite stores along the way and kept the conversation simple and safe. She didn't want to spook her new, young friend with the hollow eyes. Beth looked as if she was running from something, and she had a habit of glancing around, especially at corners. Maybe there was an abusive man in her past? That would be a good reason for a scared girl to relocate to a new town.

Soon Willyn spotted the telltale brown sign with a goose on it. The café and bakery was a favorite of hers and Tadd's, with friendly staff, great food, and a fun environment. They entered and got in line. Sunday at eleven-thirty was always a busy time.

Beth had only asked for a black coffee, but after some encouragement, she relented and ordered some food as well. She stared down at the black and white checkerboard floor, like the acceptance of lunch from Willyn made her feel guilty.

Instead of mentioning it, Willyn asked, "Would you mind getting us a table? I can order while you grab one, even if it's still dirty. Someone will be by to clean it in a minute."

Beth chose a table in the corner, as far away from the action as she could. Willyn hoped she could help the girl, because it was evident she was in some kind of trouble. After paying and getting their drink, Willyn joined her and laid plenty of sweeteners and creamer on the table. Large posters with a European feel covered the pale yellow wall behind Beth, and a picture window allowed a view of the street and the swarming mix of locals and visitors.

"What sort of church do you usually attend?" Willyn asked as she loaded her coffee, making it as sweet and light as toffee.

"Baptist, but I haven't been in a long time." Beth tapped her short, clean nails on the sides of her cup.

Willyn wondered if staying away from church had been Beth's choice or if someone had kept her home, isolating her from others. She took a mental step back, realizing she was jumping to conclusions. For all she knew, Beth could be running from the police as easily as she could an old boyfriend. She studied the girl's big, blue eyes and simple dress. A criminal? Nope. She just couldn't see that.

"I guess we must have been destined to meet," Willyn said.

Beth looked wary. "Why do you say that?"

"We have a lot in common. We're both recent transplants to Savannah. Then there's the fact we're two Baptists going to a Catholic church. And here's the real proof," Willyn added as their food was set before them. "We both have a weakness for burritos and whoopee pie."

The smell of chicken and salsa rose up, making them both take a deep sniff to savor the aroma. "There is that," Beth said before allowing an actual grin to spread across her face.

After a few bites, Willyn pressed for more info. "Do you work in town, or are you looking?"

"I have a job." Beth took a swallow of her drink before continuing. "I'm a tech at one of the hospitals."

"You're kidding. I'm a nurse." Willyn started to peel the cellophane from her dessert. "I told you. I'd like to mark our shared health profession as exhibit D. What floor?"

"Oncology," Beth said in a matter of fact tone, her expression losing a little of its brief and unexpected luster. "I like it fine, but the work's hard."

"I'm sure it is. It takes a special person to care for cancer patients."

"No, that's not what I meant. It's just a really busy hospital. Lots of stress." Beth tore into her own chocolate pie.

The flippant comment sent a ripple of concern through Willyn, but she dismissed it. Her imagination was working overtime today, and she had enough of her own to worry about without creating fictional problems for a person she didn't really know that well. "I hope we can do this again. It's nice having company."

"What about your little boy? Don't you bring him here?"

"I do, and Claire, a friend of mine, also joins us sometimes." Willyn shrugged. "I'm sure you'll meet plenty of people your own age soon enough, but the offer stands." In a quick decision, she grabbed a napkin and wrote her number on it. "This is my cell. If you need anything, I'm almost always available."

Beth picked the paper up and stared at it before shoving it into her purse. She seemed on the verge of saying something, but the bus boy came over to clear their plates, his arrival sending her back into a flat, unreadable state. No smile. No joy. What on earth could she be carrying around with her? What would make her so nervous and suspicious of everyone?

As if she suddenly felt threatened, Beth drained the last of her coffee and stood. "Thanks for lunch, Willyn. It was nice to meet you, and I might call. I'm not sure."

"Maybe I'll see you in church next week." Willyn stayed seated.

Beth gave two short and quick bobs of her head. "Maybe." She started to walk away but looked down at Willyn one more time. "If I don't see you again," her eyes clouded over then she swallowed hard. "Thanks."

Willyn watched her leave then waited until she passed by on the sidewalk outside. Beth rushed by with her purse clenched in her hands and her head tucked down to avoid meeting anyone's eyes. She didn't look up, and she didn't wave goodbye. In no time at all she was out of sight, leaving Willyn with an odd mixture of hope and anxiety.

She glanced back to study the abandoned cellophane and chocolate crumbs on the table, undeniable proof that she'd shared lunch with someone. Without it, Willyn might have found herself wondering if the strange, young girl had ever really been there at all.

4

Paige hit the puree button on the blender, causing slices of strawberry, kiwi, and banana to bounce around before churning into a medium brown sludge. It was the raw egg that changed the color, Willyn was sure, so she looked down at her new blue coffee cup instead of the concoction. Paige made shakes morning and night with the eggs, for habit as much as protein.

The sleek blender fit perfectly into Anna's modern-medieval style kitchen which boasted a stone arch overhead that matched the masonry of the far wall and its fireplace. A farmhouse sink of cobalt and hanging lights in jeweled tones gave the room a punch of color. Crystal vases were scattered about with carnations and roses, all white or cream, making Willyn pause to consider their meaning. She wondered if Anna had put them out in silent support of the current witch up to bat. They were Willyn's color.

Before, when Shauni had been challenged, they had held a variety of blooms with no apparent theme. Then again, her color was green, and even Anna didn't grow green flowers.

Looking over at Paige's disgusting shake and its lovely hue, Willyn asked, "Why don't you try some of that powder they make? Surely it would taste better."

Paige flashed a mischievous grin. "Then I wouldn't get to enjoy the professor's looks of disgust." She winked at Claudia, who'd just walked in. "I so enjoy my daily lectures on enterobacteria."

The redhead in question spread her long, pretty fingers and wiggled them to check her manicure. "I'm sure your digestive tract is as tough as the rest of you, so you're probably exempt from concern." Claudia took a stool next to Willyn and sat at the crescent-shaped island of gray granite. "Paige is our own pretty version of Superman."

In response, Paige flexed an arm like a pro and showed off a well-defined triceps. She had been a soldier in the Army, but these days she was the coven's warrior. Her tight, black pants and sleeveless shirt revealed her lean yet powerful, military-honed physique. The super-speed and strength she possessed? That was all witch.

Just then, a blonde, long-haired cat flounced into the room. It was Sassafras, who not only belonged to Kylie but also shared the college girl's golden locks and diva personality. She was called Sassy for short. Enough said.

Right behind the gorgeous cat was an orange tom with a puffed up tail. He'd evidently been in a scrape with another feline and was making a break for human population and protection. Kiko belonged to Viv, but he scooted under the nearest shelter he could find, Claudia's stool. He tucked his tail close to his body as yellow-green eyes stared out at the rest of them, begging for help.

"Where did he go? My poor baby." Viv rushed into the kitchen and kneeled down when Claudia pointed to his hiding place. She cuddled him up with coos and kisses then headed straight for the pantry to get a kitty snack.

"What happened?" Willyn asked.

"Yeah," Paige took a sip of her sludge, "and what does the other guy look like?"

When Viv only shrugged and turned away, Paige slammed her glass on the counter. "Was he after my girl again? He was wasn't he? You better lock him up in your room."

Viv's head whipped up. "No. You need to lock up Tiger Lily until she's out of heat. She's got all the males in the house going crazy."

Before Paige could fire back a response, Shauni walked in with her hand up and shook it at the two other women to quiet them down. She spoke into the silver phone in her other hand. "Tuesday? Good. I'll tell the others." She snapped the cell closed and met Paige's angry eyes first. "That was Michael, and he's going to allow some extra time this week for any of his extended family who'd like to have their cats spayed or neutered."

As both biologist and animal whisperer, Shauni continued in a firm voice. "None of us knew we would all come together the way we did, but now that we live in the same house, so do our cats. Since we're all animal-lovers here, we need to do the responsible thing and make sure we don't end up with any unwanted kittens." After saying her piece, Shauni blew out a breath and sat on the stool on the other side of Willyn. Her black hair was in its usual braid, hanging halfway down her back.

Paige grimaced then emitted a grunt. "You're right. Damn. The cats all get along so well, I guess I took it for granted they would all, you know, behave themselves."

"Even humans have a hard time fighting that specific urge," Claudia said with half a smile.

Viv relaxed and nodded. "And we don't give off an undeniable scent the way cats do, so I guess we're really not being fair. Fine. Tuesday it is." After putting Kiko down to enjoy his kibbles, Viv gave a few to Sassy, who was sitting in the doorway. "I wonder what made this one run in. Surely Kiko wasn't after her, too."

Shauni coughed a little. "No. She just got caught watching and made a hasty retreat when she heard you coming. I guess she didn't want us to know she was a voyeur."

Willyn had to laugh. "Not possible. There are absolutely no secrets in this house. Not with Anna and Shauni around.

One sees all we humans do, and the other hears everything the animals think. Maybe I'll make one of those aluminum foil hats and see if they can really block transmission."

Claudia joined in with the joke. "Then we have Hayden, who can ask her ghost friends to spy on us if she wants too. Willyn, I think I'm going to join you. Get out the tin foil."

"What are we doing with tin foil?" Kylie pranced into the kitchen much as her cat had a few minutes before. "Are you cooking?" she asked Claudia with a wide-eyed expression. "I didn't think you could cook."

Claudia shook her head so the fiery waterfall down her back glimmered under the lights. "Correction. Won't cook. There's never a time that culinary creation will override self-maintenance."

"Huh?" Kylie asked, moving to the stainless steel refrigerator to pull out an apple juice.

"What she means," Paige explained, "is she's not messing up her nails just to make food. After all, that's why the microwave was invented."

"True dat," Kylie said, making them all groan. She'd once hated the expression, and now it was stuck to her tongue like taffy.

"*Neccesito aqua.*" Lucia came in wearing shorts, T-shirt, and a glow that spoke of recent and strenuous exercise. She put two hands on Kylie's hips and gently removed her from where she stood blocking the fridge.

Hayden trudged in next, panting and eyeing the water bottles with an almost maniacal gleam. "Me, too. Lucia. Please. *Por favor.*" Her caramel-colored hair was in a ponytail that appeared to have been de-constructed, and she barely made it to a chair before collapsing.

"I was getting you a drink," Lucia said before plunking down next to her. "No need to break into my mother tongue."

"Couldn't risk it," Hayden said before slinging the bottle

back and drinking it whole.

Willyn took in the two of them then noticed Kylie's workout clothes. She knew right away what had happened. "I see you've been put through Kylie's wringer. Don't feel bad. She got me with that, too. Once. Only once."

"What? Aerobics?" Paige made a disgusted noise. "That's way sad. You two look beat."

"It was px90," Kylie said in their defense. "It's a tough workout."

"I could show you a tough workout. In fact, I've been thinking about..."

"Greetings, my sisters," Anna said as she breezed in wearing loose jeans and a white v-neck shirt. She always managed to pull off casual elegance, no matter what she wore, even now with bare feet and iridescent purple toenails. She was with her feet the way Claudia was with her hands. "Good. We're all here. I can tell because the room feels alive." With her sable hair hanging loose and long, Anna could have passed for eighteen.

Viv crossed her arms over her chest. "Yes. It is hard to miss that hum when we're all together. I'd say the frequency is somewhere between a jumbo jet flying by and an angel's harp." Her mouth pulled tight as she suddenly got serious. "Actually, I'd like to measure it next time. See if it registers." Viv the physicist never truly stopped working.

"Sure," Anna said. "I'm game, but tonight we have other matters to discuss." Willyn felt as if a frozen fist punched into her diaphragm. "Why? Has something happened?"

Anna met her eyes. "Be at ease, Little Mother," she said, using her pet name for Willyn. "We haven't come together as a whole since the choosing last night, and we have to be prepared."

"We've been through this once," Hayden said, before accepting a second bottle of water from Lucia. "Surely we're better prepared than the first time."

"The Amara will have gained knowledge and experience as well, and you can expect them to use it." The deep voice that answered surprised everyone in the room and caused an array of female gazes to land on the one who'd spoken from the doorway. While most looked at Dare with curiosity, a few couldn't hide the intrigue that had nothing to do with a stranger showing up at their meeting but everything to do with a devilishly handsome man.

Refusing to acknowledge him, Willyn white-knuckled the coffee mug in her hands until little bolts of lightning shot through her fingers. She watched Dare from beneath her lashes as he glided into the room like he owned the place. He motioned to the coffee machine with a grin for Kylie then got down a mug after the younger woman pointed to where they were kept.

"While I agree with what you said, I don't know who you are, and that's a dangerous position to be in, Mister." Paige was not as welcoming as Kylie, and her stance told everyone she was primed for action. Positioning herself near Willyn, Paige's eyes grew dark and menacing as she watched the intruder. She was in full-on bodyguard mode.

Anna wisely intervened. "Everyone, I'd like you to meet Dare Forster. He's an old friend who will be visiting. I realize the timing might raise some concern, but I think the coven could benefit from his presence." She paused. "He has great power, and you all know how I feel about coincidences."

"That there is no such thing while we face the evil," Lucia purred in her enchanting accent. Her chocolate-brown eyes tightened at the corners as she appraised Dare. It was hard to say if she liked what she saw or was planning his demise. They all knew what Anna meant. His presence had something to do with Willyn's trial, and there was no way to know if they should be worried or relieved.

Anna walked over to stand shoulder to arm with Dare,

aligning herself with him and answering everyone's question one final time. Anna accepted him, so she expected the coven to do the same. "He poses no threat to any of you." She glanced at Willyn before turning to Dare. A flicker of warning danced across her face as she looked at him. "Do you," she added, though it was more statement than query.

Dare stared back. "I want nothing more than an alliance with your coven."

For some reason his words didn't give Willyn any solace. She didn't like the way he looked at the other women, his gaze lingering on each one as if assessing their worth. She held her breath when Dare's scrutiny swept her way, but he skipped over her to focus on Paige. Standing firm, he held that witch's stare until she grudgingly nodded. Once it became clear Paige wouldn't go for his throat, the entire room exhaled as one.

Except for Willyn. Those deep blue eyes had finally found her and were riveted on her now as the others fixed snacks or settled into their seats. Unsettled, she rubbed her forehead as if staving off a headache and prayed he would look away. Having his undivided attention made her shiver inside, and there was more to it than the unpleasant encounter she'd had with him. Sensing his scorn, his judgment of her, Willyn found herself in total disagreement with Anna. This man definitely felt threatening.

"I've brought Dare up to speed on the first challenge, and what we know so far of the Amara." Anna remained standing near the counter. "Ronja and her followers weren't expecting defeat and have had to regroup and re-strategize. Her wounded pride and humiliation will make her more determined than ever."

"Because Shauni and her furry friends opened a super-sized can of whoopass on them." This from Paige who was now Shauni's biggest fan after her unexpected show of strength.

Willyn smiled along with the others as Shauni blushed.

Shauni had struggled with the idea of fighting or using the animals to do so, but when it became clear that was the only way to save herself, the coven, and Michael, she'd put aside her misgivings.

Willyn could only hope to do as well. She already had enough trouble raising her son in brand new surroundings while learning to throw a decent fireball on the side. Being the one to face the newly-enraged Ronja? Well that was just the rotten cherry on top.

"She'll also be more dangerous," Anna said. "Let's not forget she's been around for almost a thousand years, and that's more than likely why she thought we would go down easily, prophecy or not. She owes her immortality to Bastraal and will do anything to ensure the demon's resurrection." Anna caught Willyn's eye. "The Amara won't be playing anymore. They'll use anything to their advantage."

For a moment Willyn only sat and stared, knowing Anna was getting at something. When she finally understood, the implication swept through her, and she exploded off the stool. "You think she'll come after my son! Is that what you're saying?" Willyn started to pace and rubbed her palms together, though they both burned from within. Emotions were the key to making fire, and right now she was going supernova.

"It's only a possibility, but we should all be cautious. That includes the Attingers and Joe's family." Anna managed to stay calm, speaking to everyone as if she didn't notice Willyn coming undone.

Willyn found it impossible to be still. She quaked inside and out as fear for her child chased levelheadedness straight out the back door. Maybe she could leave. Pack up tonight and take her son to the far end of the planet. There was only one sacrifice she wasn't going to make, even to save the world. One she couldn't make.

Anna came over to put her hands on Willyn's shoulders, a

cool sense of calm flowed from head witch to panicked mother. "Be sure of this," Anna said, breathing deep and pulling Willyn back from the edge of chaos. "Tadd's safety will be top priority. For all of us."

"You know it," Paige said, clapping a hand on Willyn's arm, just below Anna's hand that hadn't yet let go.

Claudia stood up and came over to the trio. "Absolutely," she said, lowering her head to rest on Willyn's, another show of support.

Nods and words of agreement flowed all around, but it was the "Damn straight" from Hayden that shocked them all into silence. Even Willyn stilled as she looked at the woman who was usually the serenity of the coven. Hayden's face was set in stone.

The unity and shelter of her sisters was a comfort, and Willyn suddenly felt a new sensation. She was burning again, but this time it was in her eyes. She drew a stuttering breath and blinked to clear the tingle that came from trying to hold back tears. As she gathered herself, Anna, Paige, and Claudia simply held on. They held her up.

When Willyn was settled and able to speak, she nodded and echoed in a strong voice, "Damn straight."

~

Dare wasn't sure what he'd gotten himself into. Female bonding didn't come close to describing what was going on in that kitchen, and the gentle hum of the gathered nine had steadily crescendoed until he thought he would have to leave the room. When the blonde finally relaxed, the rest of the witches did too, and blessed tranquility returned.

Willyn. That was her name. Dare hadn't forgotten, but due to the intense annoyance she caused, he preferred to think of her as the blonde. As far as he was concerned, she was nothing but a sheep in wolf's clothing and surely had to be some sort of mistake. A Christian trying to be a witch? What the hell was the world coming to?

He'd watched as the drama unfolded and had to allow her a small amount of respect. The nine women in the Savannah Coven had a daunting mission before them, to vanquish the Amara and their demon, but Willyn had been tagged with an additional burden. She evidently had a kid to worry about.

While the women chatted and milled about, he considered the petite woman. With light, golden hair and innocent eyes that could only be called sky blue, it was hard to see her standing up to that bitch, Ronja. But then again, Dare thought, looks were almost always deceiving.

At least that had been his experience.

Shaking off the temporary insanity that almost made him feel sorry for a Bible-thumper, Dare scouted the room for someone more deserving of his attention. The Spanish witch practically oozed sexuality, but she was still reserving judgment of him, at least until she knew him better. Smart but unnecessary. He'd only come to make friends, and as it turned out, Anna's coven had a fine selection of potential buddies.

Then there was the redhead. Her hair was straight as paper and bright as flame, not to mention legs that made a man want a road map. She looked like high maintenance, though, so Dare continued his perusal. He was about to start cataloguing the hot Asian's assets when Anna snapped her fingers in front of his face.

"You with us, Forster?" She stepped in front of him and blocked his view which, judging by the look on her face, had been her intention. "Are you interested in the discussion?"

Dare had a feeling Anna knew exactly what he was interested in, but chose to play it safe. She was one witch whose fury he didn't want to be on the receiving end of. He'd known her in her teens when she'd been hormonal as hell, and it was so not a place he cared to revisit.

He gave her a wink and smiled. "Sorry. What were we discussing?"

Kylie stretched her legs out in front of her and rotated her ankles. "Oh, fate versus coincidence. You know, the usual stuff. Willyn met a girl at church, and we're deciding if she's important."

"Beth," Willyn said. "And I do think she's important. Maybe even part of my test."

The blonde formerly known as Willyn had returned to her stool and was clenching her mug again. He was well aware she resented his presence and didn't think he belonged there. Well that made two of them, so he cocked a brow at her and waited for her to go on.

She paused in her story like she wasn't sure what his next move would be but relented after a few seconds and let her eyes fall to the drink in her hands. Instead of talking, she leaned forward and peered into the cup. A wrinkle formed on her forehead while her mouth worked without making a sound.

"What is it?" Anna asked, clearly alarmed by the blonde's behavior.

"There's something in my coffee," Willyn said, her voice raspy with awe.

"Clouds?" Claudia asked before breaking into a Carly Simon rendition with Kylie lending harmony.

"No. No. People. It's people." Willyn's head shot up and the room fell silent. "There are people in my coffee."

5

Reflective surfaces were always good mediums, if one possessed the ability to use them correctly. Judging by the look on Willyn's face, Dare guessed this was the first time she'd ever taken a peek into the world of secret knowledge. Either she was actually having a vision, or she had something stronger than coffee in her cup.

"Tell me what you see," Anna said, coming up behind Willyn to look over her shoulder. "Breathe, focus, describe."

Doing exactly as instructed, Willyn inhaled deeply and concentrated on the latte-flavored visual aide. "A...bull. Yes. Definitely a bull. It's not lifelike but an outline. I can make out its horns and enough of its shape to be sure."

"You're doing well. Just stay relaxed." Anna shook her head when Viv opened her mouth to say something. "Breathe in and out and let it come to you. Don't try to force it. Just let it in." Anna's tone was low and rhythmic as one might use to lull themselves into meditation.

Dare stepped closer but treaded in silence so as not to disturb. The scene was captivating and exciting. One of the nine was harnessing a new trick, and it was the gift of sight no less. There just might be more to the little blonde than he'd given her credit for. He watched her chest rise and fall then realized he'd do better to put his eyes somewhere less distracting.

"It's changing now," Willyn said. "The lines are disappearing and leaving behind spots, or...points. I'm not sure." After a few seconds of intense scrutiny, her brows lifted with recognition. "Stars. They're twinkling like stars. Oh. Oh. There they go. They're fading away. Slowly." With a great exhale she murmured, "They're gone," and leaned against the wrought-iron twirls of the stool's backrest.

Willyn laughed before looking up to Anna. "Amazing. I've never done anything like that before." Her face was alight with the joy of discovery, eyes bright as the stars she'd just described and pink lips curved into a beautiful smile.

Dare was struck dumb. As a man who usually went for obvious attractors, like long, curvy waists and needle-thin stilettos, the pure delight in Willyn's expression was something fresh and new. It sailed through him like a summer breeze. No smooth talk or expensive perfume would impress this gentle soul, but he imagined she was a sucker for young flowers in the forest or the sweetly scented air after a good rain.

Where is this coming from? Dare took a slug of almost-scalding coffee in an attempt to break the flow of tranquility surging from the woman. Her goodness was almost tangible, and he needed to remind himself why he was here. Another look at her light blue eyes and Dare was certain. Willyn was definitely too sweet. She wouldn't do at all.

After shooting a questioning look to Anna, Viv waited until she got a nod to go ahead and asked the question she'd held back earlier. "What about the people you saw? Who were they?"

Twisting her mouth into a crooked frown, Willyn said, "I didn't recognize them, but they were women. The figures were transparent, but they wore robes or dresses and..." She drove her stare into the gray granite. "I'm pretty sure they all had their hair braided, and I have no idea why that sticks in my memory."

"It must be important," Hayden said. She, along with most of the other women, had eased closer to the island where Willyn sat.

"That's right." Anna hugged Willyn from behind and pressed close, cheek to cheek. "Congratulations, sister." She pulled away and became all business again. "You'll learn to catalogue what you see in your visions, and anything that jumps out at you is usually thanks to your subconscious. My inner witch tends to grab certain things like a baton then beat me over the head with that particular piece of info until I make sense of it. Hopefully yours will be less temperamental."

"Surely this is only a one time deal because it's my turn," Willyn said. "I've never had a vision in my life."

"Yeah and I never made fire with my hands until I came here," Shauni said with a laugh. "And I've still got that."

Anna moved to the opposite side of the island. "Once a gift like this is unveiled, it doesn't go away unless you purposely suppress it."

Dare spoke up. "And that would be a bad idea." His words drew Willyn's gaze to him, her eyes flickering like she'd just recalled he was there. He ignored the resentment and continued. "It's no coincidence you had this happen now, during your trial, but since that's the case, you would be wise to heed the message. If you want to protect your son, you need to figure out what the spirit world is telling you."

Did he think her eyes had flickered? What an appropriate term, because now they were flaming.

"I wouldn't be that foolish, and if I tried, Anna wouldn't let me," Willyn said. "She is the clairvoyant one here, unless, of course, I'm missing something. Exactly what sort of power do you have?"

Dare wanted to pick that gauntlet up and toss it right back at her pretty feet, but Anna, ever the diplomat, changed the topic abruptly and without apology. "Willyn, did you say you saw the outline of a bull and then stars?"

Willyn slowly turned to her. "Yes."

"If the stars were points with lines through them to draw the bull, then it must have been referring to the constellation, Taurus."

"That's what I was thinking," Viv said, agreeing with Anna. "But what do the women have to do with anything?"

Claudia stood and headed toward the door. "Women and bulls, robes, constellations. I'm going to do a search," she called as she walked out. "Maybe there's something on the Internet."

Willyn jumped up to follow her. "There were seven women."

"How do you know?" Dare asked, moving to walk beside her. They reached the doorway at the same time, so Dare stepped through sideways to allow her room.

She stutter-stepped in response but went on through. "Uh, thanks." Her cheeks pinkened, almost imperceptibly. "I just know."

"Then I won't question it." Dare fell back and let her move ahead, watching as she disappeared into the library with Anna and the redhead. The perfect-10 with black hair and Spanish blood passed him as he stood there, but for reasons he couldn't name, she didn't hold the same mystery as before. And damn. It hadn't been the redhead's short skirt and long legs that had held his attention as he'd walked behind the women. Or the serious but sexy, Asian scientist.

Despite all the treats laid out before him, only one thing was stuck in his head, and it was a body part that hardly ever garnered his notice. At least, not for long. Dare hoped there was something stronger than sherry in that room, because he would need it to help drown the image of innocent, sky-blue eyes.

~

Books were everywhere, neatly lined on shelves that covered almost every wall and towered far above Willyn's head.

She knew she'd landed in luxury the first time she'd come to Anna's house, but the library with the rich textures and hues straight out of an Agatha Christie novel was her favorite. She adored books and the escape they provided, so this room was a bibliophile's fantasy come to life. All that was missing to complete the scene was a grumpy but distinguished old man with a white moustache and puffing pipe in his mouth.

The library was spacious enough to hold three large desks, all equipped with computers. Claudia plopped down and began typing at one while Anna did the same right across from her. Though the others chose to sit in leather chairs or peruse the books while they waited, Willyn stayed close and leaned against the third desk.

Hoping to appear casual and relaxed, she glued her eyes to the gold dragon sitting on the corner, marveling at the detailed structure. The scales and claws were intricately carved, and its emerald eyes gleamed with threat. She ran a finger down its lovely back, transfixed by the texture and sensation. The metal felt warm, as if actual lifeblood pumped beneath. The serpentine creature glimmered under the lights, beautiful but fierce.

Now why did that make her think of Dare?

Movement near the door told her someone had entered the room, but it was the flush cascading over her that confirmed who it was. The man seemed to cause a visceral response in her body, and Willyn found herself both resentful and intrigued. She'd never had an uncontrolled reaction to any man before, even Mason. With him, she'd fallen slowly and surely in love, with his easy nature and strong heart.

Dare was everything Mason hadn't been. Nothing about the stranger was tender, and she was seriously beginning to doubt anything but obstinacy coursed through his veins. If he had a heart, it was dark with hate, and she seemed to be the primary recipient of his animosity. She didn't like him either, so his attitude shouldn't bother her.

But it did.

Willyn caught herself peeking at him from beneath the wave of her hair. His arms were crossed over his chest, stretching the black material of his shirt tight against his form. She could make out the curve of his shoulder and a fascinating display of muscles that corded when he tensed.

With a growing warmth in her belly, Willyn continued her investigation and let her eyes travel up to his face. As if corresponding to Dare's personality, the structure of his jaw and cheekbones seemed to be made of stone. Firm lines offset deep blue eyes and a too-tempting mouth. It didn't seem fair for such a harsh man to have the striking features. Those lips and eyes had probably lured many a foolish female to heartbreak, and Willyn was determined to keep that in mind. She couldn't afford to be deceived by good looks.

Lost in her musings, Willyn didn't realize she was staring at Dare until his eyes suddenly snapped back to hers. She sucked in a breath before resuming her assessment of the dragon. The dragon on the desk, anyway. Its glare was a lot less frightening than what she'd sensed from the man across the room. Dare had been aware of her perusal the whole time. He had enjoyed it, and now he was mocking her.

"I've got something," Claudia said, tapping her finger on the monitor she was using and creating a welcome diversion. "The Pleiades is a cluster of stars within the Taurus constellation." She raised her head to find Willyn. "They're also known as the Seven Sisters."

"It fits so far," Anna chimed in. "Anything else?"

"Plenty." Claudia focused on the computer screen again. "Different cultures have developed stories involving this group of stars. They relate to the seven sages of Greece, seven wise masters in medieval times, and in China they were worshipped by young girls and known as the seven sisters of industry.

The Persian name for the stars is Soraya, and in Japanese," Claudia paused to grin, "they're called Subaru."

"The sisters of industry?" Willyn echoed. "Somehow I don't think that's right. What else do you see concerning females?"

Claudia squinted and read some more. "Here's a link. Let me see where it goes." It only took a few seconds before she found something. "Wait a minute. The seven sages I mentioned? Well, they also came with seven wives who, according to an ancient Hindu myth, were all separated from their husbands because the women were unfaithful. All except one who was loyal."

"I don't see a connection," Paige said from where she sat.

"I'm getting there," Claudia replied, lifting her hand to indicate they needed to give her minute. "Seven women may not be enough to go on, but I find it interesting that whenever they were portrayed in scripts or work of art, their female character was designated by their long, braided hair."

"Like what I saw," Willyn said. "That's who they are, but why?"

"I think I can answer that." Anna had been typing on her keyboard during the discussion. "I followed up on Claudia's mention of the Seven Sisters. Only six of the stars are visible to the naked eye."

"Right," Claudia added. "They correspond to the six women who cheated on their husbands."

Anna nodded. "The seventh star is the key. It isn't as easily seen and is the basis for many of the legends. What's important to us, though, is that it's often referred to as being lost."

Willyn gasped. "The lost one." She put her hand to her neck. "It's part of the riddle Anna was given before, when Shauni's challenge was completed. We're supposed to find the lost one."

Hayden walked away from the book shelves and ran a hand through her caramel-colored hair. "And maybe you have," she said. "Think about it. You were talking about Beth right before you had your vision. And when you described her…"

"You said she was wearing her hair in a long braid," Paige said, finishing Hayden's thought.

Pacing again so she could think better, Willyn shook her head. "Hold on. We may be getting ahead of ourselves. Just because someone is wearing their hair a certain way doesn't tie them to us or the Seven Sisters. It could be a coincidence."

Willyn's frustration was making her twitchy, and it didn't help when Dare sauntered over to take the empty seat next to Viv before favoring her with an easy smile. A searing and prickly emotion rolled through Willyn. She refused to acknowledge its underlying meaning but couldn't deny the question poking at her brain. Why didn't he look at her that way?

"You told us you were drawn to Beth," Anna said, dragging Willyn back to the main issue. "You even took her to lunch, so your gut must have been telling you something."

"Yes, but it still doesn't make sense, even if she's involved." Willyn tossed her hands up. "Why the need for all the hidden meanings? What does the story of seven women have to do with Beth or the coven and our prophecy? There are nine of us."

"It's not about us." All heads turned to Shauni, who had been silent until now. "Anna, remember when you went into that trance as we approached the Amara plantation?" That was how they thought of the crumbling old house where Ronja and her twisted followers lived. "When we were walking up, you zoned out and started talking. At first you said she had all of them, but you changed your mind."

"I remember," Anna whispered, her eyes dilating as if she were mentally transporting to that day. "Then I told you there were seven, but there would be another before it was done."

"The seven sisters," Claudia said. "If I remember correctly, that's how many females are in the Amara, Ronja included. But if we're saying Beth is the lost one and has something to do with the Amara, her addition to their ranks would make eight." She tossed her red hair over one shoulder. "I don't understand."

"Neither do I." Willyn put her hands on her hips. "I bet I can guess who does know what it all means. And she won't be willing to share."

~

Ronja flipped a golden wave of hair out of her face and evaluated the construction of the basement. Technically the area was above ground due to Savannah's swollen water table, but with the walls having been rocked in, the first level finally resembled exactly what she'd had in mind.

A dungeon.

Some habits died hard, and Ronja had always found good use for a chamber that held in screams along with the chilly air. The dirt floor had been paved and sealed as well, leaving a drain in the lowest portion of each room. Clean-up would be much easier that way.

Restoring the grand southern home was her current project, and though she had extensive magic skills and a demon on standby, some things were better served by a personal touch. A human touch. That's why she'd hired masons to create this lower chamber. Filling it with furniture and her preferred accessories, i.e, torture toys, that she would take care of herself.

It wasn't a good idea to waste her stores of energy on trivial matters, not now when that damn coven had convened on Anna's little island. Though the witches were a sore spot for her, she doubted they would be a long-term problem. The first witch had bested her, true, but only because Ronja had been unprepared. That wasn't going to happen again.

From what she'd seen that day, some of the witches had only recently been introduced to the full scope of their power, and it was in Ronja's best interest to take full advantage of their inexperience. Her pride was important, but defeating the coven and calling forth Bastraal from the netherworld was crucial.

The how didn't really matter to her, but she viewed the conflict with Anna and her witches the same as she did a good Blackjack game. You weren't going to walk away with anything if you didn't play to win. No scared money on her table.

Footsteps scraping down the stone stairs had her turning to greet the two responsible for the sound. She knew it was Tyr and Scarlett before she faced them, but sharing your blood with someone caused that kind of connection. Her very cells seemed to pulse and shiver when either one of them drew near. And it always turned her on.

Tyr was her preferred lover, with his cinnamon skin and sharp, dark eyes that bespoke of his Native American lineage. She had recruited him for his gift, his ability to see what others couldn't, herself included. As a prophet or a seer, Tyr provided her with a much-needed service. As a well-developed warrior and cruelly handsome man, he provided another.

Scarlett strode beside him, as fine boned and elegant as Tyr was brutish. When Ronja was in the mood for a softer touch and a different level of communion, she called on her long-time friend with the delicate skin and stoplight red hair.

If she craved the fulfillment of strength combined with finesse, then she called on them both.

Tyr and Scarlett were the only two Ronja gave her blood to. The demon, Bastraal, had granted Ronja immortality in exchange for her promise to assist him and bring him back to the corporeal world when the time was right. That time was now, and she relied on her two closest confidantes more than ever. They would continue to feed from her and maintain longevity, for strength in the forthcoming battles as well as to keep their places in Ronja's shriveled heart.

"You've come to bring me good news, I hope." Ronja raised a brow at Tyr as she ran a hand over Scarlett's silk-clad arm. The woman had been working in a saloon when Ronja found her, so it was understandable that her tastes had run toward couture ever since.

"It is as we predicted. The eighth woman has come to Savannah," Tyr said, his features flat and unreadable. The man knew to keep pleasure and business separate at all times, a principle that had saved his life more than once.

"How do you know this will work?" Scarlett asked. She was one of the few who would risk affronting Ronja with such a question.

"Because I plan to short-circuit destiny. In case you haven't noticed, I don't follow every rule and ordinance like Anna. Hence my part as the bad guy." Ronja laughed at her joke along with Scarlett while Tyr remained serious.

Ronja had a prophecy in common with Anna and the coven, that their forces would confront each other in a classic good versus evil scenario. Both sides were aware of the time and the place. Savannah. Now.

But neither could be assured of the outcome. The fates tended to hold on to some secrets like greedy little kleptos, and all the earthbound players had to go along for a blind man's ride. That's where Tyr came in especially handy. He helped her locate mystical loopholes, as it were, and she intended to use every advantage.

What she planned now concerned her own private prophecy, a prognostication that revealed one of Ronja's own turning against her. It was to be the upside-down version of the seven sages' wives. There were to be seven women in the Amara, and one who would betray her, thereby cancelling out the magical number. The change could lead to Ronja's downfall, or so Tyr had explained, so she had determined a way to manipulate providence.

Why take a chance on the fairness of gods or spirits? The witch hunt that had driven her to the dark side almost a millennia ago was proof she couldn't trust in "benevolent" beings. At least with a demon she knew what she was dealing with. The soulless creatures were similar to serpents, often beguiling with their beauty then striking unexpectedly. So she did as Bastraal bid her, offering up her soul and devotion, giving him no reason to curl up and hiss.

"We need to bring the girl into our fold. She has come to Savannah of her own accord, so her connection to us has been validated. She may not have been meant to be here, but I called for the eighth sister, and here she is." Ronja moved to slide her palm down Tyr's jaw. "And for that bit of advice, I am grateful to you, my brilliant, all-knowing warrior."

"How do we proceed from here?" Scarlett asked, edging up to Ronja from behind, stroking the black witch's hips as she continued to caress Tyr.

"Find her." Ronja kissed Tyr gently on his lips and let him take her breasts in his hands. "Bring her to me." She pressed her groin into his while Scarlett's hands began lifting the gray, satin gown Ronja wore. She moaned when Scarlett kneeled and slid her hand up the inside of one thigh.

"And before she has a chance to deceive us..." Ronja reveled in the powerful blend of sex and evil, spearing her tongue into Tyr's wet, warm mouth as Scarlett's began an assault of its own. "I'll tear out her beating heart."

6

"If only there were a way to spy on Ronja," Willyn said, staring into space like she was considering breaking into Ronja's mansion to do just that. "I can't let her get to Beth. She's too young and wouldn't stand a chance against that witch." She looked around the room to the others. "No offense."

"What about it, Anna? Is there a way we could spy on Ronja?" Paige was tapping her heels on the floor, expending some extra energy. "Telepathically, I mean."

Dare considered the woman with white-blonde hair and model-good looks. She was definitely a candidate, gorgeous and packing a no-nonsense demeanor, but he had no idea what her special gift was. He didn't know that about any of them yet, and if he was going to make a match with one of Anna's witches, the nature of their magic would be a factor.

Anna looked up from where she still sat in front of the computer. "It's possible, but…"

"But it's too dangerous," Dare said, finishing for her. "It's not something you should try, Anna. Even you."

She let her shoulders slump and sighed. "You're right. I already got caught peeking once, and it felt like my brain started hemorrhaging."

"What if I helped?" Willyn asked, stepping forward with her hands out in supplication. "Or I could do it myself after some practice. Maybe it's what I'm meant to do."

Anna was already shaking her head, but it was Dare who answered. "Forget it." He swiped a dismissive hand through the air. "You've just had your first vision tonight. There's no way you can do it. Not if you want to survive. Ronja would catch you before you got through the door, so to speak. Besides, your searching through Ronja's head for something useful would be like a blind man looking for diamonds in a pile of gravel. A waste of time."

Willyn wheeled on him, pointing her finger at his chest. "I've had about enough of you and your ill-conceived, not to mention uninvited opinions. You have nothing at stake here, and I have everything to lose." She dropped her hand but inched closer to him, shaking with anger. "You may be a guest here, as I am, but this is my destiny and it doesn't concern you."

He watched as she stomped out of the room, cheeks flaming and eyes glittering with rage. Though most of that ire was directed at him, Dare couldn't stop himself from storming out after her. If any of the people in this room hoped to have a future, himself included, Glenda the good witch was going to have to man up. Or woman up. She wouldn't be of any use if she let her compassion make all the decisions.

"Willyn. Wait." He called after her again, but her only response was to pick up her pace. And that really fired up his bad side. Dare had never been one to chase after a female, most likely because he never had to. He grinned slowly. Wickedly. *You want to play games? Then try this one.* He stopped and narrowed his eyes on Willyn's back, willing her to cooperate. *Slow down, Sweetheart. That's it. Turn around.* He smiled to himself when Willyn shook her head then pivoted to face him. *Now wait there.*

Willyn frowned as she glared at him but didn't move another inch. "Did you just call me Sweetheart?" she asked, frowning and tilting her head as if questioning herself.

Dare took his time, strolling to the center of the grand hall where she stood looking upset and confused. She didn't care for directives, especially from him. Considering his treatment of her, he couldn't say he blamed her. He decided to use a different approach this time, given how livid she'd been mere seconds ago.

Willyn's weak spot practically glowed a vivid red bulls-eye, so that's exactly where he'd aim. Right in the middle of her tender heart. "Just give me a minute. I'm not the enemy."

"You sure about that?"

Her question gave him pause. Technically, they were on opposite sides, but the fates had thrown them together anyway. Willyn was an enigma, definitely not the typical witch, and he wondered why he found that more and more intriguing.

Dare put his hand to the center of his chest, to the area that throbbed with memory. With warning. Then he remembered who he was dealing with. Willyn wasn't a typical witch, and he couldn't let himself forget it. Schooling his features to look passive and his voice to sound calm, he said, "I know you're worried about saving everyone else. The coven, your son, and this girl, Beth. I also know you have absolutely no reason to trust me."

Willyn fingered the silver cross at her neck absentmindedly, probably remembering the way he'd lunged at her earlier. Her nails were long but unpainted, feminine and clean. That seemed to be her MO. Mother, savior, goody-goody. Everything about her seemed so warm…soft… Why the hell was he still looking at her hands?

Dare cleared his throat and continued. "I wanted to apologize. I was surprised by your…" he pointed to the necklace, "affiliations. Actually, if I'm being honest, I was taken aback."

"Ya' think?" she asked with a smirk. "I thought you were going for my throat this morning."

The grin caught him off guard. "Suffice it to say I've had a bad experience with some of your kind."

"My kind?" Willyn asked, losing the barely-there smile. "I'm a Christian, Dare. Not an alien. You act like we harvest organs or something."

Dare felt one eyebrow go up. "That wouldn't surprise me." He saw the quick change come over her face and knew he should back-pedal. He didn't want to be at odds with her, despite the scars left by his past experiences. Willyn wasn't to blame. Hell, most people of faith were basically good. Dare knew that, but he was used to protecting his own beliefs out of necessity. Having a church-goer as one of the nine still felt wrong to him. It hit too close to home.

"Sorry. Sorry," he said, stepping closer, holding a hand out to her. "I have a dry sense of humor at times."

"Try bitter. It's a more apt description."

Dare couldn't help smiling. She was a constant surprise. Maybe she wasn't all sugar and honey. Or maybe he just brought out her spicy side. "Since we're trying to be friends, why don't you tell me about yourself? I know you don't understand why I'm here, but I just might be able to help you. We do share the same goal. The complete annihilation of Ronja and her thugs."

Willyn eased to a nearby couch of green velvet that was remarkably in tune with the posh surroundings and Anna's collection of fine art. "In that case, I'll take all the help I can get. My pride falls very low on the totem these days, below my son, the coven, my challenge, saving the world." She tilted her lovely head. "So. How are you going to help?"

"I'm not sure, yet. Let's start with the basics. What is your gift? Your power?" Dare told himself he was only asking for the reason he'd told her. If he was interested in the information due to other motivations, what could it hurt? He'd already decided she wouldn't be the one. He needed more snap and fire, and Willyn was like a nice, slow burn. Reliable and steady, but not the kind to napalm her targets. And that was what he was looking for.

"I'm a healer."

Of course you are. "I can see that. Have you used your skill often? Harnessed it?" Dare thought it best to keep some distance between them and continued his interrogation from several feet away.

"I'm a nurse, so, yes. I've put it to a lot of use." She leaned back into the plump cushions and crossed her legs.

Dare took inventory of those legs. Not long and mean, but nicely shaped. Just enough for a man's hands to... he snapped his eyes back to her face. "The doctors never suspected anything? Surely they saw a pattern. Nurse Willyn's patients all healing faster than normal?"

She shrugged. "I spread it out and only gave a push to those who needed it most. They weren't always my patients."

"Right. What about your son? Do you heal his wounds?"

"No. As much I want to sometimes, it would be a disservice to him in the long run. He's going to get knocked around in this world, and I won't always be there. Besides." She smiled a special smile that told him she was thinking of her child. "Tadd would probably drain my powers on a daily basis. He's a bit rough-and-tumble."

Dare approved, of her good sense and the description of her son. "What about your husband? How does he feel about everything that's happening? Did he come with you to Savannah?" At her stricken look, Dare added, "I assumed you were married. Don't take this wrong, but you don't seem the type to..."

"No. Tadd was born long after our wedding, if that's what you're getting at." She still had a faraway look in her eyes. "Mason was killed two years ago in a car accident."

"I'm sorry. I didn't know." Dare had never apologized so much in his life. "You don't have to talk about it. I'm no master strategist, and Anna is the woman in the know, but I appreciate your'e telling me all this. It can't hurt to have one more person on your side."

She let the corners of her lips lift slightly. "No. It can't." After heaving a great breath, Willyn slapped her hands on her thighs. "Now your turn. Why have you come to the island? And I mean the real reason. I can tell there's more to your visit than just catching up with old friends."

Dare froze where he stood. He'd just gotten her to relax a little where he was concerned, and if he were to make full disclosure of his intentions, the door would be slammed in his face again and locked tight. "I have an interest in the coven."

"What sort of interest?"

"I'm not sure you'll understand or approve, since you're new to the craft," Dare hedged, hoping she'd give up.

"Try me." No latitude there.

"Let me put it a way you might find more familiar. Your late husband, or any man you've dated in the past, did they have certain qualities that were important to you? Hobbies, things in common, shared likes and dislikes?" Dare eased closer.

"Of course. Like most people, I wanted to spend time with those who were compatible. Who doesn't? Especially if you want a real relationship to develop. A lasting commitment has to be built on much more than initial attraction or even, as you said, things in common."

"Exactly. Core values being one of the most important pieces of the foundation."

When Willyn's eyes tightened at the corners and grew dull, Dare knew she grasped his meaning. "You're here to look us over?" The amount of scorn in her tone couldn't be measured.

Might as well jump off the cliff and see where he landed. "I'm here to find a mate, and though it may not happen with any of you, when it comes to witches, some of the most powerful are gathered here under one roof. That you all turned out to be beautiful, well that's just a side benefit." He shifted his stance, legs spread to shoulder width and arms crossed in defiance. "I won't apologize again, not for this. As I explained before, I'm only interested in those who are like me and will share my vision and aspirations."

"Are you talking about a romance or a business venture?" Willyn hopped up off the couch, jaw tensed. "I can assure you none of my sisters will be interested in such a charming proposal." She crossed her arms in a reflection of his body language. "And to put it in terms you'll be sure to understand, they all deserve better than to be judged like cattle."

"Spare me the morality lecture. College girls meet college boys, families set their daughters up with appropriate husband material, and some cultures pair the male and female when they're still infants. I know the kind of woman I want and am not afraid to say so."

Willyn gave him a look that said, Oh, really? "Then why is this the first I'm hearing of it?"

"Possibly because it's the first time you've let me get more than a sentence out before biting my head off." Without realizing it, Dare had moved in, his arms mere inches from bumping into her chest. His gaze landed on her mouth. In her hesitation to respond, her pink lips had parted slightly, and he realized he was curious about more than her magical capabilities.

Dare dragged his dark blue gaze back to hers of sky and saw the knowledge there. She was fully aware of his thoughts, her breath hitching in response. He noticed her hands tightening where she gripped her own upper arms. "Willyn..." he began.

"Hey, Mom! Look what Ms. Claire gave me!" A smaller, male version of the woman Dare wanted to kiss darted into the room. There was no mistaking the golden hair and light blue eyes. This had to be her son.

Dare took a step back, silently berating himself for his lack of control and good judgment. The excited child bearing down on them like a miniature ninja was another reason to stay clear of Willyn. No sense adding more to the mix than necessary.

"What do you have hidden behind your back, Tadd? And if it's breathing, loosen your grip." Willyn was fully recovered and in mother-mode.

"Aw, how'd you guess?" The little boy twisted his mouth in such a rueful manner that Dare couldn't stifle his low laugh. Two identical sets of eyes turned to him in response.

"Your mother may know what you've got there, but I still don't. Why don't you let me have three guesses?" Dare looked at Tadd and waited for his approval. He liked the kid already.

"Who are you?"

Smart boy. Probably intuitive, too. Now Dare was worried, because he didn't want the small one to pick up on any of the fully-adult vibes he'd just been having. Especially since they were all about the boy's mother. "My name is Darius." He kneeled now. "But my friends call me Dare."

That seemed to delight Tadd as his eyes and smile both exploded. "What? Like truth or dare?" He doubled over laughing, inadvertently revealing the mystery guest behind his back. Willyn had been right about Tadd having a live creature in his grasp. Moms could be scary that way.

What neither of them expected, though, was that the animal would be of the scaly, forked tongue variety. Willyn gasped. "A snake? Tadd, are you sure Claire gave that thing to you?"

Dare intervened when Willyn went to take the reptile from her son. "Hold on. It's just a garden snake," Dare said. "They're pretty harmless really."

Tadd nodded. "Uh-huh. That's what Ms. Claire said, too. She told me I could keep it and show it to you."

Willyn lifted her golden brows as if expecting more of the story.

Tadd sighed, knowing he was busted. "And that I should take it back outside as soon as you got to see it."

"Right answer," Willyn said, ruffling his hair. "Now you've met two new friends today." She looked over at Dare, giving him full warning that he'd better live up to the classification.

"Yeah. Mr. Snake and Mr. Dare." Tadd started giggling again. "I'm going to take him back to the woods now."

"I hope you mean the snake?" Dare teased him.

More giggles. "Yup." Tadd ran a few steps then stopped to look back at Dare. "See you later, triple-dog-dare," he said before disappearing the way he'd come in, laughter rippling in his wake.

Willyn grinned. "I guess he doesn't think you're too bad."

"Maybe I'm not." Dare gave her a meaningful look.

For the first time, she seemed unsure of herself. "Uh...I should make sure that snake gets back to where it belongs." She blushed beautifully, and Dare was oddly pleased by her flustered state.

Without another word or a backward glance, she followed her son out, once again treating Dare to a view of her backside. He stood and observed, grateful the room was so large. He hated to see her go, but liked watching her leave.

Unfortunately, he didn't get to appreciate her retreat for as long as he'd intended. A very-male throat-clearing drew his attention to the top of the stairs. Anna's brother, Quinn looked down at Dare.

And he wasn't happy.

Dare and Quinn went back a long way. As young, male witches well-versed in the prophecy and knowing they might both have a role to play in its fulfillment, the two had bonded and sworn lifelong allegiance. If either one had ever been in need, the other had always been a phone call away.

Their reliable friendship made the censure on Quinn's face even more troubling. "Uh-oh. Looks like I'm being called on the carpet," Dare said, hoping his friend would relax. When he didn't but strolled down the stairs with determined steps, Dare added, "I see we're serious."

Quinn grunted and motioned for Dare to come with him

down a dark corridor toward the back of the house and the large wooden door that would open to reveal stone steps. As boys, they'd spent many a day in the tower that, at some point, had been added on by one of Quinn's St. Germaine ancestors. It looked like they were headed there now.

Quinn evidently wanted privacy for whatever he felt the need to say, and Dare wasn't going to argue. The grand hall allowed sound, voices included, to echo up to the second floor living quarters. Dare wasn't ashamed of his intentions, but he'd rather have the opportunity to divulge them to whomever he decided might be amenable to his plan. To whichever woman he chose to approach.

Looking back on his discussion with Willyn, he wondered why he'd opened up with her, telling her everything the way he had. Well, almost everything. She was probably running to the coven now to warn them about Dare and his nefarious plot. Willyn to the rescue. For such a gentle person, she sure did put herself out there for others. Self-preservation didn't seem to be her strong point. Another mark against her. For Dare, self-protection was essential.

Quinn stopped at the door and faced Dare. "I know what you want," he said, glowering. "And I don't think I like it."

"You don't think? Does that mean you aren't sure?" Dare asked. He was getting tired of being put on the defensive. In fact, he was pretty much over it. "You know some things aren't up to us. I'm supposed to be here now, and you know it."

Quinn's left eye ticked once. Then again. "You can't be sure what you're supposed to do for the prophecy, and there's no reason to think your grand plan is part of it. You need to take a step back and re-evaluate. Let things unfold as they're meant to."

"That's what I'm doing."

Quinn moved in and met Dare head on. "That's not what you were doing with Willyn."

Fiery waves rolled over Dare and collided in his spine. He stiffened in response and took a step forward as well. "What do you have to do with it? Do have some claim on her?" He didn't care for the direction this discussion was taking. "Is there something you need to tell me, Quinn?"

For some reason, Dare's resentment made Quinn bark out a laugh. "No worries. Willyn and I aren't like that."

"Then what are you like?" Dare couldn't rein in his inner monster. Damn, he'd never felt this before. Surely he couldn't be feeling territorial. He'd just met the woman. And he had to keep reminding himself that he wasn't supposed to like her.

Quinn grew serious again. "She's a friend, and I don't want to see her get hurt. I don't want to see any of them get hurt. The girls have nothing to do with your vendetta."

Dare wanted to drive his fist into the stone wall but held himself in check. Too many mixed emotions rolling around together in his gut. He needed to stay calm. "I wouldn't use the word vendetta, and they are grown women. It's not as if they won't be able to make their own decisions."

"That's what I'm worried about," Quinn said.

Dare deflated instantly, hurt overriding the other sentiments battling for control. "You know I would never do that. I don't abuse the gifts I've been given. Never have. Never will." He shook his head. "I can't believe you would even think that."

"Sorry, man. You're like a brother, but that's why I had to lay it out for you." Quinn put his hand on Dare's shoulder. "I know you too well."

7

The preacher's breath reeked of rotten flesh and sulfur as he bent near her face. Though pale and thin, he loomed over her, and the grip on her jaw confirmed his strength. He was too strong for a man his age. Something was very wrong. The moist heat against her cheek combined with the smell made her gag. She jerked her head to the side in an effort to escape the foul breath but only provided entertainment for him and his followers. His laugh was deep and phlegmy.

God help her.

The once kind and generous group of travelers had turned into a maniacal mob, screaming and chanting for her death. But why? How? She'd done nothing to reveal herself as a witch. When she'd helped heal the young boy's illness, it had been naturally, with herbs and plain common sense. Maybe her skill with medicinal plants had given her away. Sometimes it took very little. Darting her eyes to the angry faces in the crowd, she had to believe there had been another reason.

And he was bearing down on her now. The preacher clenched his hand, digging his dirty nails into her flesh until she felt the sting of being punctured. He wanted to draw her blood. He thrived on it. Staring into his twisted expression of hate, she realized the people were only pawns in a game. His joining the band traveling west had been no accident or coincidence.

This was all about her.

With clarity and a surprising sense of peace, she accepted her fate and knew she'd done all she could. Their plan had worked, but the small detail of her being accused, convicted, and sentenced without a trial had been unexpected. The possibility had been overlooked. And the enemy underestimated.

Working her wrists to ease the chafing from the ropes that bound her, she allowed a tiny smile to play across her lips. She spoke soft and low, the words intended only for her tormentor's ears. "You'll never find it. You're too weak. Too witless, even with the assistance of a thousand tormented souls." She bared her teeth and hissed, "You will not triumph."

The preacher slammed her head against the wooden stake behind her, driving his nails deeper into her skin. The centers of his eyes yellowed, burning stronger than the torches lighting the grass and trees of the small, secret corner of the world where she would meet her end.

Foam gathered in the corners of his mouth, and the atrocious breath covered her once again as he shoved his face closer to hers. "How you die is up to you. Quick and relatively free of pain." His other hand clenched her breast, sending agonizing splinters of the very pain he mentioned streaking though her. "Or we can make it last until the sun casts its rays on your maimed and battered body.

"There are no rules when it comes to the punishment of witches. Anything can be done if I deem it necessary." A perverted leer showed her the extent of his sharpened teeth as he glanced around at the men in the crowd then centered his gaze on her. "And I do mean anything."

What was one night worth in the measurement of destiny? Her soul was pure and her heart devoted. No man or devil could ever take that from her. She didn't have the answers he sought, but even if she had, she would never let them pass her lips. There was too much at stake, and the witches of Savannah always stayed true to their word and their honor.

The slow shake of her head was all it took. Her refusal ignited the preacher's rage. He hit her hard and bit into her bare neck, mauling and ripping before pulling back to lick his lips. He shook with fury, glaring at her and snarling. She saw her own blood in the cracks of his teeth as he put his hands around her throat and shouted, "Where is the book?"

The ground started quaking beneath her feet.

"Willyn, wake up. You're having a nightmare." The world continued to shake, rattling her teeth with its persistence. "Wake up. Willyn."

Hearing her name being called, Willyn popped her eyes open. She was still disoriented from the dream but knew the tremors she felt were real. So were the hands on her shoulders and the man beside her on the bed. Dare?

The smell of the preacher's breath still lingered, as did the nagging fear that what she'd had was much more than a simple dream, but it was no longer her first concern. "What are you doing in my bed?" she asked, her voice low but intense. She sat up and jerked the white sheet up to her neck like a maiden whose tower had been breached.

Dare removed his hands but stayed seated on the edge of the mattress. "Easy. Calm down. I come in peace." His words were soothing but the look on his face was anything but. "Judging by your screams, you were having one bastard of a nightmare."

Willyn patted her face checking for blood from where the preacher's fingers had dug so cruelly, the pain lingering as it had before. Then she registered what Dare had said. "Screams?"

Her eyes darted to the door to Tadd's room, but Dare put a hand up when she shifted to get past him. "I'll check," he told her before going to crack the door open and look in on her son. He smiled as he walked back. "Sleeping hard from what I can tell. Does he always pull the sheet over his face like that?"

Willyn released a breath she hadn't realized she was holding. "Yes. He feels safer, I think." Running a hand through her hair she closed her eyes to relax but tensed up again when she felt the familiar weight settle beside her. Her lids drifted open to half-mast, a flag of caution to her late night visitor. "Since we've established that I'm okay and no longer in danger of waking the household, I don't see any reason for you to still be in my bed."

He didn't offer his typical smart-ass smile in response. "I'm not satisfied that you *are* okay." He actually edged closer. "You sounded as if you were being tortured."

Willyn scoffed. "I doubt that. It was only a nightmare." She wasn't sure why she was lying, because it had been more like a second reality. She was just thankful someone had pulled her out of it. Even if it had to be Dare. In the few days that he'd been here, nothing had helped mend the breach between them, and after their intense conversation when he'd looked like he was going to kiss her, she'd tried to keep out of his way.

"Why would you care if I'm being tortured? My guess is you'd throw me to the lions if you had the chance." The words had been flippant, but she caught the darkness that entered his gaze, if only for a fleeting moment. She saw the muscles working in his jaw as it clenched.

"Tell me about it," he said roughly. "About the nightmare. While it's still fresh."

"I'd rather forget about it. It was too horrible." Willyn looked beyond him to the balcony door and realized it was ajar. "You came in that way?" she asked. "What were you doing out there?"

He rolled his eyes. "Are you suspicious of everyone or just me? My room happens to be next door, and you were screaming like a banshee. Would you rather I'd left you to be murdered? Because that's what it sounded like."

Overcome by the memory that slapped at her and too tired to argue, Willyn fell back against her pillow. "That's because I was." She cast terrified eyes up to his. "I was being murdered."

Of all the things she might have expected, his fingers brushing gently over her temple wasn't among the list of possibilities. The warmth and unexpected softness of his touch eased her and lulled her into a sense of security. She let him stroke her hair back from her face as if she were a child who needed soothing.

When he stopped, she lay still, waiting for him to leave now that he'd helped her settle. Apparently Dare wasn't finished yet. "Now tell me."

She groaned. "Why is it so important to you? I told you it was awful. I don't want to relive it again. Twice is quite enough."

"Twice?" He stiffened beside her. "You've had the dream before?"

"I...sort of. I had the first part Saturday night. Tonight it picked up where it left off." She tried to smile. "Round two. Lucky me."

"You don't see any significance in that? Weren't you chosen Saturday night?"

Willyn turned his question over in her mind. The implications were frightening, but at the same time, if the dream had something to do with her trial, it was worth considering. Then another notion struck and her skin chilled. "I hope I don't have them throughout my trial." She clamped her eyes closed and shivered. "It was horrible. Horrible." Not to mention the very real pain that went along with it.

His hands were back, running up and down her arms, stirring something other than the serenity from before. She wouldn't necessarily say she was becoming aroused, she was still too distraught for that, but the heat flaming in her belly felt pretty darn good. Being near Dare, having his attention, his concern, and his caress, it all felt so...right.

She bolted up to a sitting position. "I...um...thank you, Dare. I just...you know....but I can't..." She cleared her throat, at a loss for an appropriate conclusion to the tower of babble she'd just built.

Up went one side of his mouth in a half-cocked grin. "Look, Willyn. I'm not going to attack you. I promise. I'm not going to try one thing that wouldn't be acceptable for any good, southern debutante."

His mocking tone cleared the fog in her brain. "Did you know that people who start their sentences with the word 'look' often do so because they feel cornered or are attempting to misdirect another party?"

Now he did smile. "Where did you learn that?"

"From one of my favorite TV series." She lifted her chin a notch. "NCIS."

Dare leaned forward. "You surprise me again, Sweetheart. I never miss that show."

"Please don't call me Sweetheart."

He pulled away as swiftly as he'd swooped in. "Fine. Now. No more avoiding. Who murdered you in the dream?"

The preacher's face exploded in front of her. She remembered his nasty fingernails, his nasty, yellowed eyes, his nasty breath, and his nasty teeth as they bit her. She was back to feeling cold and nauseated. The warmth had fled. Her emotions were all over the place, but she opened her mouth and the story spilled out. "It was a mob, led by a preacher, only he wasn't really a preacher. What I mean is he was no man of God."

She told him about the memories in her alter ego's mind. The traveling west and making friends. Then the friendships turning to hate and vengeance after the old man spread his vile lies. She had known she was a witch while in the dream, but a good woman, not a practitioner of black magic. The preacher. He had been the truly bad guy. Evil had run through his veins like sewage.

No wonder everything about him had been so nasty.

"You should talk to Anna. It's no coincidence you're having these nightmares now when you've just had your first accentuated cognitive experience. Dreams. Visions." A grimace briefly altered his handsome face. "And I really don't like how real they are for you. If I hadn't come in, you might still be suffering."

Willyn shuddered. "I don't like it either, but if it will give me a clue about what I need to do, then I'll take extra naps during the day if I have to. I'll dream as much as possible."

"We'll talk to Anna," he said firmly.

"There is no we." Willyn felt defensiveness rearing its head again. "If anyone makes a move regarding my challenge, it will be me. Don't forget, you told me your true motives for coming here. I can't expect you to act in my best interest when your mating call is obviously all that matters."

"Is that why I'm sitting here now?" Dare asked, his words clipped. "I could be lounging in my room with a good book if that's what I wanted. Or nodding off with images of other women in my head. There are those who would be a little more receptive to my talents and appreciative when someone offered help. Not to mention, less judgmental."

"You mean the kind who don't care who slides into bed with them?" She let her gaze fall to where he still sat. Close to her hip. Too close. "I'm definitely not your type, Dare. You've made that clear." She paused before adding, "And you're not mine."

The room was awash in moonlight, and Willyn couldn't see the deep blue of his eyes, but she could tell they had grown tense. The strong lines of his face were even more mysterious in the shadows of night, and his jaw was rough with stubble. Dark hair fell forward on his brow as he stared at her, saying nothing.

The scene was straight out of an old horror movie. Trees swaying in the distance, curtains flapping as a breeze found its way inside, and the moon high in the sky, casting its magical glow on the stone terrace. So the man in her bed must be the monster come to claim her blood, her life, or her soul.

She thought she heard him growl. "You've had a bad night, so I won't call you a liar," he said.

"What?"

"About your high moral standards. Because the way your eyes just gave me a head-to-toe and your breathing grew shallow, right now," he lowered his voice, "I'd say I'm exactly your type."

Willyn tried to swallow, but her throat felt like sand paper. She couldn't speak. She couldn't move. All she could do was watch him watch her, too afraid and too honest to deny his statement. Her tongue flicked out to wet her bottom lip and Dare moaned. "What's the matter?' she asked.

He put his hands on either side of her thighs and advanced slowly, his face eased closer to hers, giving her no option but to lean back with him. She grabbed onto his shoulders as instinct kicked in, and she drew the rapid, shallow breaths he'd mentioned before. They sounded more like pants to her, but she couldn't spare the brain power to feel ashamed. She was too busy looking at Dare's mouth as it lowered to hers. He had the lips of a male model, firm but just full enough. She couldn't believe what was happening. What she was about to let happen.

Finally, she exhaled and let her lids drift down. Dare's warm male breath mingled with hers. She could smell his natural scent, spicy and dark, and the warmth in her belly began to change, becoming deeper, more intense. As it began to flicker and spread, she waited...

Then she heard him curse.

He dropped her like a bag of laundry. She actually bounced when she hit the mattress. Her eyes flew open just before mortification swamped her, making her dig for the sheet to cover herself. For the first time she truly understood why Tadd slept the way he did. She longed to throw the white satin over her head and hide from the world.

Maybe Dare would just go away.

"You need to get some sleep," he said, lifting his hand to pull the sheet back and run his finger down her forehead, between her eyes. He did it again, then one more time. "You'll fall asleep and rest peacefully for the rest of the night."

Why was she letting him pet her like this? It was so odd, but she was suddenly too tired to point that out. The most-humiliating-almost-kiss in the world was practically forgotten as she fought to stay awake.

Sleep. Dare's command reverberated in the recesses of her mind. Tiny, hidden caverns of her subconscious filled with his voice. *Sleep, Willyn. Sleep.*

But he wasn't speaking. The realization was like a splinter in her brain. She forced herself to focus on Dare's face as she pushed his hand away. "What are you doing to me?" She was still groggy. He'd done something to her. Whacked her with some sort of telepathic roofie.

"I'm trying to help you get some rest. That's all." Dare reached for her again, but this time she slapped his hand.

"Don't touch me," Willyn said through clenched teeth. "Get out." She shoved her hands against his unyielding chest. "I mean it, Dare." She pushed again to emphasize her words. "Get. Out."

He stood and backed away. "Fine. I'm going, but get those filthy ideas out of your head. I wouldn't hurt you, Willyn."

She shook her head. "It's too much. Please, just leave. I need to think."

Without speaking he slipped out the balcony door, his silhouette visible through the glass panes as he silently pulled it shut until it latched.

Willyn put her head in her hands and rubbed her fingers against her scalp as if warding off a headache. What was she doing? All of this was so far out of the norm for her. And had she really almost let Dare kiss her? What would she have allowed after that? Because she had felt something waking within her. A sensation she'd thought was long gone. Dead and buried. With her husband.

A sob built in her chest, but before she had time to release it, a high-pitched scream ripped through the house and froze her body in place. Her lungs stopped functioning, and a lump of ice sat where her heart should be. But her mind raced to put the pieces together. *Tadd. That was Tadd.*

Willyn virtually flew out of the bed and barely managed to cut in front of Dare who had burst back in from the balcony. Together they dashed to the door separating Willyn's room from her son's and tossed it open. Tadd thrashed in the bed, his sheet down around his legs as they kicked and pummeled the bedding.

Willyn was beside him in a second, gently wiping her fingers over his temples, just as Dare had done to her earlier. "Tadd, honey. Wake up. You're having a dream." *Déjà vu.* She shook him gently and called his name until his light blue eyes gazed into hers.

"Mom. Mom." He sat up and wrapped his little arms around her, clinging to her and trembling.

"It's all right. Nothing but a bad dream," she murmured, stroking his back.

Tadd tossed his head back to look at her. "But it wasn't a dream. It was real. I felt the fire."

Steely cockroaches marched through Willyn's body. "There's no fire, Tadd. You're safe." She held her son tighter.

"But you're not." Tadd gulped and cried against her chest.

Willyn sensed movement and glanced up to find Dare standing over them, a look of concern on his face. Wisely, he only listened and didn't interfere.

Tadd was obviously distraught and terrified, mumbling into Willyn's side. Then he jerked back again, wide-eyed and pale. "It was all real. Not a dream." He cast a pleading look to Dare then back to Willyn. "They burned you," he said, tears building up again. "They tied you up and burned you!"

8

Afternoon was the hottest time of day in the Savannah summer. The city streets and stone buildings had baked for hours on end under the fiery ball in the sky, and now the multiple parks made sense to Willyn. Cool, green grass and shady trees served to soothe the weary downtown traveler and provide a respite from the burning rays.

She'd come to town to see Beth, having been surprised enough by the girl's call to immediately agree to the meeting. She was at the end of Forsythe Park, near the newly erected diner that looked more like an amphitheater than an eatery with its white arches on the back side. Still, it was a nice addition to the area, modern but with classic lines.

Tadd was with Claire today, probably being educated and spoiled in equal measure, but Willyn was perfectly comfortable with the arrangement. If Tadd confided in Claire about his nightmare, Willyn knew the older woman would keep it confidential. She and Tadd had a connection, and his needs would come first. Claire would also keep a good eye on him, guarding him, and that mattered most. Claire and Tadd also carried their enigma bags on their bodies at all times for extra security.

Kylie had named the charms when she and Willyn had watched Anna put them together. Mixing a few elements of a protection powder with her own version of an anti-scrying oil,

Anna had developed the amulets for Claire and her family as well as the Attingers. The people who worked and lived with Anna would become targets if the Amara could find them, so she'd been perfecting the bags for a long time. The wearer of the charm would be surrounded by a murky, impenetrable shield, should Ronja attempt to scry for them through any type of crystal ball or other medium. Whoever wore one of the charms could be assured their identity and location would remain a mystery, hence the enigma name.

There was no question when Tadd came as an added bonus to their clan, and Anna had made a bag especially for him. One more reason for Willyn to love her newfound sister.

Sitting under one of the oaks to wait for Beth, Willyn stretched her legs out over the grass and let the blades caress the back of her calves. She'd always loved the outdoors, feeling calmer and more at home with the plants and crawling bugs than anywhere else. It was probably the witch in her, she thought with a smile, then realized she was actually grateful for that. Grateful the idea of being a witch was something she could finally smile about.

It had shocked her to the core of her being when Anna had revealed the truth to her and the other members of the coven. They had always known they had powers, Lucia with her ability to find things, Kylie's manipulation of electricity, Shauni's animal speak, and Hayden's ghosts, to name a few, but none of them had understood why. None of them had known they were witches.

And Anna had been as surprised as anyone. She'd fully expected the coven to come to Savannah when the time was right, each woman with a multitude of tricks up her sleeve to defeat the Amara. She'd had no idea she would getting a bunch of novices who would need training from the ground up. Luckily, their union on the island had heightened their abilities, and even Anna was learning a few new things. So along with the

Savannah coven, an impromptu school for witches had been born.

Thank goodness for Anna, the calm in their magical storm. Teacher, confidante, and friend. She would help Willyn understand what was happening and why she was being terrorized in her dreams. Though Willyn knew it had something to do with the role she had to play, she would feel better getting Anna's take on things.

Anna had been gone since morning, so Willyn had been unable to seek her advice about the nightmare. Not wanting to worry the other women, Willyn had avoided them by cloistering herself in her room and reading, or at least doing her best to focus on the book hanging limply in her hands.

She'd also refused to speak with Dare when he'd come knocking at her door. She couldn't see him yet, not after last night. Instead, she'd essentially forced herself to stew all day in the memories of what had happened between them, just like the city had baked in the sun. Maybe she was a glutton for punishment, but she needed to keep her head clear and was obviously unable to do so around Dare. She pressed her lips together and mentally scolded herself again, unable to comprehend her reaction to a man she could barely tolerate.

He was actually here for a Wiccan version of The Bachelor. How could she not be repulsed? The better question was why she hadn't resisted him. Why hadn't she tossed him out of her room before he'd had a chance to worm his way closer? Well, she determined with a thump of her hand on the ground, he wouldn't be getting another chance, with her or any of them for that matter. So. Not. Happening.

To get her mind off of Dare, she leaned back with a sigh, feeling the roughness of the bark through her shirt as she watched people walk by. Savannah was a very old city with a very modern mix of citizenry. A couple with a blue baby-stroller passed, the woman cooing to the little one inside while the man talked on his phone. Close behind was a businessman pulling a suitcase on rollers and wearing a brown beret to top off his outfit. Willyn had always loved to people-watch, but Forsythe Square was proving to be a source of never-ending entertainment.

Next came two young women with their dogs. Every other person seemed to have a dog. Then a group of art students from the local college strolled by, serious and somber in their discussion. Willyn was beginning to recognize them from their clothing. They wore a uniform of anti-conformity that actually made them all look alike. Willyn raised a brow at the pink and green striped tights while still appreciating the young girl's bravery. Willyn had never made a bold fashion statement in her life, a fact Claudia and Kylie both seemed intent on changing.

She stilled and lifted her head to listen, swearing her name had carried on the breeze.

"Willyn!"

She heard it that time for sure and stood to look around. Beth stood waving her arms on the sidewalk across the street from the park. When she made eye contact with Willyn, she motioned for her to come over.

Willyn looked both ways and ran across. "Hey. I thought we might grab a snack at the cafe," she said, stepping up on the curb.

Beth shook her head. "I asked you here for another reason. There's something I want to show you." She cocked her head, indicating a huge building behind her. It was clearly abandoned and in a state of disrepair. The dilapidated structure was in stark contrast to the full, happy-looking palm trees on the street corner.

"You want to go in there?" Willyn asked, her voice sounding full of shock, even to her own ears.

Beth wrinkled her nose and shrugged. "Not inside. Exactly." Before Willyn could question her further, Beth danced away.

"Come on. It's a historical site. You'll love it. See," she said, pointing to the historical marker out front. "It's official and everything."

"Okay," Willyn said, dragging out the word. "But that doesn't tell me why we're here."

"Where's your adventurous side?" Beth asked with a mischievous grin.

"I don't think I was born with one of those." Willyn watched as Beth bounded up the curved steps on the front side of the building. The staircase was ornate in design, with posts aged to a lovely shade of lime green that meant they were probably copper. Many of the windows were broken, and attempts had been made to board them up. Plenty of holes were left for the curious eye. Round columns were on the entry-level porch and supported a balcony above, reminiscent of plantation homes.

Walking over to the marker, Willyn recited the large words across the top. "Warren A. Candler Hospital." She read the rest in silence, impressed to be standing outside of Georgia's very first hospital. She scanned a bit more of the history before Beth called out to her.

"There's not much to see. They're renovating, but it still smells old and musty, even from out here." Beth smacked her hands together to wipe them off. "Let's go around back. That's the real gold mine."

Instead of pressing for more, Willyn simply let her pass by before falling into step behind her. A couple of tourists gawked at them as they headed through the empty parking lot, like they were something interesting. At least Beth seemed excited about whatever they were here to see. It was a great improvement over the morose mood she'd been in on Sunday.

When she got a good look at the tree around back, Willyn stopped and gaped. "That is amazing! Look how big it is!" Diverting from Beth's intended direction, she crunched over pine-bark mulch to the colossal oak. Some of the large limbs had grown up then curved back down toward the earth, and the moss hanging from a few of them almost touched the ground. She couldn't begin to guess how thick the trunk was, maybe five feet or more at its widest point. She stopped at the sign in the corner of the tree's designated area.

"It says the circumference is sixteen feet," Willyn murmured. "Well, there you go. And it's estimated to be two hundred and seventy years old." She smiled at Beth. "Can you imagine what this tree has seen?"

"That's part of why I brought you here." Beth's face took on a strange excitement, a little wild. Devious. "If walls and trees could talk, right?" She walked over to pat the trunk. "Did you know that in Norse runes the symbol for the letters TH is associated with the oak tree? Also with the god Thor."

"You've studied runes?" Willyn asked.

Shrugging, Beth stepped away from the hulking base and put her hands on her hips. "I'm interested in different things. Whatever intrigues me or holds my attention." She looked at Willyn. "Ready?"

"For what? This isn't what we came for?"

Beth hiked her brows. "Oh, no. The tree is cool, but the rest is better. I'll let you be the judge. Follow me."

Willyn wondered about the mention of ancient runes and the quick change in conversation. Maybe the tree had sparked a stray thought in Beth's mind, but somehow Willyn felt the girl was better versed in the subject than she'd let on. The back of her neck tingled and ran cool, even as the late afternoon sun warmed the rest of her skin.

Beth came to a standstill by a rusty, white fence with spikes along the top to keep out intruders. Only the gate was without the sharp deterrents, but even that entryway held a warning, a sign that clearly stated *NO TRESPASSING* in neon orange. Beth was already hauling herself over.

"What are you doing?" Willyn asked in a hoarse whisper.

Beth whispered back, mocking her. "I think we'll be seen before we'll be heard."

Willyn cleared her throat. "Either way, we could get into real trouble. As in the arrested kind. That sign is there for a reason." The smell of dust and mold seemed stronger suddenly, and Willyn was compelled to move away from the building. The tree had radiated a natural, relaxing vibe. The back of the old hospital did not.

"They only put that sign up because so many people have been going down there. No one will notice us." Beth eased down the brick walk and seemed to be shrinking.

Moving closer, Willyn saw she was going down a slight decline that ended at two wooden doors of new construction. A padlock held the doors together, but a good foot and half of empty space remained at the top, just enough room for a person to slip in. She grunted a denial. "No way, Beth. I'm not going in there."

"Hmph," Beth said, crossing her arms over her chest. "I really wanted to do this with you, but if you're too scared I'll go by myself. I haven't been in before, but I read about it online." She scuffed the toe of her sneaker against the bricks and bowed her head. "I thought it would be fun to explore the city since we're both new here."

Willyn wasn't sure what to make of Beth's behavior. There was a hint of mischief about her today, and Willyn was surprised by the change. She was still young, maybe not even twenty, yet, and a little off-the-beaten-track-fun was to be expected. Willyn didn't want to bring Beth down again by denying her first request. And she definitely didn't want her going through those doors alone.

After Shauni's challenge, Anna had had a vision that presented the coven with a riddle. They had been charged with finding someone who was lost. If Beth turned out to be the lost one they were looking for, Willyn was obligated to learn more about her.

Ignoring the whispers of caution in the air, which might very well be from the unseen spirits Hayden always talked about, Willyn jumped over the fence in one agile motion and rushed to join Beth at the bottom of the slope, hoping no one saw her. She really didn't want to get caught.

"What's in there?" she asked, peering over the wood panels. "It looks like a basement of some kind." Beth pulled two thin, metallic tubes from her back pocket one pink one turquoise. When she handed one over, Willyn saw they were flashlights. "You're serious about this."

Beth flashed her sparkling blue eyes to the doors then back to Willyn. "This is one of the openings to Savannah's tunnels."

"I didn't know there were any."

"A lot of people don't. Even when the passages were built, the city tried to keep them a secret," Beth said, her excitement almost palpable.

"Why?" Willyn asked, feeling the chill on her nape again.

Beth hoisted herself up by the cement above the doors and slid her feet in first. Twisting so her stomach rested on the wood, she grinned. "I'll tell you the rest inside." Letting herself slide in, Beth disappeared into the tunnel. A moment later, her flashlight lit the walls, white cement stained green and brown with moss, time, and who knew what else.

Willyn glanced behind her and the building. In the sky a black crow and a buzzard circled each other then flew off in opposite directions, the buzzard went over the tree and toward the park. She wondered if she shouldn't follow their lead and get out of this place. She didn't have Hayden's gift for communicating with spirits, but she bet there were plenty hanging around the old Candler hospital.

"You coming?" Beth asked from inside.

Willyn's answer was to pull herself up and push herself through with the same method Beth had used. Since she was obviously going to do this foolish thing, she might as well get it over with. "Okay," she said after landing on her feet and immediately firing up her flashlight to hold in front of her like a tiny sword. "What's the rest of the story?"

Beth jerked her head and started creeping farther into the underground network, leaving Willyn no real choice but to go along if she wanted to hear more. Surprisingly, she did.

"I'm drawn to these tunnels, could hardly stay away once I felt the pull." Beth stopped to let Willyn catch up. The ground was dirty, dark, and covered with debris, so progress was slow. "The same way I was drawn to Savannah. I came here for a reason, but I don't know what it is." She turned suddenly. "But you already knew that didn't you?"

Willyn caught a glimpse of suspicion in Beth's eyes, though they were shadowed from the flashlight held at her waist. "No. I'm not really sure of anything, but in church you looked lost and afraid. I wanted to help."

"There's something else going on, isn't there?"

Willyn wasn't sure what to say or how to phrase it without jumping straight into prophecies, demons, and magic, and she didn't want to drive Beth away. "Why do you say that?" she hedged, hoping the girl would open the door for her. Maybe she was more aware of the strange goings-on in the city than she was letting on.

"Like I said. I wanted to find this place because it called to me. Sometimes I get strange feelings." With a pivot that scraped against the trash-covered floor, Beth whirled away and headed deeper into the tunnel.

"Don't go too far in," Willyn said firmly. "I don't want to get lost down here." As much as she wanted to help Beth, she had Tadd to think about and didn't want to end up a missing person for several hours. Or days. Her coven would go mad with worry.

"Did you know there were three separate outbreaks of

yellow fever here in the eighteen hundreds?" Beth continued her slow trek through the silent passage. She apparently didn't mind the smell of refuse and rot, mildew mixed with aged dirt. And something else. Willyn's antennae were tingling. This place was empty and quiet yet filled with a foreboding quality that triggered every warning mechanism her body possessed. It didn't smell like death, exactly, but it reeked of depravity.

Okay, now I'm getting carried away, but being underground when I can barely find my way around in the sunlight is simply foolish. "I'm not going any farther," Willyn said, coming to a halt. "I'm sorry, Beth, but you'll have to tell me the rest now. This isn't a good idea." She kicked her shoe at something then shined her light down to see what it was. "Right. There are syringes on the ground, and they aren't the safety-cap kind. I'm going up, and you should come with me. We don't need to meet up with anyone who hangs out down here."

"Fine." Beth practically pouted. "Just a few minutes first, okay?"

Willyn nodded, hoping to move things along faster.

Beth's face gleamed as she started speaking again, like a kid telling campfire, ghost stories. "The first time the fever hit, it killed over six-hundred people, and those who ran the city did their best to hide how many were dying."

"Why would they do that?" Willyn asked, intrigued, despite her better judgment.

"Why do people in power ever do any of the things they do? They wanted to put a good face on things. Seem like they had it all under control." Beth glanced around as if afraid they'd be overheard. "I'm not sure when the tunnels were first built, some say during the Civil War, and there are other underground systems that were used by pirates to kidnap people and force them on their ships, but that's another story. Anyway, the third time the yellow fever broke out in Savannah, it was really bad. Too many dead bodies to know what to do with." Beth held her breath, letting the anticipation build.

Willyn hated to ask, but she did. "So what did they do with them? The bodies?"

"*Lots* of things, if the stories are to be believed. They used the tunnels to sneak them out of the hospital, some out to the woods to be buried or burned while others were kept down here for secret autopsies."

"Down here?" Willyn felt her voice squeak with the question. Beth only nodded.

"That's the stuff of nightmares, and I don't need any extra incentive in that department." Willyn folded herself into her arms, guarding against the subterranean chill.

"You've been having nightmares?" Beth frowned. "Does it happen a lot?"

"Only recently," Willyn said, glancing around, hoping they were done with the day's excursion. She looked back to see Beth staring at her, face expressionless and eyes blank. "Hey. Are you okay?"

Beth shook herself and crooked her neck to the side until it popped. "Yeah. Sure. I don't have nightmares. If one starts, I just shut it down."

"Neat trick. Think you can teach me?" Willyn smiled grimly

"I don't think so, and you're right. If you're one to have bad dreams, we shouldn't be here."

The younger girl's entire demeanor had changed, and Willyn didn't know why.

"I don't want to be responsible for giving you...well, we should just go," Beth said in a flat tone. "We are neck-deep in our own version of monster-filled catacombs."

Willyn was curious about Beth's odd behavior but decided she would much rather finish the conversation somewhere brighter. And safer. "Since you put it that way, I'm heading for daylight." She turned to go back toward the exit. Luckily, they hadn't made any turns, so she assumed she'd be able to stay straight and make her way to the light. Unless she felt like trusting the directions of whoever had marked arrows on the wall with black paint and left a religious calling card with graffiti declaring "Satin Rules."

She decided to trust her own directional sense.

After a few cautious steps, Willyn stopped. She thought she'd heard something. Beth shuffled up behind her, so Willyn motioned for her to be still. "Listen. Did you hear that?"

"Hear what?" Beth whispered.

"Voices." They both stood still as stone, eyes and ears focused on the tunnel stretching into blackness before them. They'd come farther than Willyn had realized, the absence of light telling her they were deep inside. They listened as time seemed to come to a standstill, and the cool air grew stagnant and thick. Willyn felt herself easing back into the tunnel, more concerned about whomever was coming in behind them than anything they might encounter in the bowels of Savannah's hidden crypts.

Willyn blinked, sure she was seeing things. A deep, red glow was crawling along the base of the tunnel, an unnatural iridescence that covered the floor and climbed slowly up the walls, spreading until it lit the space. When it grew close enough to drown out Willyn's flashlight, she stumbled backwards, bumping into Beth's chest. "Go. Go," she said, her voice tight with urgency.

"Go where?" Beth asked, her eyes wide now with fear more than excitement.

"Deeper in, if we have to, but we have to move! Now!" Willyn knew her raised voice would carry in the stone chamber, but giving away their location was no longer an issue. She had a feeling she knew who was coming. And they were coming after them.

They ran recklessly through the tunnels, weaving left or right on a whim when a turn came up. There was no time to decide which direction would lead them out, the ruby-colored light was tracking them, advancing on them with its strange sparkle. It would have been beautiful if it weren't emanating pure evil. Willyn was afraid it might actually grab onto them if it got close enough. The illumination seemed to have taken on a life of its own, though she knew there was someone controlling it. And that person wasn't far behind.

They ran until Willyn's side stitched and her thighs cramped. She tried not to look back. If she fell or lost any of her lead, they would have her. The Amara. It had to be. Who else could master something as insidious as that bloody ooze?

"There! I see light," Beth yelled, darting toward the blessed rays of sun falling across a slab of cement. It looked like one great step they would have to climb to reach ground-level.

Willyn scrambled along after her, stumbling over loose rocks and crumbled cement until her ankle screamed with pain. She cried out as it twisted but kept going. The oddest thought popped into her head. She knew Kerri Strug would keep running, especially if the fate of the world were at stake.

Beth leaped up on the block and waited, her arm out for Willyn to grab. "Hurry! It's close!"

With a final push from her uninjured leg, Willyn heaved herself up with Beth's help and immediately gained her feet again. She could see grass and hear traffic. They were almost there, and an uneven set of steps led up to what had to be the city streets or a park.

Together she and Beth ran up the stairs and collapsed onto the grass as soon as they broke the surface. Willyn crab-walked backward as Beth stood, both of them staring intently at the hole they'd just escaped, waiting for the red light to burst from the depths behind them.

They waited, their own labored breaths louder than the cars roaring nearby. Birds twittered around them and people carried on with their day. Nothing else came out of the tunnel.

"What are you doing?" a small voice asked, bringing Willyn's attention to the child peeking out at them from behind a tall, metal fence.

Willyn took in her surroundings and the tourists milling about with pamphlets. Through the fence she could see stone markers. When she realized they were safe but saw where they were, she fell back onto the grass, groaning and laughing at once. "That's just typical of you, Beth."

The girl bent over with hands on her knees, still panting from their exertion. "What do you mean?"

Willyn lifted one hand to point then let it flop back down on her belly. "You led us right into a cemetery."

9

Someone was working a spell. As soon as Willyn entered the foyer, the scent of lemon, peppermint, and a heavier smell she couldn't quite identify floated over her. She knew she was late for the lesson but had called Anna en route to the island to let her know she was running behind, but that was all she'd told her.

Moving across the slate floor on silent feet, Willyn dreaded the multi-female interrogation squad she was about to face. She'd already healed her ankle but would still have to fill the coven in on every detail of what had transpired in the tunnels. With life or death on the line, there were no secrets small enough to keep.

Beth had cut and run almost as soon as Willyn had been able to stand. Though Willyn had attempted to talk to her, to warn her she might be in danger, Beth had only shaken her head and backed away, saying, "I don't know what this is. I wasn't expecting this." Cryptic words from a peculiar young woman. The more Willyn tried to get to know her, the more confused she became.

Willyn followed the stream of aromatic air until she found the others in what had come to be their usual state. Barely controlled chaos. Well, at least she would be able to spill her worries to her trusted friends all at once, and nine heads were better than one.

"You're putting too much. Wait. Teaspoon, she said a teaspoon." Viv, with her smart glasses on, was valiantly trying to impose the importance of precision on an unwilling and stubborn Kylie.

"She also said to follow your instinct," Kylie argued, "and my gut is telling me it needs more mugwort." Pulling her lower lip between her teeth and concentrating, she continued to sprinkle a powder into a bowl before stopping suddenly to proclaim, "There. Perfect."

The witches were all gathered in what should have been the formal dining room. After realizing her new friends had zero training in herbs, oils, or potions, Anna had re-arranged the large room, bringing in long tables and equipment to transform it into an expensively decorated chemistry lab. The women could each appreciate an authentic Monet on the side wall and other priceless treasures as they tried not to combust anything unless called for.

No one had set fire to themselves. Lately. But Anna kept an extinguisher handy just in case.

"If we're going to partner up, I think I should at least work with someone of a like mind," Viv said, blowing her angled, black bangs off her forehead in frustration. "Claudia and I are a match."

"Thanks a lot," Kylie muttered, tossing Viv a glare.

"Learning to appreciate other styles will only enhance your own," Anna said in her typical way, wise and a little mysterious.

"At least Kylie wants to participate," Hayden told Viv. "It's all I can do to get Paige to read the instructions to me."

Paige held up her hands. "Hey. I know my strengths and it's not this."

"Which is why you need practice," Hayden said, tossing her caramel-colored hair back before squinting at the book lying between them on the table. "You forgot the yarrow."

"What's cooking?" Willyn asked, wincing at her own bad

joke.

"There's my partner," Lucia said, her accent laying a little heavy on the *rrr*. "We're trying our luck with a few psychic enhancement spells in honor of our new clairvoyant."

When Lucia wiggled her brows, Willyn put a hand to her chest. "Oh. You mean me?"

"Who else?"

Willyn looked to Anna. "It may only be temporary. I'd hate to waste everyone's time."

Their lovely teacher sat on a table at the front of the room, swinging her legs. "Nonsense. We all have a bit of the oracle in us, and you never know when a third eye will come in handy."

"That's true," Claudia said, looking up from the bowl she shared with Shauni. "Plenty of people have untapped cognitive extrasensory skills."

Kylie cocked a well-toned hip. "Right. Now say that again, but not in Claudia-speak," she said, bringing a smile to all their faces.

"How about this? Maybe if I hit you hard enough on the head, it will release your psychic potential." The red-haired witch lifted a pestle and mimed a knocking motion toward Kylie, her grin belying the threat.

Willyn wished she could join in the playful antics, but she had too much trouble to share. And she'd only been the chosen for three days. How much more could go wrong? "We were attacked by the Amara today," she blurted, bringing the action and laughing to a dead halt.

"Are you okay?" Shauni rushed over and gave her a quick head-to-toe. "Are you hurt?" The two women had bonded early on, each with the odd handicap of being too compassionate. It was only an issue when they were forced to fight or kill someone. Darn morals even rose up when dealing with the bad guys. Shauni had conquered her fears, though, fighting with her animal friends to rescue the man she loved. That had been part of her lesson.

Willyn had no idea what would be required of her during her trial, but she kept circling around to Beth. Maybe she was meant to save her? Keep her out of Ronja's hands and whatever evil scheme the black witch was concocting. If that was the case, she was doing a bang-up job so far. Thank goodness Beth could run so fast.

"I'm fine. I twisted my ankle but..." Willyn didn't get the chance to finish before multiple hands were steering her toward a chair.

"Get off that ankle," Hayden said. "Um, which one was it?'

"I'll get some ice." Kylie darted out the door.

Shauni pulled up another seat. "You're a nurse. You know to elevate it."

Willyn huffed. "I'm also a healer." She frowned at the lot of them, though she knew they were only trying to help. Everyone always protected her the most, even Kylie who was the youngest. Sweet little Willyn. Poor defenseless Willyn. She was evidently going to have to start proving herself. "I said I'm fine." The gruff response had several sets of eyes widening and a few looking to each other in surprise.

"I get it," Paige said with a wry grin. "Willyn, heal thyself."

The muscles Willyn had clenched in annoyance began to relax. If anyone would understand the need to stand up for themselves, it would be Paige. "It's a little sore, but even that should clear up by tonight. I hate to waste my gift on myself, but I did need to walk." She released the last remnants of irritation and settled into the chair with a long, exhaled breath. "I never saw their faces, but I'm sure it was them. The magic stunk of Ronja's crew."

"What magic?" Kylie asked, dropping the bag of ice on a nearby table when Shauni shook her head, letting her know it wasn't needed.

"Start from the beginning," Anna said, moving closer. "You

went to meet Beth again. What did she want?"

"That's the strange part. Well, *one* of the strange parts. This whole day has been a trip down the rabbit hole." Willyn held her hand out for the ibuprofen and glass of water that Kylie had also brought back with her. "I assumed she wanted to meet in the park for a walk or late lunch, but she took me into some tunnels under the city and told me some history-laced ghost stories."

"The ones under the hospital," Anna stated, clearly familiar with the passages. "They've seen their fair share of death and clandestine activity. I don't understand why she wanted to go there when the city has plenty of other sites to see."

"I'm still not sure either, but I had just started to make my way out when I heard voices. None I could identify, but at least one female." Willyn shivered but continued. "All of the sudden there was a red glow. It looked like a light at first, but the way it moved was unnatural. The edges started coming closer but not uniformly like a flashlight would do. It seemed to crawl along the cement as if it were alive. Oh, and it glittered."

"A glittery blob?" Viv asked.

"Pretty much, but flat against the walls, floor, and even the ceiling. Needless to say, we ran, and I have no doubt the light would have done something to us if it had caught us." Willyn swallowed the pills and chased them with the water, allowing the cool liquid to wash away the acrid taste of fear climbing up her throat with the memory.

"That's strong magic," Anna said. "And after meeting Ronja's group, I would have to narrow the creator of that light down to a few possibilities. Ronja herself, though I don't see her deigning to enter a dirty tunnel."

"Me, either," Shauni agreed. She had first-hand knowledge of the immortal witch who'd tried to take her out of the picture. Ronja had hoped to kill Shauni and stop the coven on their first try. They all knew the coven and the Amara would go head to head in a classic good-versus-evil, but no one could be sure how it would come out in the end. That part wasn't spelled out in the prophecy. The witches were running on a mix of faith, hope, and devotion. Loyalty to each other and life as they knew it.

Anna nodded and continued. "I don't think Sylvie could pull that much power from her bag of tricks. She's stronger than the average hoodoo but is limited. That leaves the brunette we saw with the rest of them at the Amara plantation, who I'm still not familiar with. Then there's Scarlett." She made a face. "Who, unfortunately, I am."

"How did they know Willyn was down there? Do you think they followed her?" Hayden's face was loaded with worry.

Willyn was almost hesitant to say what she was about to. "I'm not sure they came for me."

Anna's cobalt blue eyes narrowed. "You think they followed Beth."

"Yes. I'm sure they want her. I was just a lucky benefit."

Hayden started playing with her hair. "Why would they want Beth? Does she have any powers? Is she important somehow?"

Willyn felt as if she was somehow betraying the young girl by voicing her doubts, but the Amara were definitely stalking her. Willyn had known Beth was different the first time she saw her, and even if it made sense for Ronja's goons to have actually been after Willyn today, she just didn't think that was the case. "Something is going on with her. She said some things today that didn't make sense, about being called to Savannah."

Shauni gasped. "Like all of us were."

"She's part of the prophecy, isn't she?" Viv asked. The rest of the group all started talking at once.

Anna held up her hand, a silver ring with sapphires glinting under the light as she waved for quiet. "If Willyn believes Beth is important, she probably is, but we can't make any assumptions about why she's here."

"Or if she can be trusted," Paige said, crossing her arms. "I hate to say it, Willyn, but from what little you've said, I'm not getting a good feeling about this girl."

"How can you say that? You don't even know her." Willyn sat up straighter, ready to defend Beth as well as her own judgment of character. "I can tell you she's scared and confused. That's enough for me." Her mouth worked before she found the words she wanted. "And what if I have to help her? What if it's part of my challenge?"

"To spend time with a person who has an obvious penchant for gruesome things?" Paige asked. "Something about that isn't clicking."

"I agree with Paige," Kylie said, wincing when Willyn looked at her. "Sorry, Wil, but hearing the things you told us about her gives me the creeps."

"What things? I barely have any information on her."

"Exactly." Kylie moved closer, holding Willyn's gaze with hazel eyes that were much wiser than they should have been at her age. "The tiny bit we know about her is almost all morbid. She took you into tunnels that have a dark history, according to Anna." She looked to Anna then for confirmation.

"They do," Anna confirmed. "They were used to transport bodies of yellow fever victims and plenty of other things over the years. Things that were better off hidden from prying eyes." She sent an apologetic look to Willyn. "And even you said the way she talked about working with cancer patients was unsettling. That she seemed to lack compassion."

"Yeah she does," Paige jumped in again. "Because she's only there to watch the suffering." The leggy blonde slapped her fist into her palm as if just making the connection. "If the Amara want her, it's probably as a recruit. Reason enough to stay away from her."

Willyn stood. "Reason enough to protect her. She has no idea what's going on. I'm sure of that. She even said what happened today wasn't what she expected." Willyn stopped, thinking what she'd just said sounded more like a negative than a mark in Beth's favor.

"So Beth knows she was pulled to Savannah for something extraordinary, but she hasn't shared it with you." Paige hiked one pale eyebrow, waiting.

"She might have been about to tell me, but we were interrupted by the incredible glowing blob." Willyn heard the strain in her voice and evidently so did they. Claudia moved to one side while Shauni flanked her on the other.

Anna sighed and rolled her eyes to the ceiling. "Let's all take it down a notch, and Willyn, unless that ankle's all better, why don't you sit back down. I know you'll want to appear perfectly normal for Tadd."

If the head witch had been playing emotional horseshoes, the comment would have been a ringer. "Low blow. But you're right." Willyn sat back down.

"Now, tell me everything else Beth said that you thought was odd." Anna was back to being head witch in charge. Steady, firm, but gentle.

"Um, that brings me to another issue I was going discuss with you." Willyn squirmed under the steady gazes of her coven. "I mentioned to Beth about the tunnels and their past being good fodder for nightmares, and that I didn't need any more in that department. She said she never had problems with bad dreams, and from the weird way she acted, I felt like she was being evasive. She seemed to want to share more with me but was uncertain."

"That's not terribly disconcerting," Claudia said.

"If you'd been there, you'd understand. The way she reacted to my having nightmares, she looked almost..." Willyn faded into silence.

"Almost what?" Anna prodded.

"Guilty," Willyn said, with a huge lump forming in her chest. "I'm sure I'm wrong, but surprise flashed across her face before she tried too hard to come across as uninterested." She laughed, but there was no mirth in the sound. "I probably imagined it."

"You haven't been imagining the nightmares. *Pesadillas*," Lucia said with a shudder. She'd been silent throughout most of the discourse but was very involved now. "Dreams can be portals, you know, from the spirit world and more. You need protection. With your new visions and strange nightmares, you could be exposed to whatever wants in."

Willyn turned to Anna, hoping for comfort. The pursed lips and darkened eyes told her none would be forthcoming. "Lucia's right," Anna said, "We need to take precautions. If Ronja senses your vulnerability, she'll go straight for it. I'm not sure I want you sleeping alone until you're strong enough to defend yourself there."

Willyn didn't mention her nighttime guest and certainly wasn't about to suggest Dare continue to be her bedtime chaperone. Maybe some secrets could be kept after all. "Defend myself where? In my dreams?"

Anna had walked to the front table and was flipping through the pages of a book. She stopped to meet Willyn's eyes. The grave intensity there was petrifying. "Absolutely. Don't forget who we are, Willyn. Or who we're dealing with."

Willyn's heart jolted as the reality of Anna and Lucia's warnings sunk in. Then she thought about Tadd. "Oh my God. Anna, I'll do what you say, but first, we have to make sure they can't hurt my son." She suddenly felt faint and clenched onto the chair's arm rests. "He had the same dream."

10

Willyn was taking a break in the solarium, comforted and solaced by the plants in all their splendor. Strolling around the walkways and losing herself in the enormous room was fast becoming an addiction. It was quiet here, filled only with greenery, sweet-smelling blooms, the sun from above, and her silent musings.

It had been two days since she'd filled everyone in on her extracurricular nighttime activities, and multiple precautions had been taken to protect her while she slept. Anna had given her a special "psychic bodyguard" pillow stuffed with regular filling along with dried mugwort, some St. John's wort, and a small piece of real silver. She had also helped her make special bath oils and lotions for peaceful dreams. Willyn had heard of fragrance layering before, but now she was taking the practice to heart.

In addition to Anna's suggestions, Willyn had entered her bedroom that evening to find her bedposts with new decor. Strands of red coral had been wrapped around each. The women had denied any knowledge of the beads, but Anna confirmed the stones were often used to ward off nightmares and spiritual threats.

The only other person who could have put the beads in her room was Dare. The bright, reddish-orange coral was a gorgeous addition to the creams and whites of her own conservative decorating style. It was as if Dare had left what he could of himself, since Willyn had physically banned him from her private space.

She'd spent countless minutes staring up at the glistening, moonlit strands, contemplating the man who supposedly despised her and her "kind" yet seemed bound and determined to keep her from harm. The warm, cheerful coral was a strange substitute for the cold, hard man.

But no. He hadn't been cold at all. She remembered the small space between them when he'd sat next to her on the bed. Energy waves had sizzled and cracked between her hip and his thigh, pulling and pulsing, needing a connection.

She really had to stop thinking about it. She hadn't seen Dare since that night, but he'd occupied her mind ever since. Nothing good would come of an unhealthy infatuation with a man who was so thoroughly wrong for her. She had to keep reminding herself he was trouble.

"Earth to Willyn." Shauni was standing next to her, leaning forward to catch her gaze. She laughed when Willyn focused on her. "Glad you're back with us. I've called your name a few times. Your presence is requested in the storage room. Correction. Our presence."

"The storage room?"

"You know. The doors at the far end of the breakfast area that are never open. Evidently they lead into a storage room, and Anna and Paige want to discuss something there." Shauni bent to sniff a violet flower. "If we stay true to form, I expect we'll discover an inter-dimensional doorway or something equally boring."

Willyn smiled. "Little green...no, little pink men."

"Now you've got it." Shauni put her hands in her cargo shorts. "See you in a few." She left the way she'd come, giving Willyn a chance to round up her thoughts. Or eradicate those thoughts as they would only lead her straight into a problem she didn't need. Dare was trouble incarnate.

Willyn pulled on her resolve like a coat of armor and wound her way back through the interior jungle. She made it out into the hallway, the soles of her shoes making a light scuffing noise on the stone floor, when someone stepped out a door in front of her. The last person she needed to meet in a darkened corridor.

Judging by the look on his face, Dare had intercepted her on purpose. "We need to talk," he said, closing the door he'd come out of. He stepped toward her, in front of her, blocking her path. Had his voice always held the quality of warm, melted toffee? Rich, luxurious, and able to make her mouth water? Willyn firmed her lips and sidestepped to go around him.

He moved to block her. "No you don't. You can't avoid me forever, and you're wasting your much-needed energy by doing so." His hand shot out to grasp her forearm. "We need to talk."

"Why? So you can plant a few more subconscious suggestions in my head?" She shook her arm loose. "That was the worst sort of invasion. I thought you were trying to help me, but instead you took advantage of the situation and my weak moment."

Dare hiked up one dark brow. "Don't kid yourself, Willyn. You were never weak."

Though issued as a challenge, his words rolled through her and fired an inner pride she never knew was inside her, lying in wait for a little stroking and praise. People had told her to "be strong" after losing her husband, but the directives had always been accompanied by a pat on the shoulder or sympathetic smile. It had always seemed as if no one really expected her to make it on her own.

Now here Dare was, practically calling her out for claiming vulnerability. Instead of finding it offensive, she actually felt appreciative. Grateful.

Oh, yeah. She really needed to keep some distance between herself and Darius Forster. Had she thought he was trouble? More like quicksand. Very attractive and alluring quicksand.

"I have to meet the others." Bowing her head, she tried to skirt around him again. "We can talk later."

Dare moved to intercept her again, but this time he used both hands and clutched her wrists, using his grip to gently drag her closer. "Okay." He leaned in to whisper near her ear. "Then we won't talk."

Before Willyn could process his intent or voice any objection, Dare brushed the side of his stubble-rough cheek across hers then swiftly captured her mouth in a soft but unyielding kiss. His hands slipped down to hold her fingers delicately, stroking the sensitive flesh on the underside. The easy brush of his skin on hers and the subtle sensuality of the kiss made her burn in the way she'd always been warned about. The way every good girl had been warned about.

She collapsed against him a little but managed to stay on her feet. He felt and smelled so good, like a dark secret promising something special. Something forbidden. Part of her balked at letting Dare take such liberties, but that part of her wasn't in control at the moment. The sheer fascination of him and the emotions he stirred held her in a trance.

Her mind fogged over until a stray warning flashed behind the back of her closed eyes. A trance? What was she doing? Willyn summoned her will and wrenched away from him, the broken contact leaving a void that was painfully cold. Her head and vision cleared as mistrust rushed to the forefront. "Did you make me do that?" she asked breathlessly. "Dare," she accused, "did you get inside my head?"

~

Dare had been enjoying the lingering sweetness of Willyn's soft lips when her words jarred him out of his fantasy. The suspicion and distress on her face told him how little she trusted him. And why should she? He'd been utterly transparent about both his dislike of her religion and his desire for a mating with one of the coven. Tack on the slip he'd made the other night in her bedroom when he'd tried to force her to sleep, and he was weighing pretty heavily in the negative column.

He didn't know where the urge to kiss her had come from, just that the sight of her after two days without had driven him instantly mad with hunger. He'd never gone for nice girls. Why was she proving to be such a temptation?

"Answer me," Willyn said, staring at him like a wounded animal. "Did you force me?"

As if caught in a landslide, Dare fell backward through time, to another place and another person who'd charged him with the same crime.

"Did you force her?" His father swayed on his feet, the brown bottle in his hand foretelling of trouble. The stench of cheap beer practically burned Dare's nose. It was the smell of home and of pain. Things were bad enough in the Forster household when everyone was sober. The fact his father was boozing it up on a Friday night worried Dare, but what the big man was saying terrified him.

"Speak up, boy." His father dragged out the first word so it was ssspeak. Evidence that at least a six-pack had gone down. This was going to be ugly. "I asked you a quessstion. Did you force her?"

Dare didn't need to ask what he meant. The only question in his head was how his parents had found out so quickly. Damn it. He hoped Sarah was okay.

"The preacher's daughter?" His mother was there now, having come from the kitchen with a wooden spoon in her hand. Maybe the kitchen utensil was as bad as it would get. Hopefully his father was well past a mean drunk and teetering on the pass-out-in-the-recliner phase.

Dare hated coming back to the two-story house on the edge of town. The pale yellow paint and neatly trimmed shrubbery were all part of a facade. The happy, all-American home. Except, as far as he knew, Ward had never taken Beaver out back with braided telephone wire. Braided. What kind of man took the time to create his own version of a whip?

"You played your little mind games on her dincha' boy?" his father asked, moving closer to Dare. His mouth worked and twisted with the rage he wanted to let loose. "The devil's had control of you long enough. It's time we got rid of 'im for good."

Dare withered inside. It wouldn't be the first time his father had tried to chase the demons out. His devout parents believed the only possible reason their son could plant ideas in other people's heads was the presence of pure evil.

Dare looked over his father's shoulder to the Lord's prayer written in script, hanging on the wall in a cheap wooden frame. If only his parents truly understood the words.

The unmistakable sound of the creaking back door drew Dare's attention to the kitchen. His mother looked over her shoulder then stepped out of the way. Dare's blood chilled and beads of sweat broke out on the back of his neck. Two of his father's buddies marched past his mother, retribution in their eyes and anticipation in their grins.

"Sarah is a good girl," his mother said as she clenched the spoon and shook at him. She wouldn't intervene for her only child.

"The only way you got her in the back of your cheap car was with that devil's trick of yours. Now the preacher and his wife know all about you two and your cavortin'." His father started unbuttoning his shirt, revealing the sleeveless wife-beater beneath. This was going to be worse than ugly. Dare thought about running.

"I told him I'd handle it once and for all." His father took two long strides to Dare and grabbed his upper arm. "And I mean to do just that." He nodded to the other two men and all hell broke loose.

Too late, Dare realized how much trouble he was in, but the burly men were all over him. They pulled him through the kitchen, over the linoleum where he'd banged pots and pans as a baby. They dragged him down the stairs where his mother had put the stinking, burning, Campho-phenique on his scraped knees more times than he could count. They held him down under the tree his father always said would be perfect for a tree house. One he never got around to building.

Dare thought again of Sarah. She was a good girl like his mother said and had made Dare wait longer than any of the other girls in town had made their boyfriends wait. She was a shy girl who loved children and sang in the church choir. His parents had been all for the two of them dating. They'd hoped she would make him a better Christian.

Instead, he and Sarah had taken each other's virginity in the back of his beat up truck. On a blanket under the stars. They loved each other as much as any seventeen-year-old kids could, but that didn't matter to his parents. Nothing mattered now except trying one more time to alter the nature of their worst disappointment. Their son.

Who had the devil's gift.

A fire was burning out back. Dare hadn't noticed it before. His father's movement caught his eye as the man took drunken steps toward the pit before stirring the embers there with a stick.

Then his father put another stick in the fire. "I've done my best with what I been given," he told the popping, orange glow. "That's the God's honest truth. Words and whippins ain't done it, so I figure the power of Jesus Christ is what it will take." He pulled the stick back out of the fire, but the end burned red like...

No. Please, no. Dare had all but forgotten the two men holding him down while he'd watched his father, but his struggle renewed with vigor when he understood what was coming. The thugs only dug their fingers in deeper and pressed him into the dirt.

Dare's lungs couldn't draw a full breath. His heart beat like a rabbit's. His throat wouldn't work, but even if it did, his mother wouldn't answer his cries. She was as fanatical as his father. They all talked a good talk, but they walked in an entirely different direction.

Yet they called him Satan's son.

Dare's father took heavy, slow steps in his direction. His face was blank. No emotion flickered there. Not even hate. The total lack of empathy destroyed the last bit of love Dare had for the people who had brought him into the world. But it was far too late to do him any good. He'd lost his last chance to get away from the salvation they were determined to force on him.

Smoke whirled up from the iron and into the darkness of the tree-lined back yard as his father brought it over. Now Dare could see the shape at the end, burning bright and throbbing with searing heat. It was a cross. His father held it to the side as he leaned down and ripped the front of Dare's shirt open. Then he stood, spreading his feet as if he needed to be steady. "You will walk with the mark of Christ on display, so the devil will never be able to enter your body again."

As the homemade brand descended, Dare shed a final tear for the parents who had deserted him. One of the men slapped a hand over his mouth just before the heated cross hit home.

No one in the nice, safe neighborhood ever heard him scream.

Dare jerked his head up to find Willyn's pale blue eyes staring at him with concern. He was clutching at his chest where the scar remained. After a few deep breaths his panic ebbed and he could feel Willyn's hand over his.

"Are you having chest pain?" she asked, transformed from affronted female to efficient nurse in response to his distress. "Dare. Tell me where it hurts."

"It's nothing." His voice was raspy, so he cleared his throat. "I'm not in pain. I was remembering something that's all." He lowered his hand and slipped it out of her soft fingers.

"What memory could affect you physically, because I don't care what you say, you were feeling something."

"The mind can be a powerful thing." He noticed the cross she was never without hanging above her amulet, and it pissed him off. He was unsteady at the moment and knew he was wrong to take it out on Willyn, but seeing the symbol that, for him, translated into cruelty and hate...hell, it just rode all over him. "I'm not your patient, and I don't need false concern." He all but growled at her and regretted it instantly when she flinched and stepped back.

"Aren't we a pair?" she asked. She combed trembling fingers through her hair. "Neither of us can decide if we hate the other or not."

Truer words couldn't have been said. Dare felt a pinpoint of relief to hear she was having the same problem he was. "I guess it's not ideal to try and get to know someone in the middle of a three hundred-year-old prophecy that's finally coming true." He almost rubbed his chest again but stopped mid-motion. He would prefer the spunky Willyn over the nurturing one just now. "But to answer your question, no, I wasn't in your head at all. I told you I wouldn't do it again, and if nothing else, I do keep my word."

Her posture relaxed. "I believe you, and I'm sorry I triggered a bad memory for you."

The woman was too damn astute. "You didn't. Don't worry."

"But as soon as I..."

Dare cupped her cheek. "I said you didn't." He had every intention of taking one more taste of her before she ran away, but she jerked back. She must have seen it in his expression. Too bad. But if she knew the full extent of what he really wanted to do to her, she'd have already bolted, leaving a trail of dust in her wake.

She stumbled away, coming up against the wall behind her

and the tapestry hanging there. A long table was on one side of her, and Dare shot his arm out to plant his hand against the tapestry on the other. She was good and trapped.

"Willyn," he leaned forward but held the length of his body in check. He wanted only their mouths touching, so maybe he wouldn't scare his quarry too badly. "Hold still and let me kiss you." He kept his voice low and soothing, fighting to keep the raw desire coursing through him at bay. "You asked me if I was in pain."

She stood frozen, lids lowered as if lulled or seduced. He hoped it was the latter. She licked her pink lips. "Yes."

"I'll feel much better as soon as we..." Dare cut himself off. A bright flash drew his notice to the tapestry.

"What is it?" Willyn asked, alert once again, the spell broken by his apparent distraction. She lifted herself off the wall and turned to look at whatever he was seeing. "Was it a spider?" She cringed, telling him what she thought of the eight-legged crawlers.

"Maybe I'm seeing things, but I thought I saw the tapestry light up. Like a small streak of lightning." He ran his hand across the rich colors. "Here."

Willyn reached out to do the same. As soon as she made contact, a slight blue spark slithered across a portion of the fabric then died out. She gasped. "I saw it."

"Let's lift our hands off then put them back at the same time," Dare instructed. As soon as their palms landed, another streak sputtered to life then disappeared, like a battery trying to charge.

"We need to get the others," Willyn said. "This can't be normal. Even for this house."

He nodded. "I'll walk with you."

"Okay."

They started down the hall and had taken a couple of steps when Willyn reached out and grabbed his arm. "But one thing first." She shifted nervously from one foot to the other. "After what's happened between us, even if we don't know what to do with it. I'd appreciate it if you didn't do the same to my sisters. It would be...disrespectful."

He nodded. "Of course." A thrill ran through him.

With a quick smile of acknowledgement, she turned and headed toward the grand hall. He followed silently as she hurried to find the other women. There were more pressing matters to be dealt with, like St. Elmo's tapestry, so he wouldn't say anything to her yet.

But as far as Dare was concerned, he was no longer interested in her sisters.

11

"The Tree of Life," Anna said as she examined the wall-hanging. The background of the tapestry was twilight blue and littered with tiny stars that beckoned. The tree itself was a deeper tone, its indigo trunk thick and blended with the ground. Branches spread out to cover the scene, glistening here and there with what appeared to be a mystical dust.

Willyn imagined fairies had decorated the wise old tree. There was no rhyme or reason to the flowers growing on its limbs. Different shapes and colors suggested multiple varieties shooting off independently. A falcon rested in one bough with smaller birds throughout. Other animals grazed in the distance. Willyn took in the symbolism and felt it was a beautiful representation of the earth's inhabitants and the bonds that connected them all.

"The tapestry has hung on this wall for decades," Anna continued. "I believe the rendering was done by one of my ancestors, but that's all I know." She frowned and looked at Willyn. "That seems remiss of me, but to be honest, there are more antiques and heirlooms here than I can keep up with. We have an inventory list of everything, but I don't remember this particular piece."

"Neither do I." Quinn spoke up from the back of the crowd. They were all gathered in the wide hallway to study the tapestry and investigate it more thoroughly. "That seems pretty strange to me. Neither of us is familiar with it. It's been here my entire life, but in a way, it's as if I'm seeing it for the first time."

Anna and her brother looked at other with chagrin and voiced their suspicion at the same time. "Ronja."

Dare was standing next to Willyn. In fact, he hadn't left her side since their unexpected little interlude. Willyn felt the warmth emanating from him like he was a radiator. The pull she felt to this man was startling in its intensity. Could that have attributed to her wariness of him? He edged even closer when the black witch's name was mentioned. "You think Ronja performed some sort of cloaking spell and kept you from noticing this particular tapestry?" he asked.

Anna shrugged. "It's only a guess at this point, but Quinn's right. It was shrouded in something magical. If Ronja was responsible, the entire house needs a good cleansing. I just don't know how I could have missed it, and Quinn, and our parents. The St. Germaine line goes back to the beginning, to the three original witches and their prophecy. How could something this important have been lost over time and not passed down?"

"You think it's part of the prophecy then?" Willyn asked.

"I have no doubt," Anna said.

Hayden eased forward, her amber eyes soft and knowing. "I sense remnants of a spirit here. Perhaps it's the source of energy, I'm not sure." She let her head fall back, opening herself up to the knowledge that swirled around the aged fabric, unseen to the naked eye. "My mistake," she said as her head popped back up. "The imprints of three spirits are imbued in this work. Three very strong people left a piece of their will behind."

"And I'm sure we can guess who they were," Kylie said before shifting a look to Claudia. "But why guess? Why don't we have the historian take a look?" She waved her arms like a game show hostess and mimed the commercial that always made her laugh. "Look here with your special eyes."

Claudia chuckled, as did a few of the others. Kylie could always be counted on for comic relief, and considering the tension and curiosity surrounding the group, Willyn was grateful. Claudia looked at Anna who nodded her agreement.

All of the witches had a gift they could call their own, and Claudia wasn't a history professor by chance. She'd always had an inside track when it came to accurate historical data. When she touched something, she saw where it had been, what had gone on around it, and who had been there. She described it as channel surfing. Sometimes she got a show from last week and sometimes from four centuries ago. It depended on how old the object was and what it wanted or needed to tell her.

She tossed her vibrant red hair over her shoulder and moved to stand before the tapestry. Closing her eyes, she reached out and let her fingers graze the woven threads. The moment she touched it, she got her answer. "Oh, yes. I can see them. Three women who have just completed an extraordinary task." She pressed her eyes closed tighter. "But now they're making preparations for those who will come later."

"That's us," Kylie whispered, only to be shushed by Viv.

"There will be great danger. What they face will be tenfold." Claudia stepped back suddenly and let her hand drop. She appeared shaken. "They fear for us," she said. "That's why they prepared backups. Different ways to get us the information we need." She turned to face all of them. "Something is in the tapestry. They used spells and enchanted tools to create the scene."

"How do we get it out?" Lucia asked, placing her hands on her well-shaped hips.

"Willyn," Anna said, clasping her hands together, "what exactly happened before when you saw the light?"

Willyn searched desperately for a way to explain without mentioning the fact she and Dare had almost made out on the ancient heirloom that also happened to hold a crucial piece of intel. "I was leaning against the wall and the tapestry. When Dare put his hand on it, he saw something." She ignored the multiple sets of brows that shot up. Even a barebones description made it clear something intimate had been going on. She felt her face flame. "Anyway, we decided to test it. It only happens if we both touch it."

"When two witches touch it," Quinn added, making an observation.

"Right," Dare said. "But whatever magic is in there wasn't meant for me, so we only got a misfire." He took Willyn's fingers then dropped them as quickly, giving her encouragement without making a spectacle.

The man was proving to be quite a contradiction. First he was a pit bull going for the throat of Christianity and all it stood for. Next he came to the aid of her and Tadd when nightmares were chasing them. Now he was actually showing concern for her feelings? Maybe her challenge was simply to figure out Dare, because he was confusing her more at every turn.

"Let's see what happens when Willyn and another of the coven give it a try," Quinn said.

Since Claudia was still standing close, she and Willyn met eyes and reached out as one. The lower right corner lit up with streaks that sputtered and died.

"It looks like heat lightning," Paige said, her mouth open in awe.

"Excellent," Kylie added.

"It's obvious we all need to get involved," Viv pointed out in her scientist voice. "If it was truly meant for the coven, then it will probably take the power of the nine to fire it up completely." She handed the notepad she held to Dare. "Here. You might need this."

He smirked. "You think we should take notes?"

"You never know," she said before leaning closer to whisper, "Loverboy." With a wink for Willyn, Viv moved to find a spot between Hayden and Lucia. The coven was forming a semi-circle to accommodate the large number of people crowded into the corridor.

Anna was on one end of the curved line and gestured to Willyn to take the other. "This is your time, Little Mother. Your hand should close the connection." She gave a smile of encouragement to Willyn and all the others. "Ready? Is everyone holding hands?"

"Why don't we all just touch it at the same time?" Paige protested. The joining of hands was evidently too kumbaya for her.

"This is more ceremonial," Shauni said, taking Paige's hand and kissing it for extra yuck-factor. She laughed at her friend's reaction.

Paige looked as if she'd been slimed. "Can we get on with it then?"

Anna caught Willyn's eye and raised her hand. Willyn mimed her motion and together they laid palms against each end of the tapestry. The fibers woke up like a circuit board that had received a jolt. The power of nine was the juice it had been waiting for.

"Wow," Kylie said, eyes wide with wonder.

"You said it," Claudia agreed.

Willyn and Anna smiled again at each other. There was a suspicious glisten in the head witch's eyes. Anna sniffed lightly. "I am constantly amazed by what we find and what we can do when we're all together."

"It's gorgeous," Willyn said, a surge of pride rushing through her at the power and connection she felt. She was unified with her coven. They were all different but the same, much like the life forms signified by the tree.

Another sniffle brought everyone's attention to Paige who blinked rapidly and said, "Shut up all of you. Not one word." Shauni remained silent as requested but laid her head on

Paige's shoulder briefly, acknowledging the emotional moment.

"While I'm as stupefied as the rest of you, I'm also noticing a problem." Viv was focused on the tapestry, head tilted to the side. "What is that language, and does anyone know how to read it?"

Willyn squinted, trying to make sense of the markings. There were curves and right angles, some with lines through them. It definitely looked like writing. "I have no idea, so I hope you do, Anna."

Anna shook her head. "I recognize it, but it doesn't matter that I can't read it. We happen to have a magical language specialist among us." She looked over to the two men standing behind the line of women. Dare had given the note pad to Quinn, and Anna's brother was writing furiously. "I'll have the translation done in a sec. I just want to get it all down first, in case you guys blow a fuse or something."

"Huh," Kylie scoffed. "We could run like this for days. Right, girls?" She started humming and jumbling some words together. Willyn didn't recognize the tune until Kylie belted out the chorus. *"Yes, I've paid the price, but look how much I gained. If I have to, I can do anything. I am strong…"*

Claudia was bobbing her head and fell in with the backup. *"Strong,"* she sang in a clear voice.

"I am invincible." Kylie again.

"Invincible," echoed Claudia and a few others. They were all getting in on the act now, swaying and grinning from ear to ear. Nine strong voices sang the last together, the sound bouncing off the walls and into the main house. *"I am womaaaaaaaaaaaaaaaaaaaaan."*

Dare and Quinn exchanged an aggrieved look, but wisely kept their thoughts to themselves. Quinn simply shook his head and continued to copy the script as all the women fell into laughter.

"If we fail at being witches, maybe we can go on the road."

Hayden was still bouncing her hips from side to side.

"No," Lucia said, the denial thick with Spanish influence. "I get stage fright."

Hayden rolled her eyes. "I doubt you have a shy bone in your body."

Their teasing was interrupted by Quinn who held up the pad. "Would you all like to know what it says, or are we going to be treated to another rendition?"

"Don't encourage them," Dare muttered, crossing his arms over his chest.

"Are you sure you got everything?" Anna asked.

Quinn looked insulted. "I'm sure."

Willyn and Anna removed their hands and the hallway dimmed, telling them just how much wattage they'd generated into the tapestry. A collective groan accompanied the blackout. It had been a high, that sizzle and tingle of their united abilities.

"The message was written in the Alphabet of the Magi," Quinn told them. "I can't imagine what it took to create this. We had some mighty strong forebears," he said to Anna.

"They did send a demon back to hell," Paige said. She scrunched up her face. "But why hide it this way? What if we'd never found it?"

"That's what I intend to figure out," Anna stated firmly before striding over to stand by Quinn where she tried to get a peek at the paper he held.

He slapped it against his chest. "Patience. I'll read it to all of you at once."

Anna huffed in a way that made Willyn smile. Even wise and powerful white mages could be tormented by their little brothers.

"You want it now, or should we go somewhere more..."

"Now," Kylie said, taking a threatening step toward Quinn. The two of them were almost always at odds.

"Fine." Quinn held up the pad and read what he'd written.

"By those powered three times three, must the following be found. The Tree of Life relies on the nine, the book, the blade, the burial ground."

Shauni slumped. "The burial ground again. That I never found." More than once she'd brought up the subject. Animals had passed the secret on to Shauni from the spirit world when it had been her turn to be tested. She still felt like she'd missed something,

"It doesn't matter, Shauni. You passed, so that means you did what you were meant to." Anna pinned the raven-haired witch with a look. "Stop beating yourself up. You went first. The bravery required for that was more than enough."

Willyn swallowed as her throat ran dry. "Now I have to make sure I don't drop the egg." When she saw the puzzled faces, she added, "You know, that game with the spoons and...never mind. I'm not good with similes or analogies or whatever." She was getting flustered at the thought of letting them all down. "I can't fail. That's all."

Forcing herself to concentrate, Willyn went over the message in her head. Then she thought about the nightmare. Luckily, she hadn't dreamed at all since they'd made the protective items, but now she wondered if that was a good thing. "I think I'm supposed to find the book," she said.

"Why?" Paige asked as she leaned back against the opposite wall. "Why that specifically?"

"Didn't I mention that part?" Willyn asked. The women rotated their heads in the negative. "I must have been too upset. I know I told you about the preacher and the fire. I was so concerned for Tadd after what you said about dreams being actual portals, I guess I forgot." She glanced at Dare, feeling guilty that she'd purposely avoided him. If she'd let him in on the discussion with the coven, he might have helped her remember details she'd forgotten.

"When the preacher leaned in closer, he asked me...or her...

where the book was." Willyn watched as surprise, confirmation, and other reactions formed on the faces of her friends. "Now we know it exists, or that it did exist, and according to that," she gestured to the wall-hanging, "it's something we need if we're going defeat the Amara or maybe the demon itself." She hated saying the awful name out loud. *Bastraal.* It made her feel filthy. "I'll let myself dream tonight. I might get more information."

"No. That's not an option." The harsh refusal from Dare shocked Willyn as well as Kylie and Hayden, judging by their bug eyes. Claudia, Shauni, and Viv just smiled slyly. They fully understood why he was over-reacting.

This is crazy. This is crazy. I have to get back in control. Willyn wasn't sure she liked everyone thinking there was something going on between her and Dare. And she definitely didn't appreciate their approval, for heaven's sake. They were supposed to be her friends.

She reminded herself that they didn't know the real reason Dare had come to the island. If they'd known he was here to play The Dating Game, those grins would turn to dangerous glares. They wouldn't let him near her and would launch into protective mode. As usual. Willyn wasn't sure she wanted that to happen either. Not because she hated being coddled, but because she didn't want anyone trying to keep her away from Dare. She shook herself. *This is crazy. This is crazy.*

"One of us can be with you," Lucia said to Willyn. "I can spend the night in your room and give the alarm if it looks like you are dreaming."

Anna held up her hands in an obvious eureka moment. "I have a better idea. We can all be there, and Willyn can have the vision in a safer place."

"Um. No offense, Anna, but I don't think you'll all fit in my bed," Willyn said skeptically.

Anna laughed. "I'm talking about a different method that

should get us the same results."

"I know where you're headed with this." Dare rubbed his chin as if considering what he suspected. His deep-sea eyes fell on Willyn, causing entirely too much heat to blossom in her belly. "I want to be there," he said.

Anna looked at him thoughtfully. "I think you should be." Then she glided over to Willyn and took both of her hands. "If you trust us, I'll make the preparations."

Willyn nodded. "I'd like a drink of water first."

"Absolutely," Anna replied. "Quinn," she called over her shoulder, "can you start gathering the essentials?"

"Sure." He nudged Lucia and Hayden and motioned for them to go with him.

Let's go get that drink." Anna squeezed Willyn's hands. "But before we go, do you have any questions? Are you sure about this?" She cocked her head and gave Willyn a meaningful stare. "Are you ready to go back in and face the monster?"

12

Candles and torches illuminated the great room, the heart of the home and the coven's most sacred place. The core of their power. If Anna wanted to perform the dream visitation here, then the head witch was more worried than she was willing to tell anyone. Especially Willyn.

Stone walls encircled the massive room, creating a dome. Above was a pentagram of wooden beams, a symbol of many things, but for the coven it represented unity, beauty, and enduring strength. Willyn considered the five-pointed star. She'd never known the difference between the two words used to describe it, having only seen them in horror movies. She now knew a pentagram was simply the star without a circle around it and a pentacle was enclosed by one. No hidden evil there, simply another misunderstanding thanks to a history that vilified practitioners of the craft.

She realized there may have been a time when she had been one to misjudge, but she'd never acted on hate or fear. Now that she'd been introduced to the existence of magic, how could she do anything but embrace it as part of the world in which she lived? The world created by a god she had spent her life devoted to? A god she still worshipped, despite the new dimensions of "normalcy" she'd encountered.

There are some who would call her a sinner or believed she had been deceived, but Willyn knew love and charity when she felt it. The coven was the embodiment of loyalty and compassion, and Willyn had chosen to trust her own heart over the judgment of strangers.

That's why she was here now, literally placing her life in their hands. Anna had sworn she would keep Willyn from harm, and her word was more valuable than the sum total of the St. Germaine estate's net worth. Willyn imagined that number was a whopper.

In the center of the room was what appeared to be a... recliner? It had been draped in a pale blue sheet of satin. The color was an aid for finding the truth, and that's why she was risking a trip to the horrid world of her nightmare. She needed the truth. She needed the book. And there was no doubt in her mind that the answers lay waiting in her dream.

Three shoulder-high candle sticks were positioned around the chair, and each held a candle. One red, one black, and one indigo. The necessary mixture of hues to repel any psychic attack that might come her way while she was under. The very idea of being mentally assaulted made her skin twinge as if trying to escape from where her body was taking it. No such luck. She was going back in and taking her flesh with her. The better for the preacher to rip and tear.

She halted mid-step as a gut-wrenching blast of nausea hit.

"You okay?" the female whisper came from Willyn's left. She smelled the scent of freshly-cut green apples and knew Shauni was there. "I will be," Willyn replied. "Just had a bad moment. Let's get this thing done."

She took the seat of honor in the lovely light blue recliner. The bizarre notion of Archie Bunker and his magical chair made her burst out laughing. Nerves still lingered, though, so the sound was a bit strained and unsettling. She waved away concerned looks from the others. "Inside joke. I'll share my lunacy with you later."

"We'll be right here the whole time." Dare silently appeared at her side and gave her one of his wolfish grins. "Don't think I'm done with you yet." He slid away into the shadows when Anna came and sat on a stool beside Willyn.

With her long, sable hair pulled back in a braid, Anna was the picture of a fairy-tale princess, if you ignored the faded jeans and periwinkle peasant blouse. The consternation set hard into her features told Willyn this wasn't going to be a pep talk. "I want you to know everything before we begin." She focused her blue eyes on Willyn. "I've added a few extra layers of warding to our circle tonight. More than I would have normally."

"Why?" Willyn asked, dread crawling up her throat.

Anna sighed. "I believe you have a mare attached to you." She grinned when Willyn only stared at her. "Not the kind of mare you're thinking of." She motioned for the other women to come closer so all of them could hear. "I started thinking the other day when you told us about the bad dreams you'd been having. The repetition and timing were odd, but not as disturbing as the final bit you told us near the end."

Willyn stiffened her shoulders in full expectation of what Anna meant.

"Tadd's having the identical nightmare at the same time was a red flag I would have been stupid to ignore or explain away. Only someone with a specific ability for subconscious influence could control two minds simultaneously." Anna pursed her lips as if considering her next statement. "Even if she didn't realize she was doing it."

"She," Willyn echoed. "You think you know who the mare is. One of the Amara?" Wiggling in her seat, she frowned at Anna. "You still haven't told us exactly what a mare is. I get that it has to do with dreams, but I've never heard of it."

"Sure you have," Quinn interjected. "It's why we call them night*mares*."

"Many forms of the word have been around for a very long time. The pre-Indo-European word was *mer*, meant to rub out or to harm. The most common lore contends the mare is usually female and rides around on a horse." Anna lifted a shoulder. "I don't know about all that, but I know they do exist, and rarely do they come equipped with much of a conscience."

The hesitancy Willyn had detected in Anna and the easy tone she used finally registered. "You think the mare attached to me is Beth."

Anna was sympathetic. "I do. Like I said, she might not be intentionally affecting you and Tadd, but she apparently spends a great deal of time thinking about you. Her power is focused on you and inadvertently on Tadd."

"What should I do? Stay away from her? I want to help her. She's so young, but I can't expose Tadd to more danger than I already have." Willyn lifted a fingernail to her mouth and began to nibble, a nasty, old habit kicking back in. She was supremely stressed out.

"All you have to do is relax and go get the information you need." Anna patted Willyn's knee. "I'll help you figure out the situation with Beth. I don't want her getting into trouble any more than you do. Just remember the big picture. All of us will have to make difficult choices before this is over, and there are many, many lives at stake."

She was right. If the Amara had their way and the demon was unleashed, tragedy would fall across the town of Savannah and all its inhabitants. And that would only be the monster's appetizer. Willyn had to stay her course.

Anna sat back and nodded. "Ready?"

Willyn managed to relax again and breathe out the word, "Yes," before looking around as the coven, Quinn, and Dare all moved in more tightly. For a moment she was frightened. All their faces were distorted by flame and shadow, but the touch of Anna's hand eased her back down to reality. "I'm ready."

Anna dropped her arm and pulled the lever to lower the upper part of the chair. Willyn let her eyes close and released herself from the anxiety that had plagued her since she'd entered the room. Now was the time for action. For bravery.

It was her time.

Anna's smooth voice floated into the void. She spoke of doors that were barred to evil and called for planes to open for the traveler. Words of protection and peace were the last Willyn heard before she felt herself begin to drift. Soon she was flying through blurred colors, sounds, and textures. She realized this must be what happened when a fully awake person transported to the land of dreams. It was both marvelous and terrible.

Her trip through the wormhole was nothing compared to the landing. It felt like she'd run hard into a brick wall, and the smell of smoke burning her nostrils confirmed that she'd arrived. Her one stop ticket to hell was in effect, and as soon as her vision cleared, she saw the preacher. In all his gruesome glory.

His hands were around her neck and spittle was flying as he yelled into her face. The breath, oh the breath, it was back again, too. "Where's the book?" he demanded, tightening his grip to threaten and terrorize then releasing again to allow a tantalizing bit of cool air to rush into her lungs. He knew if he wanted answers, his victim needed to breathe.

"I can't say anything. I won't say anything. It will endanger them all." Willyn felt the words inside her mind as if they were her own, yet the voice was distinctly foreign, more genteel with a touch of the Old South. She and the woman who owned this body were one. *"The book is safe. I left it with the others and packed a decoy to bring along on my trip. We'd hoped the evil would take the bait."* The voice paused. *"But none of us knew it would come to this."*

Her death. That's what the woman meant. She had never expected the preacher to hold such sway over the travelers, enough so they would stand by and watch as an innocent woman was tortured and murdered. Willyn had to act fast. Or think fast. She wasn't sure how this worked, so she took a leap of faith and thought the words. If the woman was in here with her, she would understand.

"Please tell me. I am a member of the prophesied coven. I am one of the nine. I have to find the book." Willyn waited for an answer. None came, and she feared it might not be so simple. The preacher shook her then. Shook *them* and leaned closer. He licked their cheek with a foul, rotting touch. It felt bumpy and Willyn imagined maggots as the source. *"God help me. Help us."*

"If you don't tell me where it is, I'll be forced to return to Savannah," the preacher whispered. "I believe you've left someone behind. An enchanting little version of yourself. Maybe she can tell me what I want to hear." He laughed low and lecherously. "I have a sweet tooth for pretty young things." Behind him the crowd raised their torches and screamed for blood.

"No. No." The woman's voice was in Willyn's head again. *"Not my Hally. My daughter."* Willyn ached along with the woman at the thought of harm coming to her child.

"She has the book. She has a plan to hide it. She and my sisters will hide it where he cannot go." The preacher moved to the side. *"After the fire!"* the woman's inner voice rose in a crescendo as pain swarmed through her left side. Willyn felt it too, but not as fully as the woman. The coven was protecting Willyn from the physical effects, but nothing could save her from the horror she was experiencing.

The preacher had not gotten his answer. He had moved away, ending his interrogation and with it, the woman's life. The crowd had her now. She was still tied and unable to defend herself, and the mob planned to take full advantage. As the pitchfork in her side retracted and plunged again, the woman screamed.

And so did Willyn.

The smoke was worse now, bringing with it a stench she didn't recognize. She darted her eyes around, looking for the source, and saw her skirt changing from beige linen to a smoldering yellow and orange, black at the edges as it moved. She was on fire. They were burning the witch.

"Please stop! She's innocent! She's innocent!" Willyn cried out to the poor woman's executioners, but to no avail. She could feel the beginning of separation and flight. She was being pulled back. The dying woman's last thought went with Willyn. It repeated in her brain the same way it had in the anguished mother who feared for her daughter.

Willyn woke screaming it over and over.

"Hally! Hally!" She shook and jumped as hands fell on her from all sides. She was hot and wet. Sweating. The journey to the nightmare had taken more of a toll on her body than she'd realized. Maybe that's why the coven had brought her out. She panted, desperate to relieve the scorching heat. She'd come away with remnants of the dreams before, and this time it had been the hot, licking flames chasing her back to the real world.

Anna chanted something and a white swirl rose between them. It veered toward Willyn and settled onto her skin, tiny crystals healing and soothing. She took a long, deep breath and let the balm wash over her. Through her.

"Hally," Willyn said, calmer now, eased by the gentle auras of her sisters and the tranquility of the sacred, great room. "We have to protect Hally. She's here in Savannah." She drew a few more deep breaths and shook her head to clear it. "No. that's not right. She *was* here in Savannah. Long ago. I don't know when, but she was a descendent of the witches. I'm sure of it."

The sense of being shot with a tiny arrow entered Willyn. The back of her head tingled. "Hally Daigle. That was her name. The daughter." She knew the last bit of information had been thrown through time and multiple dimensions. From the dying woman. Straight to Willyn. Why did she want her to know?

Dare kneeled beside the recliner. He didn't say anything, but his nearness was reassurance enough. Willyn would worry about that later. She was still too fuzzy to wonder why Dare put her at ease simply by being there. Anna and the others looked on in silence, allowing her a chance to sort it all out.

Willyn suddenly felt foolish. "Never mind. I must be mixing up my own history with what I gained from the dream. I used to dabble in genealogy," she explained. She put her hands to her cheeks but her palms were too warm, so she let them fall into her lap. "Hally Daigle was my great, great, great grandmother, or somewhere in there. I remember because it made me think of Halle Berry." She offered them a sheepish smile then coughed. "I did bring back something useful, though. I think."

Anna was looking at her strangely. "I'm sure you did, and we can discuss it all once you've recovered."

"I feel great." Willyn coughed again. She still smelled and tasted smoke. Smoke and charred flesh.

"You're not quite yourself yet," Anna said. Her eyes were still somewhere far away as she studied Willyn, making her wonder if she'd come back from the dream intact.

"Why are you staring at me like that?" Willyn asked, the hairs on her arms prickling.

There was a pregnant pause. "Hally Daigle is listed in our records as well," Anna said, lifting one side of her mouth in a wry smile. "She was a descendent of the original three that banished Bastraal."

Willyn's head started spinning. "What are you saying?"

Anna laughed and stuck out her hand. "It's nice to meet you." Now her eyes sparkled with mischief and pleasure. "Cousin."

13

Willyn was as pale as the white satin sheets on her bed. Dare frowned. Bed sheets? Now why was that the first comparison he could think of? Better not to look too closely at the wanderings of his dirty mind or why they always headed straight for R-rated territory. With a neon sign of warning flashing in his subconscious, he paused to inspect his theory. And found it lacking. He didn't think fondly of Willyn's bed because of what *might* happen there.

It was simply the first place he'd ever touched her.

Cut it out Forster. She's important because of her fate and the fact she has to help save the world. Nothing more. Stop putting a romantic spin on it. Dare's internal discussion halted abruptly when he saw Willyn stagger. She didn't need any more excitement tonight. What she needed was rest and nourishment. *And I'm only worried about her because it's her turn to pass the cosmic test. Yeah. Right.*

Channeling his irritation and banishing any musings that weren't to his liking, Dare stepped up behind Willyn and slid an arm around her waist. They were near the bottom of the wide wooden staircase in the grand hall, so he tried to steer her up the steps. "You need to lie down for a while. Like about eight hours." He pushed a little harder when she dug in her heels. "We can get something brought to your room for dinner."

"I'm not going to my room," she said, chin jutting and lips

firmly pressed together. She was the picture of mulish. While donkeys might respond to a kick in the rear, he didn't think that would get the desired response from her.

"The prophecy, the Amara, and that damn book will all still be around tomorrow. You'll do better if you revisit everything after you're rested," Dare said, nudging her again.

Willyn's mouth fell open as she cast her eyes around to the other women, all of whom were waiting and watching. "Can you believe this guy?" she asked her friends. Dare hoped the other witches saw reason, because as strong as he was, his power was no match for them all, even if they were still novices.

"He might have a point," Hayden said. "You look a little peaked. None of us have eaten since lunch, but you've been through a lot more. We'll send you up a tray."

"And we promise not to try to figure anything out before tomorrow morning," Shauni said, as if realizing Willyn's pride was on the line. She stepped forward, intense green eyes curving at Willyn as she smiled. "I had a hard time knowing when to stop, too. It's exhausting. Your mind is running constantly, trying to figure out what to do next. And never mind the countdown flashing in front of your eyes, ticking off the days one by one. Am I on schedule or running behind? Have I already failed but just don't know it yet?"

Willyn exhaled and nodded. "It does wear you out." She looked at Dare again. "I'll grab something to eat in the kitchen and will be ready to get back to work straight after. I just need some foooo..." She didn't finish the sentence, her breath whooshing out of her when Dare tucked his other arm behind her knees and swept her into his arms. He beat a trail for the stairs before anyone could object.

Walking from the kitchen and observing with a curious eye, Paige munched on the chips she'd gotten from the pantry. "What did I miss?" She munched some more. "And should we save her?"

Anna laughed. "No. She's not in any danger."

"You sure about that?" Kylie asked with a wiggle of blonde brows. "I think he's starting to like her. If you know what I mean."

"The guy who abhors church-goers hooking up with our Willyn?" Claudia was less than convinced.

Anna sighed. "It's time we let Willyn fight for herself. Magic has its reasons. She was chosen second because the fates believe in her." Eyeballing Paige's chips, she added, "I'll have two trays made ready, and as far as Dare and Willyn being a match," she shrugged, "I've seen stranger things."

Quinn sidled up to his sister and grinned boyishly. "An odder pairing than the witch and the Christian?" His eyes, the same cobalt blue as Anna's, twinkled with mischief. "Hmph. Name it." He looked up to follow the movement of the fierce, dark man with the golden woman in his arms. Every curious female in the room did, too.

Upstairs, Dare made it to Willyn's bedroom just in time, since her vigorous wiggling almost made him drop her on her shapely backside. He man-handled her inside and shut the door behind him. A streak of white flew from on top of a loveseat in the corner to underneath it, and Dare had the impression of a cat.

Of course it was. All of the witches had a cat. Why kill a good stereotype?

The pummeling of his chest tore his thoughts away from folklore and back to the volatile woman in front of him. "Move out of the way, or I'll do it for you," she threatened, her pale blue eyes roiling with thunderclouds. "You have no say-so over me, damn it!"

Dare gave her a hard smile. "Tsk. Tsk. I would have never pegged you for a curser, Willyn. What would your church family say?" He leaned against the heavy oak door, making his body a barricade. When she glanced over her shoulder to the balcony doors, he lowered his voice, filling it with a warning of his own. "I will take you down and plant you in that bed if I have to. Don't test me."

He put a finger to her lips to still the fury she was about to vent, "Besides. The other girls are making you some food, I'm sure. They are as worried about you as I am, so don't...what is it your kind says? Oh, yeah. Don't steal their blessing."

Willyn pivoted and stalked to the loveseat, sitting on the creamy fabric harder than necessary. She was in a full blown pique, but at least her cheeks were blooming again. He hadn't liked the wan look on her face downstairs. Not at all.

Tapping her foot on the floor, Willyn asked, "Why are you worried about me? Or were you just saying that to get your way?"

Dare grimaced inside. Had he actually admitted that out loud? He needed to exercise more caution. He never showed his hand, but she constantly seemed to be catching him off guard. "You're gunning too hard, that's why. And no. I wasn't just saying I was concerned. I meant it. I told you I don't lie."

She actually snorted in response.

Choosing to overlook it due to the fact he had literally hauled her in here like a sack of mandrake, he continued. "And this girl, Beth. You're not thinking clearly when it comes to her. She's bad news. I can feel it."

"All the more reason for me to help her. Maybe she just needs a little guidance. Why else would she have called me?" The cat was easing out from under the loveseat, now that the voice of its mistress was calmer. Willyn reached down to rub its head. "She's obviously crying out for help, and I can't ignore her."

"Even if it interferes with your duty to the coven?"

"I won't let it."

Pushing away from the door, Dare homed in on her like a heat-seeker, stopping just shy of the cat's tail, so that it jumped into Willyn's lap with a disgruntled sound. "You already have. You let her drag you into those tunnels and put you in danger. Your behavior regarding her has been careless and naïve."

"She's a young girl who's lost her way, Dare. I have many obligations in this life, and I won't short-change any of them."

Dare scoffed. "You Christians. Always trying to save someone, regardless of whether or not they want you to."

Gently pushing the white cat to the side, Willyn stood and met him toe-to-toe. "Don't worry, I would never try to save you. I know a lost cause when I see one, and you're beyond redemption."

Dare hadn't cared about the opinion of anyone else in a very long time, but Willyn's contempt stung. "Funny. That's what my mother said after I got Sarah Poole into the back of my truck. Like you, my mother was supposed to be a kind and faithful woman." His tone reeked of sarcasm. "You're determined to see the good in Beth, even though she's probably responsible for tormenting you and your son." He leaned in closer. "So where's my benefit of the doubt? You've already found me guilty. No trial needed. Just like that mob did to your ancestor, more fine, church-going citizens."

She sucked in a breath at the comparison. "I would never...I didn't mean you're..." She gulped, obviously awash with guilt from her harsh words. She put a hand to her forehead and closed her eyes. "I don't know what's wrong with me. I'm never like this."

Dare watched her try to stay in control of herself, experiencing a good bit of his own shame and self-recriminations. This wasn't going the way he'd planned. He'd brought her, well, forced her up here to relax. Now he was piling on more stress. He felt a tug of guilt, but it didn't stop him from noticing how sweetly her upper lip bowed and how the lower one trembled with her anguish. He couldn't help wanting to kiss her again, to fill her up with his energy and warmth. To take away her pain.

Hell, he wanted to override every emotion she had and replace it with passion for him. It was only fair she be as consumed with it as he was. Dare paused, his hand on its way to her cheek again, intent on finding that soft spot right below her ear. He'd imagined following with his mouth. Taking a tender bite.

What's wrong with me? Dare frowned and lowered his hand to her shoulder, a gesture meant to console instead of caress. She was vulnerable, and though his intentions were good, she'd never forgive him if he took advantage of the moment.

From behind her, the cat stood on the edge of the cushion, pawing at Willyn and offering a mournful meow. Then she, and there was no longer any doubt the cat was a she, gave him a look that clearly said, "Now look what you've done."

Dare put both hands on the crown of Willyn's head, stroking the golden waves that fell to her shoulders. She was all blue skies and sunshine. He felt like the storm cloud that had moved in to darken her day. "Don't be upset. We both just need to..."

"Mom! Hey, Mom!" Tadd burst in the room from his connecting door, a bundle of unsuppressed energy. He came to a dead stop as if slamming on his brakes and crinkled his little face. He cocked his head. "What's wrong with my mom?" he asked Dare before putting his hands on his hips in what had to be an imitation of Willyn. He stared directly at Dare. "What did you do?"

~

Willyn simultaneously brought her head up and pasted a cheery smile on her face in one deft move. "Hey, sweetie," she told Tadd, going to him and kneeling down to his level. "I just had a headache, and Dare was helping make it better." She felt bad enough about ripping her son out of the life they'd known before and exposing him to the dangers they faced in

Savannah. The last thing she wanted was for him to worry about her and Dare.

Tadd scrunched his face even more. "He was playing with your hair." He rolled his eyes and blew out an exasperated breath, most likely thinking how weird adults could be.

"You came in here fired up about something. What's so exciting?" She swiped his silky blonde bangs away from his eyes. Time for a haircut. She could smell that special mixture of little boy, dirt, and sunshine. She wondered what adventures he'd had today and what she'd missed.

"Claire said you were going to eat dinner in your room and were really tucked out..."

"Tuckered out?" Willyn asked.

"Yeah. That." He pulled his head back, clearly telling her to knock off the mom-love she was still showering all over him. She took her hand away from the side of his face, slightly saddened by the glimpse of future days when she wouldn't be the most important thing in his world anymore. "So can I go home with Claire and Joe tonight?" he asked. "Joe said we could camp out in the back yard."

Willyn grinned. With the enormous manor here on the island and Anna's swanky house on the mainland that Joe and Claire cared for, Tadd was most excited about sleeping in a tent. She considered that a good sign.

Then she remembered the Amara, the nightmares, and how Ronja would use any weapon she could to get to Willyn. It seemed pretty unfair. Each of the witches had to pass a trial, yet the Amara only had to beat one of them. If a single woman of the coven failed, Ronja and her followers would win the war and raise the demon Bastraal from the underworld.

"I'm not sure you should leave the island just now," Willyn said, aching inside when Tadd's face fell.

"Whyyyyy nooot?" Tadd was gearing up his temper mode. He was a good boy but was still just that. A five-year-old boy.

Before she could say anything, Dare stepped in. "Maybe we can think of a way to make it happen, okay, Kiddo? Why don't you run downstairs while your mom and I finish talking. Then I'll come down and tell you what she said." When Tadd fell quiet to consider the large man and his offer, Dare pressed on and whispered in a conspiratorial voice, "Give me a chance to work on her." He winked for emphasis.

The message from one sneaky boy to another was clear. Tadd whooped and jumped into the air. "All right, Mister Dare!" He ran back the way he'd come, pulling the door behind him and grinning as he went. As an afterthought, he peeked back around and said, "Hope your head stops hurting, Mom." Then he was gone.

Willyn wasn't sure what had just happened. She was not used to having a mediator between her and her son. She didn't like it either. She swung around to pin Dare with a look, forgetting the remorse from before. The man was infuriating. High-handed and controlling. She. Hated. That. "What do you think you're doing?"

He shrugged. "Don't mention it. I like kids." He lowered his head and his voice. "I want to have a couple myself."

Willyn understood his meaning and couldn't decide what angered her the most. "First off. I wasn't thanking you. I can take care of Tadd and do not need your interference. So in the future, stay out of it." She advanced on Dare, and he had the good sense to take one step back. "Second, I don't know what kind of game you're playing with me, talking about having children with that 'come hither' look in your eyes." She nailed herself in the chest with a finger for each word she said next. "I'm. Not. That. Easy."

Seeing his jaw clench, Willyn maintained the offensive position, unwilling to let him get a shot in. "First you practically assault me. Then you try to tell me what to do about... everything. Now, you've decided I'm actually good enough to...

to..." she searched for the appropriate expression, "to breed with?"

"I'm not sure I like the analogy," he said through gritted teeth.

Willyn slapped her arms across her chest. "If it walks like a dog, barks like a dog, smells like a dog."

"You know what? Forget it." Striding across the room to stare out the French doors that led to the balcony, Dare spoke with his back turned to her. "You're right. I don't know what I was thinking. Our being together in any way is a bad idea. We couldn't be more different, and we obviously despise each other. We can't agree on anything."

Willyn had told herself the same things over and over, but hearing the sentiments from him felt like burlap scraping over her heart. What he said made sense. So why was she noticing the picture he made standing by the door with the waning moon rising in the sky over his right shoulder?

She'd noticed when he'd carried her upstairs how thick and strong he was, in all the right places. His chest had been granite, and the arms holding her had been sturdy as steel, unaffected by her weight. Yet, he wasn't built like a bruiser. With the muscular shoulders that tapered to his waist, she imagined he would fill out a tuxedo perfectly. He would make a dashing figure with an edge of darkness.

Despite how he'd tried to help her, there was still a lingering mist of doom around Dare. He still wasn't telling her everything. "I know. You're right," she said. "We don't get along. So why do you keep pushing? Why don't you just stay away from me?" She glanced at the red-coral wrapped around her bedposts. *And why can't I stop thinking about you?*

"Somewhere along the way my judgment got cloudy." He put his hand on the wall. "We believe different things. I'm not the kind of man you need." He turned swiftly to face her. "And you have absolutely no faith that I could be."

Willyn didn't respond. How could she say anything when she wasn't sure if she agreed with him or not? She was attracted to Dare, but could she ever fully trust him?

"You go ahead and fight the Amara. I'll stay out of your way. Even if I think you're gunning for trouble with this Beth." He shook his head like he was telling himself how ridiculous Willyn was being about the girl.

"You don't understand and that's fine, but I have to try. I was alone once and had my whole world crumble from beneath me while I fought to find my balance. For me and for Tadd." Willyn wished she could find a way to get through to Dare. Maybe he could let go of some of his hate. "I didn't do it alone. I needed help and He was there for me when it counted most. I'm sorry you don't believe, but God saved me. I have to live my life as a reflection of that. I have to make it worthwhile."

Dare's features calmed, but the void left behind was worse than the tension it had replaced. He was completely withdrawn. A stranger again. His hand went to his chest momentarily before he walked past her and to the door. He didn't spare a glance as he left, saying, "I guess that's the difference between us. You must have been good enough."

She called out before he was gone. "What do you mean?"

Steel-blue eyes blazing with fury, Dare stared at her. "I'll never change, Willyn. And why should I? Why should I believe?" He lifted his head defiantly, lips lifting with the hint of a snarl. "Your God didn't save me."

14

Even Kylie's magic coffee machine and the tantalizing aroma it created fell short of what Willyn needed to wake up. She decided to go for one of the bolder choices Lucia preferred, selecting one appropriately named Jet Fuel. If anything was going to clear the mist from her head, surely that was the one. She mumbled something resembling a morning greeting to Claudia and Kylie who were at the crescent-shaped island. The two were bonding over their mutual addiction as they flipped the pages of a clothing catalogue.

"That skirt would look great on you," Kylie gushed to Claudia. "It would show off your mile-long legs."

"And that green top would set off your eyes." Claudia glanced at Kylie. "Then again, it might clash with your hair and coloring." Kylie pulled a long lock of honey blonde hair around to hold it against the picture. "You're right. I don't want to look sallow."

Willyn cast a weary look toward the two women who'd become her family and thought... *Blech*. She was in no mood for fashion this morning. In fact, she was in no mood for anything other than the potent brew in her favorite mug, light green with red tulips dancing around the bottom edge. It was her happy cup and always made her feel better.

She was still waiting for it to work.

Tossing and turning all night had left her feeling grumpy,

and it would have been understandable if the problems jumping hurdles in her mind all night had been about Tadd, or the Amara, or any other respectable issue. Yet, the pea under her mattress all night could only be attributed to the tall, dark, stranger who'd thrust himself into her life. Dare.

She was constantly trying to block him from her daydreams. No matter where her musings took her, he always seemed to be there waiting for her. It was getting to the point where she started thinking of him as "Dammit Dare." She'd muttered the phrase often in the night as she'd tossed and turned, trying to forget the sweep of dangerously dark hair over mesmerizing eyes that were deeper and bluer than the Atlantic.

Assaulted by the images once again, Willyn blew on her hot coffee and muttered under her breath, "Dammit, Dare"

"What'd you say?" Claudia asked, pulling her nose out of the catalogue to look at Willyn. "You need something?"

"Only a lobotomy," Willyn answered, leaving both her friends with muddled looks.

Viv walked into the room decked out in gray, capri-style sweatpants and a matching shirt. Like all of them, she was dressed to "get physical" as Ms. Attinger had told them all early this morning when she'd knocked on their doors.

With a shining cap of silver hair, Ms. Attinger was as fine-featured and lovely as the average fairy, or so Willyn imagined. She and Mr. Attinger, her husband, kept the household running, and apparently, neither of them ever slept. Early or late, they were somewhere making sure nothing was left unchecked, unlocked, or uncooked.

"I've been told we should have some carbs and protein but to not overstuff." Viv was without her glasses and had her sleek, black hair in a short ponytail. Even without makeup she was a stunner. A Japanese empress come to have breakfast with the serfs.

Is that what they were called way back when in Japan?

Willyn didn't know, but the gist was the same. "What are we doing?" she asked Viv while the other woman sliced a grapefruit and sugared it before slipping it on a plate with scrambled eggs and a bagel.

"I heard something about clearing out the storage room we never got to see. Maybe we'll be moving something." She looked at Willyn and frowned, then she loaded some eggs and a strawberry muffin, Willyn's favorite, on a plate. She put it on the island and pulled out the stool, motioning for Willyn to take the seat. "You need to eat. I think you look worse than you did after your dream-trip."

Willyn grunted and marched over. "Thanks, Empress."

"Huh?"

"Never mind," Willyn said. "Thanks for the food, Viv. I just didn't sleep well."

Kylie jumped on the perfect opening. "Did your guest have anything to do with that?" She wiggled her blonde brows over a glass of orange juice as she drank.

Willyn spared enough energy to give her an are-you-serious look, which only made Kylie reach over and pat her arm. "It's okay. I'm holding out hope for you. And they say it's like riding a bicycle."

"Coming from someone who probably never went without long enough to forget," Claudia said, ducking when Kylie scooped up some jelly with a finger and aimed for her face.

As always, they made Willyn laugh. She was still exhausted and anxious, but the day had begun to brighten. Just a bit. She held out her empty coffee mug to Kylie. "Why don't you go stir up your little machine for me? I think you owe me a cup." When the college girl took it with a wink, Willyn called over her shoulder, "And make it Jet Fuel."

~

It looked as if Mrs. Attinger's magic elves had been hard at work already. The so-called storage room had been emptied out and sparkled in a way only newly cleaned spaces did. And what a space it was.

The ballroom was a stunning two-tiered room featuring a mezzanine, grand staircase, eight massive columns, and ornate wooden ceilings two floors above. Showcasing the style and grandeur of a bygone era, marble floors of a delicate white and eggshell swirl gave the impression of a vast sky opening before them. Visitors would have felt like they were literally dancing on the clouds.

Willyn wasn't the only one stunned by the elegant room. "Storage room, Anna?" Claudia asked, spinning with her arms as if she were a little girl turned princess. "Why have you had this hidden away?"

Also in exercise clothing, though hers was black and stretchy, Anna sauntered across the floor. "My parents started storing things in here when I was little. It was an adventure land for Quinn and me, with the heavy furniture and other draped items creating a maze filled with hiding places. We made a new fort in here every day, and I would climb into some of the pieces hoping to find my way to a magical land of snow with a great lion and white witch." She hugged herself and flushed with happy memories. "I loved this place and never thought to change it."

"So why now?" Willyn asked.

Anna smiled at her. "Because Paige has made a good point."

"Which is?" Willyn asked as a loud slapping sound drew her attention to the corner where Paige had dropped a large blue tumbling mat and was rolling it out. She was afraid she had her answer.

Anna gestured to the mat. "That we shouldn't always rely on our magic to get us out of tight spots. A combination of our abilities and physical competence is the smartest way to go."

Paige looked up with a grin of anticipation. "She means that I get to teach you all how to kick some Amara ass."

Hayden came to stand by Willyn. "And have our own backsides beaten in the process?"

"You know what they say," Paige answered, leaving them to guess the expression she was referring to.

"I think she's letting us know there will be some pain," Shauni said, a frown on her face and hands on hips that were covered by her favorite item of clothing, cargo pants.

"You going to get down and dirty in those?" Hayden asked her, pointing to the gray pants.

Shauni nodded. "I was told to dress comfortably, and it doesn't get any better than this. Besides, if we have to face off with any of Ronja's hacks, they're not going to let us run change our clothes first."

"Tru dat," Kylie said, and everyone groaned.

"Oh. Before I forget," Shauni said pointing a finger at Willyn then Viv and Claudia. "Michael will be able to get a couple more cats in this week for their...ahem...procedures, so get with me later and let me know what works for you."

Willyn bit her lower lip. "I keep forgetting. With all that's going on..."

"Hey. I understand." Shauni slung an arm around her shoulder. "That's why I'm reminding you. But if we can get all the boy cats taken care of, your Snowball will have a little more time." She pinned Viv and Claudia with a look. "Specifically your two boys."

"Okay. Okay." Viv sniffed. "Kiko will probably never forgive me, but it's the right thing to do." She elbowed Claudia. "Let's partner off, and the first one to land on her butt has to take her cat in first."

Claudia's eyes gleamed with aggressive intent. "Deal. But no using your telekinetics on me. That's cheating."

"Actually," Anna broke in. "We want you to use everything

you've got, so you won't be grasping for ideas when the time comes."

"So what am I supposed to do to defend myself?" Claudia asked. "Grab her shirt and tell her where she bought it?"

Anna tilted her head to the side. "Get creative. That's the purpose of the training. If you can't pull from your own personal gift or the magic you've learned from me, you'll have to fall back on good old fashioned street-smarts."

Claudia looked at her long nails, newly painted a passion plum purple. "Great. Just great."

Anna pointed to the ornate wooden ceiling and the chandeliers dangling with a million points of light. "Quinn, Dare, and I have already cast a spell on the room, so feel free to fire away with any elemental spells." She patted one of the large columns. "The protective spell will absorb anything you throw at it, so don't hold back." She grinned. "We considered making it a reflective surface that would send your magic back at you, but we can save that for later. When your reflexes have improved."

Willyn felt her brows go up as she glanced at Hayden. "We might be in more danger here than out on the town with the Amara." The two laughed lightly then stilled when the large doors behind them opened again to admit two more party-goers. Quinn and Dare.

"Okay. Everybody's here now, so pair off with a partner and get ready to start with the basics." Paige gestured to the men. "You two pick a witch. You need to get used to breaking that cardinal guy rule of not hitting girls." She motioned with her head when they just stood there staring. "Move it. I'm in charge of these sessions, and by the time we're done today, you'll be sore and tired but much better prepared."

Willyn sensed Dare's eyes on her and sighed with both relief and regret when he stopped next to Lucia. "How about it, Lucy?"

Lucia narrowed deep, chocolate eyes at him and quickly wrapped her long brown hair in a messy bun. "If that little dig with my name was meant to get a reaction," she fell into a fighting stance and smiled, "it worked."

The two of them moved to their own spot away from the others and began basic punches and deflections. Dare's laughter mixing with that of a female's, any female's, seemed to grate on Willyn's sense of calm. She felt her bad mood rearing its head. *It's only Lucia. Even if Dare tries to flirt with her, she wouldn't rise to the bait. She knows he and I...*

Willyn felt the words drop from the front of her mind to the bottom of her stomach as they trailed off. She and Dare what? Absolutely nothing, that's what. She had no claim to him and didn't even want to face the fact that the lack of a connection bothered her. When had she started to think of him as being hers?

"Hey, girl. You want to go a round or two with me?" Shauni was still there beside her, everyone else already with another partner.

"On one condition," Willyn said. "Don't even think about going easy on me."

Paige called out, "Anyone afraid of falling on the hard floor can come over and use the mat." She waited but no one moved. "Excellent," she said before rolling the mat back up. They'd all passed her first test.

Paige started with some basic punches and kicks, demonstrating how to get the most power behind each and the proper way to make a fist. Claudia had not gone gently into that particular night and had required some tough love from Paige. Broken nails were quite the issue.

Then they all practiced with one person punching or kicking while their partner blocked. Willyn channeled all her tension into the thrusts and began to feel the annoyance working out of her muscles. Out of the corner of her eye, she saw Quinn and

Hayden sparring while Kylie tried to hit Anna. The matches all seemed fairly safe and controlled.

Two claps from Paige and everyone relaxed. "If you've all loosened up enough, let's start free-style fighting. Use any move you've got in your arsenal. We've got a healer on hand if we need one," she added with a grin that clearly stated her love for a good knock-down-drag-out.

Now the fighting started for real, with grunts and gasps breaking out all around the room. The first were from Quinn and Dare who'd both been treading lightly with their female partners. A good blow to Quinn's abdomen and one to Dare's kidney had them rapidly re-thinking their strategies.

Soon a stray fireball whizzed past Willyn's ear before Hayden's voice yelled, "Sorry!" just before Quinn took her down and feigned a chop to her neck.

"Stop being so damn polite, Hayden," Paige ordered. "You lost your focus, now you're out for the count or dead."

A scream from Anna, made them all pause and look, though they kept their arms up in defense. Her hair seemed to have more static than it had before. "Good one," she was telling Kylie. "I forgot that your good friends with electricity." She shook her hands before clasping them together. She chanted something Willyn couldn't hear before a puddle formed beneath Kylie's feet and hardened into rubber. The younger girl was good and stuck. And she was also grounded. Anna backed safely away and sent a wave of distortion toward Kylie, making the blonde's head snap back.

"You punched me!" Kylie cried. "From way back there! That can't be fair!"

Anna laughed and shrugged.

"Deal with it, Blondie," Paige said before moving on to referee Viv and Claudia.

Since she was still watching to see what Kylie would do, Willyn never saw the roundhouse coming. When Shauni's kick connected with her chin, all Willyn could think was, *Thank goodness she's not wearing her hiking boots.*

Willyn went down but channeled her own power of healing before her torso hit the floor. When Shauni leaned over to ask if she was okay, Willyn grabbed her hand and placed a foot in her belly. Shauni went flying and landed with an "Oomph!" behind her.

Rolling over on her belly, Willyn started laughing along with her partner, both of them panting in between giggles. "Why don't we stay down here a minute? Get our breath back."

Shauni let her head fall back on the floor. "Sounds good to me."

"Ow! Medic!" A male voice sounded out in the distance, prompting Willyn to jump to her feet. She was the medic, after all. Quinn was holding both hands over his left eye, and Hayden had hers clamped over her mouth, her own eyes wide with panic.

"I'm so sorry, Quinn," Hayden said.

He swept a leg out and knocked hers out from under her, still covering his eye. "You're still being too polite," he told her with a grin.

Willyn rushed to his side and peeled his hands away. "What happened?"

"I'm not sure but, it felt like someone poked me in the eye," Quinn blinked rapidly, trying to keep his lid open for Willyn's inspection.

Placing her own hands around the injured eye, Willyn sent a cooling and healing wave to the site. After a few seconds, Quinn took her wrists and brought them away. "You do good work. It's completely gone." He looked at Hayden, who'd joined them. "So what did you do? Your hands were nowhere near my face."

"I think I learned a new trick," she told them all, dancing a triumphant jig. "There were a couple of ghosts hanging out watching the fights."

"That's always so comforting," Viv said dryly.

Ignoring her, Hayden continued to explain. "I didn't know I could do it, but I sort of imagined one of them poking his finger in Quinn's eye to help me out, because he was really backing me into a corner, and the next thing you know, one of them did exactly what I wanted!"

"You've always been able to talk to spirits," Willyn said. "What's so different?"

"I've never had them act on my thoughts before. It opens a whole new level of communication. Plus, it shows that some of them can make parts of themselves corporeal with my help. The uses for this are endless!" Hayden's caramel-colored hair had come unbound, so she re-clamped it in her barrette. "It's like I have an ever ready posse at my disposal." She grew serious suddenly. "I would never abuse them, though."

"Of course you wouldn't," Quinn said, patting her on the cheek. "It was brilliant of you. But now...I'm taking a water break. Feel free to ghost-bust anyone else."

Lucia stepped forward. "I want to try."

She was fearless, Willyn thought. It was hard enough to deflect the things you saw coming. Invisible combatants? She wasn't ready for that.

"I'm going to grab some juice," Shauni told Willyn. "We'll get back to it in a few, okay?'

"Sure." Willyn nodded but was disappointed. She'd been enjoying the sparring more than she would have expected. She'd never had the opportunity to spar with anyone. It was actually pretty fun.

She froze when she felt a presence behind her. "Looks like we both lost our partners," Dare said. He was standing close enough for her to feel the warmth of his breath.

She turned slowly, lifting her face to look into deep, blue eyes that challenged. It probably wasn't a good idea, given their brief but volatile history, but something in the smug set of his lips made her go out on a long and wobbly limb. "I won't be gentle with you," she said with deceptive calm.

Dare laughed low and harsh. "So what else is new?" He feathered a finger over her lips and gave her a dark look of longing. He fell back into a defensive pose and notched his chin at her. "Show me what you've got, Sweetheart."

"I told you not to call me that." Growling low in her chest, Willyn punched hard, coming to a snap a couple of inches behind where his face should have been, but he'd snaked to the side, and she'd missed. She had to keep her anger under control or she was a goner. *Block, breathe, anticipate.* She recognized the bunching of muscles that indicated he was about to move to her left. As soon as he did, her fist shot forward, making a solid connection with his cheek.

Dare didn't slow down, but she was sure he'd felt the punch more than a little. He'd flinched for a second with his eyes crinkling at the edges. Her hand was throbbing like a bruise, but it had been *so* worth it. He seemed to think she was some frail blossom blowing in the breeze. Hapless, waiting to be snatched up by any man who stopped to notice her. *Poor lonely little flower.*

A slow smile spread over her lips as she envisioned herself another way. The hawk swooping down to latch onto the back of the man's stubborn head as he bent down to pluck the innocent bloom. She woke up from the daydream when a flat hand struck her solar plexus, knocking her breath clean out of her lungs.

Stunned, she did nothing when Dare slipped around to her back, supporting her weight while she recovered. As soon as she started drawing in cool, deep air and regained some of her wits, she realized she was trapped. Dare had her arms locked behind her with his strong ones looped under the bend of her elbows. He edged closer, making good use of her immobility.

The heated moisture of his breath was on her neck as he whispered, "You've got pretty good form, Sweetheart." He pushed his pelvis against her lower back, grinding side to side in a small, controlled motion. The point of contact between their bodies was in no way suggestive, but the rhythm of his strokes was pure sex. The smooth friction stirred up ancient and instinctual cravings somewhere south of her belly.

Willyn wiggled and jerked her arms, but they remained tight in his grasp. "I hate the way you say that. I am not your sweetheart, and coming from you, it doesn't sound like an endearment."

Dare continued as if he'd never heard her. "You're smaller than Lucia, but fierce for your size." He smoothed his palms up over her shoulders and down her back to settle on her waist, leaving a trail behind that blazed with sensuality. Willyn did her best to ignore it.

"But Lucia's hips," he said with what sounded like a smack of his lips. "Now they were made for breeding."

Willyn sucked in a breath. She didn't see red, exactly, but her vision did go hazy around the edges. Then her mind cleared, snapping into sharp and perfect clarity. Shifting her apparently-lacking-hips to the left, she swung her right arm down, back, and up in a perfect arc, landing with a dull *whump*...dead-center in Dare's scrotum.

The breath coming from him now was in the form of strangled wheeze, but she refused to turn around and check on him. She stomped over to a nearby cooler, grabbed a bottle of water, and headed out the door. Still fuming, she decided a good, hot shower was in order. Followed by some type of alcohol. Her knowledge was severely lacking in that department, so she'd have to get one of the girl's to give her some tips. *Dammit, Dare.* The man was driving her to drink.

After Willyn stormed out, Quinn strolled casually over to Dare with a pained look of male commiseration on his face.

"Man," he said. "You all right?"

Dare coughed, fighting with the inevitable nausea that was trying to gain ground in his stomach. Doing his best to concentrate on the detailed, wooden ceiling far above, like those focal points women in labor used, he swallowed hard and groaned. "Not the first time. Won't be the last." His voice was thin and wheezy. "But this agony isn't the worst of my problems."

Bending over and planting his palms on his knees, Quinn squinted at his friend. "What are you talking about?"

With a jerk of his head indicating the open door Willyn had escaped through, Dare laughed, then grimaced at the added muscle contraction. He blew out a long, moaning breath, and said, "I'm crazy about that woman."

15

Everyone gathered in the library to discuss the message Willyn had received when she'd traveled to her dream. Since they were looking for a book, the room seemed an appropriate place to start. Dare sat in a large leather chair, waiting for things to get under way.

The rest of the women seemed to be warming up to him, for the most part, but as far as Willyn was concerned, he was still *persona non grata*. She had joined them a few minutes ago but had yet to make eye contact with him. He consoled himself with people-watching, or in this case, eclectic-and-amusing-collection-of-witches watching.

"This is the Kama Sutra?" Kylie asked, face contorted and obviously annoyed. Leave it to her to blurt out her thoughts, however anomalous they may be. "I thought it was supposed to be about...you know. Positions."

Claudia laughed at Kylie. The younger girl was clearly disappointed by the book in her hands, black satin with a red tree on the cover. "That's a common misconception," Claudia said. "There are seven books in the Kama Sutra, and only one is about the act itself. The manuscript is actually a collection of instructional prose regarding all manner of courting and relationships between a man and a woman."

Kylie flipped some pages, determined to find what she'd always heard about. "Ah. Here it is." She studied and flipped.

Studied and flipped. "Hmmm. They describe the different types of kissing." The smile on her face told them she was finding humor in the subject matter. "There's a bent kiss, a straight kiss, a pressed kiss."

As Kylie counted off the ways to meld mouths, Dare shot a look to Willyn. She seemed unaffected. And was still ignoring him.

"Ooh. There are also instructions on marking someone's skin with your nails in a crescent shape. They actually have a name for that." Kylie's eyes got big. "Biting?" She closed the book. "Maybe I'll take this up to my room later."

Still watching Willyn, Dare saw her blush at last. He'd have to remember her response to the use of teeth and find out if it her flaming cheeks had been out of embarrassment or the desire to try the method for herself.

"The gang's all here," Paige said, walking in to flop down on a couch in one of the sitting areas. The library was huge, so there was more than one place to relax and prop up one's feet.

Everyone had showered and changed after the morning's training bout. Then they'd all enjoyed a restoring lunch prepared by Mrs. Attinger. Willyn had slipped in, made a plate, and left again without ever speaking to Dare. He wondered how long he'd be in the hot spot. Or the cold spot, considering the shoulder she kept giving him.

"We should start with the message, though short, I believe it will tell us what we need to find the book." Willyn stood in the center of where they had gathered, a general rallying her troops. She was rigid, hands on hips and a sternness to her features he'd never seen before. The ordeal was taking a toll on her. That much was obvious.

Dare just hoped he wasn't adding to the strain.

"The woman in my dream was my ancestor, who we now know was Beatrice Daigle, mother to Hally, thanks to Anna's family archives. I'm sure Beatrice told me exactly what I needed and though simple, her words hold more than we might realize." Willyn nodded at Claudia. "You've been to the tapestry again?"

"Yes. I thought I might get more from it if I was alone. No other energy to distract me." Claudia retrieved a large tome from a nearby table. "The book I saw was about this size and color. I thought a visual might help. There was a drawing or some sort of writing on the front, but I couldn't make it out."

"I have a feeling we'll know it if we find it," Anna said. "It's meant for us. We need it for the prophecy and to vanquish the demon. I have to believe the book, the blade, and the burial ground are all things we'll need to keep Bastraal from attaining human form." She turned in a slow half-circle, meeting everyone's eyes. "If you feel the slightest tingle from a book, or even get an odd sensation in your gut, bring whatever you find back here."

"You're talking as if you know where we should start looking," Kylie said. She was standing near her buddy, Viv. Though the blonde, college girl and the Asian scientist were on opposite ends of the personality spectrum, they seemed to have formed a fast and deep friendship.

Dare mused. Two weeks ago they had both been on his radar, now the only thing in his sights was a tenacious yet delicate female with a natural gift for nurturing those in need. Willyn was *so* not his usual type. Plus, she was already a parent, and he'd always thought to avoid that particular complication.

So it was even more surprising to find himself enjoying the kid's personality, looking forward to spending time with him, and anticipating whatever crazy thing was about to pop out of his mouth at any given minute. Tadd seemed to have a nose for mischief and mayhem. Dare really liked that about him.

It was Willyn who answered Kylie's question. "In my dream, Beatrice told me her daughter had hidden the book somewhere the preacher could not go. The island has been home to the original St. Germaine witches and their descendants since the first banishing. The family has always known to be on their guard."

"And there have been fires here in the past," Anna explained. "A small one in the tower and one that destroyed a barn that was out back. This all transpired decades ago, and only the barn fire lines up with the right time period, but we have to try looking elsewhere, too. I don't want to make assumptions."

"If they hid the book on the island or in the house, why send Beatrice across the country as a decoy?" Viv asked. "I mean if it was that safe here, why the ruse?"

Anna wrapped her long, brown hair up in a tail, evidence she was getting ready to start the search. "Maybe they needed to buy time for some reason. Beatrice said her sisters and daughter had a plan. We can't be sure the book is here, but we should rule it out."

"What about the blade and the burial ground?" Paige asked. "When will we start working on them?"

Anna's face took on that mystical quality they'd all come to recognize. "Those are not for Willyn, so they are not for this time, this trial. I'm sure of it."

Except for Shauni and Willyn, all of the witches traded apprehensive looks with each other. They were all thinking of their own trials to come. Some of them would be charged with locating the blade and the burial ground, and no one cared to speculate about what those investigations would entail. The burial ground part sounded particularly gruesome.

"We should break into groups," Anna directed. "I'll start in the tower. It's not been used for years, and I'd hate to ask any of you to venture into the dust and cobwebs."

"I'll go with you," Hayden said. "I'm used to cobwebs. I've had to clear out more than a few ghosts from old houses no one wanted to live in."

Quinn stepped forward. "I'll take Dare and Willyn to where

the old barn used to be. Since one of the fires was there, it makes sense to search the storage cellar."

Dare didn't protest. He also thought Willyn should visit the location of the fire, since it fit with the clue from Beatrice. It was Willyn's task to find the book, so she would be more sensitive to it if they got close.

Unlike Dare, however, Willyn did object. "I'm sure you and I can handle it, Quinn," she said coolly. She obviously saw the wisdom in her need to go but didn't want Dare tagging along. It looked like he wasn't forgiven. He'd been crass when he'd teased her about Lucia, but the spark of jealousy he'd seen had been well worth the trouble. Even if it had left him aching on the ball room floor.

"It will take both Dare and me to lift the steel door covering the entryway. Sorry, Kiddo," Quinn said.

Willyn turned on her heel and hurried out, but not before Dare saw the mortification on her face. Quinn's apology made her realize how transparent she'd been about not wanting Dare in her group.

As Dare followed after her, he caught a few grins from the other women as well as a couple of warning looks. Regardless of whether each woman was in the supportive camp or the suspicious one, the message was the same. Tread lightly with our Willyn.

He knew these witches banded together like a pack of wolves in designer clothing. They would have to. Dare had a gut feeling jeopardy was lurking around the corner, waiting to strike if given the chance. Other than their presence in the tunnels with Willyn and Beth, the Amara had been fairly quiet since Willyn's time had been announced. Too quiet.

He hoped they weren't saving something special for her. If so, he'd just have to make sure he was by her side when the other shoe was thrown in her direction. Prophesied or not, he was officially inserting himself into the line of fire.

Was he actually contemplating a selfless act? Damn. Egocentrism had been one of his favorite personal faults. Willyn was turning out to be a good influence on him. Now why had he gone and let that happen?

"You coming, Forster?" Quinn asked, raising impatient brows from the doorway.

Stick to Willyn. Like superglue. Dare's hands curled into fists of their own resolve. "On my way."

~

The summer heat was so thick it could almost be heard creeping across the land and weaving through the thick stand of pines. The trees had grown in over the years, since nothing had been built to replace the barn that had burned to the ground in this very spot over a century before. Willyn was grateful for the shade and that it was too hot for the no-see-ums to be active. If there had been one great adversity to living in Savannah, other than facing off with black witches and other monsters, it was the presence of gnats so small they could hardly be seen. But oh, were they ever felt.

She looked into the blazing sun and let it warm her face one last time before she stepped into the shadows to watch Quinn and Dare clear a few optimistic weeds that had tried to cover the large door in the ground. After exposing the seam on the side of the handle and twisting a knob to open the latch, the two men pried their fingers under the steely mammoth's edge and lifted.

After a grunt or two, they managed to lift it enough to get some leverage, counting off to three before tossing up and back where it landed in a cloud of displaced grass and last fall's pine straw.

Willyn couldn't help but feel a certain fascination as she watched Dare's shoulders flex with the effort. The female in her was very impressed. And a little turned on.

When Dare's eyes shot up to find her staring, she felt the intensity of his manliness rush straight from him, in through her parted lips, and all the way down to her toes. She buzzed and tingled in response, suddenly wishing Quinn wasn't there with them.

I'm mad at him, remember? She silently remonstrated herself. *He's nothing but a womanizing warlock with the morals of an alley cat.*

Remembering how much she liked cats, Willyn tore her gaze from the prime male specimen in front of her and looked instead to the huge rectangular hole in the forest floor. What was down there? And would she find the book?

Somehow this seemed far too easy, but she wasn't going to toss away hope. Maybe some of them would have a short and sweet challenge. Maybe she'd be one of the lucky ones.

"The ladder is rotted through. We'll have to use a rope," Quinn said after poking his head inside.

Maybe she wouldn't be so lucky after all.

Quinn spoke to Dare. "I'll go down first and catch Willyn if you'll help her up here."

Dare nodded and helped Quinn tie the rope through an opening in the steel door frame. Having expected issues with the old storage space, Quinn had brought the rope with him. As it turned out, he'd been right. Willyn considered the metal door. It appeared to have been installed more recently, probably as a safety measure. Anyone who didn't know the cellar was there could easily disappear beneath the earth and sustain serious injuries.

Stepping closer, she peered over Dare's shoulder while Quinn lowered himself over the edge and down the line. She heard the sound of boots meeting ground shortly after. "It's not a bad drop," Quinn called up. "Use the rope, though."

Willyn felt Dare's eyes travel up her legs, bare beneath

the hem of her white shorts. "You think your arms are strong enough?" he asked. "I can lower you down instead."

The noise Willyn made told him exactly what she thought of his offer. Channeling her skills on the uneven bars from... *Lord, how long had it been?*...her childhood days as a gymnast, she backed to the opening and kneeled before gripping the metal to shove herself back and down. She hung in mid-air for a split second before sensing the space between her feet and the ground. She let go, ignoring the rope entirely.

"I'll take that as a no," Dare said under his breath. "Clear out below," he added before performing the same maneuver Willyn had.

"I don't know about you two," Quinn said, flicking on a flashlight, "but I'm still using the rope to get out. My special gifts don't include flying."

Willyn smiled at him. "Don't worry. Mine don't either." The temperature in the room was at least ten degrees cooler, maybe more, creating an eerie contrast to the warm, summer world above. She scanned the underground storage area that had once been beneath a barn. It didn't take very long. "This is it?" she asked, waving dust out of her eyes. Their presence had stirred up dirt, must, and other unidentifiable particulates that had been left undisturbed for quite some time.

"They probably stored grain down here. Maybe feed for the horses." Quinn shrugged. "I wouldn't know myself, but that sounds close enough."

Dare pointed to the wall behind Willyn. "Whoever dug out this room never got to finish it."

Turning to see what he meant, Willyn followed the beam of Quinn's flashlight to a partially constructed brick wall. Only three-quarters of the job had been completed. She gestured to one side of the chamber then the other. "The rest of the walls are supported by wood. Maybe they started bricking in for more stability, or to guard against water seepage. I'm surprised anything was built below ground at all."

Dare's features lit up. "If we wouldn't expect a cellar to be built on this island, maybe whoever was after the book all those years ago wouldn't either."

"The preacher," Willyn said with a sudden chill. "And Ronja." She lifted wary eyes to the men. "It's always been Ronja."

"That immortal bitch is going down this time," Quinn said, surprising Willyn and Dare with his vehemence. "She's caused too much pain and suffering, and now we know she's been doing it for centuries."

"That's what happens when someone makes a deal with a demon," Dare uttered as he crossed to the brick wall. "I expect she'll be getting her due, and hopefully one day soon." He ran his hands over the masonry, pulling and pushing on the occasional brick. He finally stopped in one particular area. "Willyn, why don't you come check this out."

Intrigued and promptly forgetting her annoyance with him, Willyn moved in beside him, crowding close enough to press her shoulder into his arm. "What is it? Did you find something?"

"I'm not sure, but a few of these bricks were placed out of pattern." He took her hand and placed it over the cool, rough blocks.

They were old-style bricks, slightly coarser than those found in modern structures. "They're loose," she said, before pulling and wiggling on them in earnest.

"Here. I'll do it. You'll hurt your fingers." Dare pushed her hands away.

She pushed them right back. "I can do it."

"Just let me get them out and you can…"

"Hey. Kids," Quinn said from behind them. "Why don't you try working together." He huffed. "I'll hold the light so you can see."

Like a child who'd been caught making faces, Willyn offered Dare a sheepish look. "Do you have anything to scrape the mortar away?"

"As a matter of fact," he replied with a lopsided grin before reaching in the pocket of his jeans. "I do." He flipped open a Swiss army knife that had seen better days.

She laughed. "How old is that thing?"

Still holding it in his hand, Dare stared at the knife, but something dark flickered over his face. "My father gave it to me when I was ten."

When he stood there without elaborating, Willyn whispered to him. "We don't have to use it." The knife meant something to him, but she wasn't sure he was simply feeling nostalgic. He was hurting, and she didn't know why. The urge to take him in her arms and comfort him hit her like a landslide.

"No." Dare said sharply, jolting her from her secret impulse to hold him. "It will hold up. My father believed in buying quality tools." He started digging around the bricks. "Nothing but the best."

His words had bite to them, and Willyn perceived a tension directed at his father. He'd never mentioned his parents, but then, she'd never given him much of an opportunity. Soon the first brick slid out, and Willyn took it to place aside. The other three in the outline Dare had carved crumbled apart quickly afterwards.

"Bring the light over," Dare said to Quinn. "It's not reaching inside."

With every step Quinn took, Willyn could feel her heart beating faster. There was definitely something back there, but dirt kept falling down and the constant stream of loose earth made it difficult to tell what was what. Impatient, Willyn reached in just as the flashlight illuminated the area she and Dare had exposed. Her hand progressed a few inches before striking something hard. "There's something here." She dug around in the packed soil, trying to get a grip on whatever it was. Her fingers closed around a long, misshapen object.

Her heart sunk. "Roots," she said glumly. "That's all that's back there. The book's not here."

"That's why the bricks were loose," Dare said. "The roots were working their way into them."

Quinn let the light fall a little, taking the shine out of their eyes. "Maybe it's somewhere else down here. We might have to take down the whole wall to be sure."

"No," Willyn answered. "I'm sure." She dusted off her hand. "The book isn't here."

A scraping filled the room just before Quinn yelled, "Watch it!" Willyn jumped away from the unstable wall and barely missed being hit by the falling bricks.

Dare wasn't as fortunate. Only two bricks had toppled from above the tiny excavation site, but both had landed squarely on his forearm, leaving scrapes behind that instantly swelled with blood.

Willyn tried to take his arm but he refused, lurching away from her. "Don't," he said. "I'm fine."

"You're not. Let me heal you."

"Willyn." His tone stopped her in her tracks. "Let it be." His jaw was stern and his eyes grave. "I appreciate it, but some things need to heal on their own."

The denial felt like a slap. She'd only wanted to help. It was what she did. What came naturally. She couldn't think of a justifiable reason for him to refuse. Add one more to the pile of things she didn't understand about Dare.

"Fine." She threw up her hands and headed for the rope. Quinn was already halfway up, so she waited until he broke the surface and started climbing. Quinn reached down and put his hands around her waist to tug her over the side of the door frame.

Kneeling to the side to catch her breath, Willyn looked into the hole and watched Dare hoist himself up, making record time. Again, she noticed his flexing muscles, but then her gaze fell to his bruised and bloodied arm. *Stubborn man.*

On the heels of her frustration came a blast of cold, hard shock that pulsed through her veins as her mind froze and tried to make sense of what she saw. Dare's button-up shirt was only hanging open a little, but from above, Willyn could see his chest clearly. There was something on his skin, a scar.

She could tell by the puckered, pale texture that it had been made by a burn. That alone wasn't what made nausea and sympathy rise together and shake her to her bones. The shape of the scar. *Oh, my God. Please. No.* It was a cross.

The implications of what that meant, the possibilities of how it had gotten there, all of it swarmed Willyn, causing her to hold her breath and inch away from the door. She didn't want him to look at her now, or he would realize she'd seen it. Compassion would pour out of her and he would know. As little as she understood about Dare, she knew it giving him pity would be the wrong thing to do.

She turned away, standing up to walk toward the house. If she could take a minute and decompress, she could reel in the emotions that threatened to break free and make her wail and scream for the pain he'd obviously suffered. *Who would have done such a thing?* An answer leaped into her mind, but every cell of her body repudiated it. *No. Never.*

She forced her eyes to the green grass as she went, searching the far reaches of her mind for any other explanation. She felt as if she'd swallowed a bowling ball, but it was simply the weight of her remorse and disgust over what had been done to Dare. So many things he'd said made sense now.

Focusing on taking deep breaths and staring intently at the ground, Willyn didn't see anything out of the ordinary, but she heard someone yelling. Her head jerked up. That was Joe's voice. Her stomach clenched as the pieces locked into place. Joe and Claire were taking care of Tadd.

She broke into a sprint, leaving Quinn and Dare behind,

calling after her. She didn't stop until she broke free of the woods. It was then she saw Joe, running to the house and yelling for Anna. He disappeared behind the corner of the house as he entered the front yard, racing for help.

Willyn started moving again, searching desperately for any sign of Tadd or Claire. She should never have let him leave the island. She should have been more careful. Self-recriminations battered at her insides as she picked up her pace. The only thing holding her together was pure adrenaline. Her heart was slamming into her ribcage, and each breath seemed to tear a hole somewhere deep inside.

Then she saw Claire. She was carrying Tadd in her arms. He was alive. And crying. But her child's tears weren't what made Willyn go on full alert.

It was the dismay on Claire's face. When her wild eyes found Willyn, the older woman shook her head and spoke, her lips trembling so hard Willyn could barely make out the words that spilled in a torrent. "I'm sorry, Willyn. I'm so sorry." She hurried closer. "Ms. Anna put a ward on the mainland house. We stayed there all weekend, safe and sound.'" Claire started crying then. "But we forgot about the boat."

Willyn and Claire met in the middle of the green grass decorating Anna's lawn. She tenderly took Tadd in her arms where he buried his head against her neck to sob.

Claire rubbed his back, her mocha skin awash with tears that wouldn't stop. "He fell asleep. He fell asleep in the boat." She sniffled and looked at Willyn. "Joe's gone to get Ms. Anna, but I knew he'd need you first. You've got to heal him."

Willyn tightened her grip on Tadd. "What do you mean?" Pulling him away so she could get a better look, she put her hand under his chin and lifted his face. The world fell out from under her. *Help me. Help me. Not Tadd. Please, God, not my baby.* Panic flared and her mouth failed to make coherent sounds as she looked into her child's light blue eyes.

They were bleeding.

16

Calling forth every ounce of motherly love and curative power she possessed, Willyn concentrated on sending everything she had into her son's small body. There was no room for anger or panic. All she saw and all she imagined was a glowing white light of soothing energy flowing into Tadd.

When he stopped crying, she looked to see if the treatment had worked, but blood still dripped from the corners of his eyes. He didn't seem to be in any pain, but the crimson stains on his cheeks had transformed his normally innocent face into a vision if the macabre.

Dare was suddenly beside them, kneeling to put one hand on Tadd's shoulder. "What happened? Are you hurt?"

Willyn wasn't sure whether she should be annoyed or impressed that he was questioning her son instead of her. But it didn't matter. Tadd opened up to Dare and the story tumbled out.

"I guess I was taking a nap. I don't remember." Tadd took two hiccoughing breaths, still recovering from the crying jag. "Then there was this woman. I couldn't see her face, because she was in fog. She told me I had to bleed. She was sorry, but for her to get what she needed I had to bleed." He wiped his small hand across his face and held it out to look at the wetness. His eyes got big, but instead of letting the sight of blood scare him, he glanced up at Willyn as if asking her opinion on the stuff.

"You're going to be fine, sweetie," she soothed. "We just have to figure out how to make it stop."

Tadd nodded and wiped his hand across the grass to clean it. "Gross," he said.

The sound of trampling feet registered just before Anna, Joe, and Paige came to a dead halt and assessed the situation. Seeing Tadd and the condition he was in, Anna and Paige both sucked in a breath but said nothing. They glanced at Willyn, letting her take the lead.

Trying to hide the fear still crashing through her, Willyn spoke to the adults in as calm a voice as she could muster. "I pushed the most powerful healing surge into him that I've ever created. He doesn't seem to be injured, but I don't know how to stop…" unable to vocalize the rest, she tilted her head to indicate the bleeding. "Tadd said a woman came to him in a dream and told him he had to bleed."

"A subliminal suggestion," Anna said. "Her words had such an impact on his subconscious that his body manifested what she wanted it to."

"Like stigmata or something?" Paige asked.

Anna shook her head. "I'm not sure, but if you subscribe to the theory that the mind is strong enough to cause such things, I guess anything is possible."

Having joined the group quietly, Viv spoke up. "It's called psychogenic purpura. Spontaneous hemorrhaging with no obvious physical cause." She had her glasses on, evidence she'd been working on her research. If anyone here understood the power of the mind, it was the coven's telekinetic wonder.

"I just want to know how we fix it," Willyn said, feeling the break in her voice that was about to cut loose. She and Claire had been taking turns dabbing at Tadd's eyes, and two of the older woman's cloth handkerchiefs were saturated. If he was actually losing real blood… "We need to stop the flow. Now."

"If a subconscious influence caused the problem, then that's our best bet for solving it." Dare took Willyn's hand and tugged until she looked at him. "Willyn," he said, holding his deep blue eyes steady on hers. "You have to let me help him."

At first she didn't comprehend what he meant, but then it registered. He was asking permission to get inside her son's head, to probe around and manipulate his free will. The idea did not sit easy.

"You have to trust me," he urged, glancing at Tadd and back to her. Steady, patient, yet unmovable. With his warm hand enveloping hers and concern etched into the tension of his features, Dare was united with her in a way she'd never expected to feel again. He was offering to fend for her child while respecting her at the same time.

Willyn's chest flooded with sweet release. She would trust him. She *did* trust him, despite his black sheep façade. There were more layers to Dare Forster than she'd realized before. One of those layers constituted a man who cared about her and Tadd.

"Yes," she whispered. "Help him."

With one last squeeze to her hand, Dare let go and focused on Tadd. He didn't say anything to draw her son's attention; he simply stared intently as Tadd swept his hand back and forth over the blades of grass.

Willyn knew Tadd was scared, but he was acting like a champ. When all of this was over she was declaring an official pepperoni pizza and homemade brownies celebration. Tadd's favorites. She'd have to be sure they also had plenty of Dr. Pepper on hand.

"Yes. I do." Tadd was talking in a small voice, still looking down at his sweeping hand. "No." He was quiet for a moment, then again. "No."

It was like he was having a conversation with an invisible man or imaginary friend. Willyn looked at Dare and knew exactly who that friend was. He was pushing Tadd to recognize his own subconscious abilities. And her son was hardly even aware of it.

"I don't like it," her son said in a louder voice. "Okay." He looked up into the sun, blinking as the bright light met his pupils. He giggled and stood up. "Okay." Running off before Willyn could say anything, Tadd yelled over his shoulder. "I'm going to go find Skid and get his ball. He likes to play outside."

"Wait." Willyn started after him, but Dare pulled her back down, telling her, "He'll be right back. Don't worry."

"But how will I know if he's okay? I have to see if he's still bleeding."

"You will and he's not." Dare gave her a dazzling smile before planting a kiss on her parted lips. He winked before standing and helping her to her feet. "How quickly you forget," he said in a teasing tone. "I could have sworn you were going to trust me."

With a smile of appreciation for Dare, Willyn explained that trusting him with herself was one thing, but a good mother always double-checked. However, Tadd was back in a flash with his face all cleaned up and no sign of blood. Thank goodness for Claire.

Though Willyn's internal organs still felt like Jell-O, her son appeared to have recovered completely. He bounded back toward her and Dare with a carefree smile. She decided to take a few deep breaths and follow her son's lead.

With ball and Frisbee in tow, Tadd demonstrated Skid's catching abilities for the crowd, though the young dog still had issues coming to a clean stop. The sun was high in the sky, a blazing yellow ball, so everyone decided to spend a couple of hours playing. They could all use some fun time.

Willyn watched her child run and laugh then looked at Dare as he blended easily into the peaceful scene. She couldn't help noticing the change that had come over him. Man, boy, and dog all seemed to function on the same wavelength, sharing jokes and nuances that left Willyn mystified. It was good to see her son with a male figure again. The men who lived or worked at the island home had always made time for him, but Tadd had never looked at any of them with the same sparkle as he did Dare. Should she view it as a blessing or more heartbreak that would be waiting down the road for both her and her son?

Right now, she elected to enjoy the day and the company. She wouldn't steal this moment from any of them. All of her friends needed a break, and after seeing the smallest of them attacked, they were determined to take one. They surrounded Tadd with an impenetrable wall of love. Revelry and joy made their own special kind of white magic, one strong enough to banish the darkness.

If only for a little while.

When the frogs started calling and evening crept closer, Quinn and Joe went to the mainland for pepperoni pizza while the women made plenty of brownies, no nuts per Tadd's preference. They feasted on cheesy goodness and chocolate squares, washing the feast down with what had to be barrels of Dr. Pepper.

When bellies were full and Tadd's lids were starting to droop, Willyn knew the sandman had come calling. For good measure, all of the charms around her son and his room had been reinforced. No one was taking any chances. "Sleepy, Champ?" she asked, expecting his standard denial. He fought sleep nightly, but never managed to vanquish that particular opponent. Instead of protesting, Tadd only nodded and slid out of his chair.

Then he walked over to Dare and stretched out his little arms.

Willyn's heart dissolved into a pool of affection, and her eyes stung as she watched Dare pick Tadd up and walk out. She didn't go after them, because an inner voice told her to let them have their time.

After the dishes had been cleared and evidence of the impromptu party disposed of, Willyn made her way to the second floor and eased silently along the walkway. The door to Tadd's room was cracked, and Dare's deep voice drifted from within, rising and falling as needed to give life to the story he was reading to Tadd.

Letting her head rest against the wall, Willyn listened, allowing her memory to take her to another time. Another voice. Mason had been a wonderful father, a caring man, and a passionate, considerate husband. And he would want Willyn to grab happiness with two hands if she got the chance. He wouldn't want her to let fear make her choices or prevent her from jumping into love again. If that's what was developing between her and Dare.

She couldn't deny the flutter in her stomach when he walked into a room, or the way her eyes searched him out whenever his voice echoed throughout the large house. And when he kissed her, oh, when he kissed her. Imagining where their physical relationship might lead made her tingle all over. Made the breath catch in her throat.

On the other side of the door, Tadd asked a question about the story, forcing Willyn to clean up her imaginings. It had been ages since she'd yearned for a man this way, and if the goings-on in her child's bedroom were any indication, Tadd had also given his stamp of approval.

Lost in thought, she turned to head toward the stairs, but stilled as another realization occurred to her. She remembered Mason and his circle of friends. Her late husband had been an infallible judge of character, accepting people for who they were instead of what they might represent. Listening to the young giggles that chased after her, she knew one thing with absolute certainty.

Mason would have really liked Dare.

~

After days of calling Beth with no result, Willyn had finally gone to the hospital where she worked. Though she'd been avoiding Willyn, Beth was still concerned enough about her losing her job to agree to meet her the following night. Taking control of the situation, Willyn had insisted on the rendezvous site. She'd chosen a pub downtown that her friends visited whenever they needed a night out. Kylie and Lucia had assured her the staff and regulars were friends and the bar would serve as neutral ground. Even the Amara didn't behave rashly in public.

Modern music from well-placed speakers somehow melded with the antique furnishings. Imprinted tin ceilings in a creamy color were the real thing, having graced Savannah's oldest bar since the year it had been built. Willyn assumed the place had once been a speakeasy, but she couldn't say for sure. It was too bad Claudia wasn't here the give the place a reading. Regardless, there was plenty of old-style charm, and Willyn could see why her friends liked the bar.

With a sigh, she checked her watch again. Beth was late. Willyn wondered how much the girl knew about her powers as a mare and that she'd been affecting her and Tadd. Since Beth had been doing her best to avoid a discussion and possible comeuppance with Willyn, the answer seemed obvious.

Willyn considered Beth's possible motivations while sitting at a table in the corner of the pub with Kylie, Viv, and Claudia. The others had stayed behind, particularly Paige and Anna, who Willyn had instructed to keep an eye on Tadd. Paige was the expert when it came to physical security, and Anna's magic could be an H-bomb when necessary. The two of them would be a force of reckoning. While the coven might have to abide by rules for each witch's trial, when it came to Tadd's safety, the gloves had officially come off. He would stay on the island with his guardians until Willyn's test was over.

Just as her son had acquired a few more shadows, Willyn suddenly had one of her own. Dare slid into the bench seat beside her, pressing his thigh against hers as he set down his beer.

"Did you get lost?" Kylie asked, referring to how long he'd been gone to the men's room.

Dare nodded toward the bar. "I met the owner on the way back and got caught up talking. Nice enough guy. Since he kept glancing over here, I thought I'd scope him out."

"Our protector," Viv said, clinking her glass of cider with his mug. "Cheers."

Kylie reacted true to, well...Kylie form. "Is he cute?" she asked, craning her neck in an attempt to see over the crowd.

Curious, Willyn looked as well. She felt Dare's hand slip into her lap and take hers before he said, "I'm afraid you'll have to make that decision. I'm not going to speculate, nor do I care to know, what specific qualities make a guy *cute*."

"Is that him talking to Jen?" Kylie asked. She was pointing at the female bartender, Jen, and a man with brown hair whose back was to them. He was gesturing to the line of bottles behind the bar as Jen nodded with her hands on her hips. Then the man turned in their direction.

"Oooh," Kylie gushed. "Hunka, hunka." She sipped her prissy, pink drink. "He looks like the hot guy from that video a long time ago." When they all stared at her, she added, "You know. The song was about vibrations or something." She started mimicking a rapper. "Feel it. Feel it."

Viv dropped her head into her hands. "*Dame.*"

Willyn didn't know what the Japanese term meant, but it often fell from Viv's lips when Kylie was around.

"The guy from that video happens to be a pretty well-known actor these days," Viv told Kylie. She supplied the name when the younger girl still didn't know who she meant.

"That's the same guy?" Kylie asked in disbelief. Then she

squinted at the bar owner and said, "Oh. Yeah. He kind of looks like him, too."

Willyn and Dare glanced at each other and laughed. Their actions and responses were becoming more and more in sync, just like a...*gulp*...couple. She pushed down the doubts as they started to rise again and rubbed her fingers against his. There was still so much left unsaid between them, secrets and fears yet to be uncovered, but she was taking things as they came. One kiss at a time.

She was still basking in the pleasure of Dare's nearness, his shoulder and leg rubbing against her, when unexpected company arrived at their table. Beth wasn't among the latecomers. Only Lucia and Hayden stood there, but given the expressions on their faces, they had information about the nightmare girl.

"Anna had a vision," Hayden blurted. "Beth is going to the Amara tonight. Anna doesn't know where exactly, but she described what she saw and heard. If those leads don't help us find her, then we always have the next best thing." She hooked a thumb at Lucia.

"I might need help getting a lock on her, Willyn," Lucia said. "I've tried, but she's being blocked."

"Ronja," Willyn and Viv said as one.

"That's what I'm thinking," Lucia confirmed.

Dare pushed aside his drink. "Tell me what Anna saw."

"She said the building was dark, both the lighting and the place's aura, but it's a dance club of some kind. The music was heavy and what sounded like a mix of metal and alternative." Hayden shifted her eyes to the side in thought. "She also said the front door had a tall gate attached to it, but I'm not sure what that means."

Dare stood. "I do. There is a club that fits your description. *Bedlam*. Wrought iron gates are affixed to the entrance and the severity of the décor only gets more intense inside. A lot of Goths hang out there, but it's primarily a..." he fell quiet, wrinkling his brows as he hesitated.

As Kylie quickly tossed back her drink and Viv jumped up, Willyn also rose from the bench. "A what?" she asked, not sure why she felt a sinking hole of dread in her stomach.

"According to rumor," Dare answered, his eyes going dark, "the place is a vamp bar."

17

The sounds of the city at night died to a low murmur as Willyn, Dare, and the others walked along the cobblestone street to one of the many buildings lined up side by side to face the river. As they headed to the far end and a lonely brick edifice, the scent of fresh pralines and other delectables wafted out of a nearby candy store. The warm, sweetness was enough to tempt even the most vigorous health nut.

The enticing smell was soon replaced by that of clove cigarettes and brown liquor. Willyn couldn't identify the brand, but she'd know the distinctive bouquet of southern whiskey anywhere. She peered up at the balcony where people sat in silver chairs, enjoying their discussions, drinks, and smokes beneath the summer night sky.

They had arrived at their destination. The word *Bedlam* was spelled out above the doors in crooked letters, giving an impression of chaos, just as the name implied. As they passed through the open doors, the black metal bars with spikes on top were precisely as Hayden had described. Willyn didn't know if the message was for people to stay out or a warning that once you were inside…there would be no escape.

If the woman selling tickets was any indication, Willyn prayed it wasn't the latter. Her ink-black hair was in a spiky, Mohawk style with the left side of her scalp shaved bald down to her ear. Several chains ran from the lobe of that ear to her nose, and Willyn grimaced inside. Without a word, the female version of Alice Cooper snatched the money Dare tossed down to cover their group and motioned impatiently for his hand which she stamped hard then shoved away.

"Do you think it's us," Kylie whispered, as she motioned to Willyn's yellow T-shirt and her own of Barbie pink, "or is she just in a lot of pain?"

As Willyn stepped up to get her own hand marked with a strange black symbol, she noted the stretching of the girl's ear and nostril and decided it was probably a little of both. The club's hostess was pretty scary, and Willyn shuddered to imagine what they might find inside.

Paige had been right. Beth definitely had a dark side, and Willyn was afraid it might be too late to help her. Despite the trauma inflicted by the nightmares and Tadd's physical response, Willyn couldn't give up on the girl. She was still convinced Beth was part of her test, and if helping her was the goal, Willyn had hit a significant snag. Apparently, Beth wasn't interested in being helped. She'd come to meet the Amara, and Willyn could only hope it hadn't been a willing choice. If they were somehow forcing Beth, then there was still hope.

The second set of doors was farther in, painted black, and emitting loud, shuddering thumps. As soon as they opened, music crashed over the group like an avalanche of nails and boulders, both jarring and piercing at the same time. A woman passed Willyn as they entered, drinking some sort of dark liquid from a vial. *Please don't let that be what I think it is.*

The vibe of the club was one of unrepentant rebellion, a middle-finger to everything in the world that was soft and light. The décor was in the style of an ancient castle, complete with faux stonework for walls and a few well-placed columns. Skeletons hung from heavy cuffs along one wall, and Willyn hoped they were fake as well. She knew the people here weren't all necessarily evil or dangerous, but she'd bet her last spell book there were some who were.

In single-file, she and the others pushed through the crowds looking for a place to re-group, but the club was packed. Finally they made it to the far side of the dark room and gathered near the wall. A few clubbers were sending Willyn and Kylie scathing looks, clearly sensing that the pastel girls didn't belong. Lucia wore black jeans and a leather vest, so she blended, as did Viv with faded jeans and a simple, wine-colored tank. Hayden wore a sheath dress of dark blue and could have passed either way.

As Willyn searched the mass of swaying bodies for Beth, her eyes were drawn to a couple in the corner who were moving against each other in a suggestive way. She took another look and gasped when the woman lifted her leg and wrapped it around the man's pumping hips. There was no suggestion. They were having sex to the hard and fast rhythm of the music. In public.

Dare grabbed her shoulder and pulled her near, his heated stare having followed hers to the couple's display. "Stay close to me," he growled, wrapping an arm around her waist. His demeanor had completely transformed, and the man who'd gently held her hand and read her son a bedtime story had vanished. In his place was a warrior, alert and savage, ready to defend what was his.

Willyn's womanhood responded with a surge of primal longing. The erotic atmosphere called to a hidden part of her that wanted to succumb, to let desire rule over decency. And the way Dare looked was not helping. His chiseled face was in shadows, lit only by the pulsing stage lights of crimson and blue. A patch of his dark hair hung in his face, lending a bit of wildness to his appearance that contrasted with the sleek black shirt he wore. The sleeves were rolled up to his elbows, revealing strong, sinuous forearms and thick wrists. His jaw clinched while he surveyed the room, and his stance was that of a man ready for a fight.

If Willyn didn't know him, she would have given him a wide berth. The man she was falling for was positively menacing. Intimidation factor ten-out-of-ten.

He was so hot.

Noticing Dare would fit right in if not for her presence beside him, Willyn reined in the sexual mutiny going on inside of her and let her inhibitions slide back into place. Her passions had briefly eclipsed her senses, something she couldn't allow to happen while they were here.

A murky impression pushed at the edges of her sixth sense. Returning to a focused state and opening herself up, she detected an undercurrent of malevolence but couldn't pinpoint the source. "The Amara. They're here," she said to Dare and her friends. "At least a few of them."

"I can feel it, too," Kylie replied, with Viv and Lucia nodding in agreement behind her.

Hayden had been perusing the extensive first level as well as the second floor above where more people, dressed mostly in black, leaned against the railings. "I'd say there have been a number of dark ceremonies performed here. Someone has opened a door." Her concern was apparent. "And it's allowed too many foreign entities to walk right in."

"You see ghosts here?" Lucia asked.

"A few, but they aren't what worries me." Hayden eased between Kylie and Viv, her face entering a spot illuminated by deep red light. "There are things here I don't recognize." She lifted a finger. "And two of them are hovering around that girl, who I'm going to guess is Willyn's friend."

Willyn found the girl Hayden had picked out but had to study her for several seconds before recognition clicked. The brown hair which was normally in a simple braid was unbound with a dark streak running down one side. Blue eyes that had once come across as innocent were now strikingly sexy thanks to black liner and smoky shadows. Her siren-red lips suckled the straw of a cocktail in a sensuous manner, but her body language warned others not to trespass.

Beth had morphed into a Goth goddess, and Willyn felt as if she were truly seeing her for the first time. The young girl seemed much more at home in the navy leather dress that hugged her curves than she had in sedate church attire. Gone was the impression of a lonely, lost youth, and Willyn wondered if it had all been a ruse.

But why would she disguise herself? Or had she been clinging to the last vestiges of a persona she felt she had to project? There was only one person who could provide the answers, and Willyn was more determined than ever to get to the truth. Her heart always went out to the suffering and the needy.

But she didn't like being played.

"Bogies at nine o'clock," Kylie said, nudging Willyn's arm.

Glancing over, Willyn could make out the three bodies moving in a direct line toward Beth. They were on the opposite side of the dance floor, but their overwhelming quality of depravity gave them away. She recognized the Native American man from the day Shauni had battled the Amara on their own stomping grounds, the plantation of great neglect. Behind him was another favorite, Ross the shape shifter. The most frightening form he ever took was his own. The guy was a maniac, in the truest sense of the word.

And swinging her elegant hips through the crowd behind the men was none other than the creator of the dazzling, red blob. Scarlett surely took her name from the ruby tresses surrounding her pretty, white face. Or maybe from the color of her beautiful but toxic magic.

Willyn broke away from Dare and started shoving her way through the crowd. With murderous intent on her face and purpose in her step, pastel girl was beginning to fit right in. She heard Dare call her name but pushed ahead with the single-minded goal of getting to Beth first. She wanted to know why the girl had tortured her and her son, or if she even knew what she'd done. Beth had focused on Willyn for some reason, and she wasn't going to fall into the Amara's clutches without a fight from the coven.

"Beth!" Willyn yelled to get the girl's attention when a cluster of laughing men blocked her path. Beth straightened up at the sound of her name and pivoted her head until she spied Willyn. Her red lips fell open and guilt flashed in her eyes just before she shut it down and hardened her features into an expression of willfulness. It was clear she'd chosen her path, and didn't want Willyn's interference. She shook her head and pushed away from the wall, moving in the direction of the coven's enemies.

"Willyn, wait." Dare was beside her again, moving to shield her from the rowdy horde of drunk males. He barged ahead, clearing the way for her and taking the lead as they pursued Beth.

"Damn it!" Willyn cried when Beth rushed headlong into Ross's arms. The shifter gave his captive an ominous smile before hugging her tight and picking her up to spin around. He set her down in front of him and shoved her, compelling her to go back the way he and his associates had just come. "We can't lose her," Willyn said, urging Dare to move faster with a small shove of her own.

She could feel the other witches behind her and hoped they were able to keep up. There was going to be a confrontation when they caught up to Beth and the thugs who were forcing her to leave with them. Willyn was well aware of Scarlett's strength as well as Ross's ability to change into a variety of deadly animals, and if the dark-skinned man, Tyr, was truly Ronja's lover, he surely possessed his own brand of evil.

Willyn prayed she and Dare wouldn't be facing them alone.

The trio veered down a hallway, dragging Beth along

with them past bathroom doors that were painted black and appropriately labeled *Beasts* and *Beauties*. At the end of the corridor was another door, silver metal of some sort. It swung open to admit the Amara members and their captive before slamming shut.

Willyn and Dare finally broke free of the crowd and raced toward the door, only to be intercepted by two towering hunks of male muscle. The men wore black T-shirts with the red skull and cross bone symbol for poison on the front. They were the club's security.

One of them had shaved his head totally bald. He grinned, purposefully exposing his long, sharp incisors. Correction. They were the vamp version of security.

Dare situated himself between the bouncers and Willyn just as Viv, Lucia, Kylie, and Hayden caught up with them and fanned out to guard from the back. Lowering his head slightly, Dare shot a look of concentration at the two men and shook with repressed fury. "I've never met an actual vampire before, and I'm guessing you two are a couple of posers." He bared his own teeth. "Let's see if I'm right."

The bald one quickly lost his grin while the other giant traded his threatening expression for one of bewilderment. They both stepped politely to the side, like a human gate swinging open for admittance. Dare stepped through without a glance for the bouncers, telling Willyn they'd both been introduced to one of his mind-control specials.

But they weren't through with obstacles, yet. Dare jerked on the handle of the metal door then hit it once with the flat of his palm. It was locked.

"Let me have it," Viv said, moving into the spot Dare had vacated. She held her hand out toward the lever handle, rotating her fingers in one direction then the reverse. If the moving locked made a sound, it couldn't be heard over the music still pumping from the main room. Viv knew her stuff, though. With a quick twist of her wrist, the handle shifted and the door swung open. "Next," she said with a smile before barreling ahead.

Willyn practically leaped through after Viv, leaving Dare swearing behind her but right on her heels. They passed through a non-descript room with two chairs and a row of filing cabinets then through another door that opened into an expansive office. Whoever worked behind the large desk had very expensive tastes. On the far end there were ceiling-high bookshelves, yet one of them didn't look quite right. It was off-kilter.

"There's a hidden exit behind the books," Dare said. "They didn't shut it completely."

"Because they didn't expect us to get past Dee and Dum," Kylie said.

Willyn surged ahead and slid her hands behind the wood panel. It glided open with ease. "We have to catch up with them. Whatever Beth has or hasn't done, she didn't leave with them willingly."

Cement steps dropped off into a lower level, and the musty odor drifting from below reminded Willyn of her last subterranean adventure. "They've gone into the tunnels, and there are lighting fixtures as far as I can tell."

"I saw a flashlight in the front room. I'll grab it," Hayden said.

A clambering noise like running footsteps echoed down the tunnels followed by Beth's voice demanding to be let go. It sounded like she was trying to get away. "We have to get down there," Willyn told Dare, before they started down, taking the steps two at a time with the other women following. They turned a single corner and found themselves face-to-face with Ross who was struggling to hold onto Beth.

"She doesn't seem to like your company," Dare told the shifter, before lowering his head as he had with the two bouncers to control their minds. Ross's eyes were eerie enough, their color the bright blue of a swimming pool, but he could have passed for a zombie when they went blank and his arms fell to his side.

Beth stumbled away from Ross and glued herself to the dirty wall, her red lipstick smudged and eyes wide with fear. Willyn held out a hand to her, but a smooth, cultured voice carried through the shadows. "Not so fast." A transparent blast of magic hit Willyn and her friends, knocking them all to the ground. The spell smelled like cinnamon and made her eyes burn. *Scarlett.*

With her vision blurred, Willyn made it to her knees then to her feet, reaching out toward Dare. He was already up. "Careful, Willyn," he said in a quiet voice. "She's packing some serious heat."

Healing her eyes so she could see, Willyn saw that Dare's power over Ross had been disrupted by whatever Scarlett had thrown at them. He stepped toward Beth, so Willyn did as well. "Beth. Come here," she urged the girl.

Beth shook her head and shoved her hands into the roots of her brown hair. Her face was a crumpled mess bordering on total breakdown. "What is all of this? What's going on?"

"I'll explain everything, but you have to come with us now." Willyn eased closer, but Ross did a two-step toward Beth and laughed with his normal level of derangement. "You don't want to take us all on," the shifter said. "You think Ronja sent us just for fun?"

Ross surprised Willyn then by lunging forward and swiping for her throat. She jerked back and evaded his hand by mere inches. Only the appendage was no longer human, and she realized the tiger's claws had been meant to end her life. The failure didn't faze Ross. He simply grabbed Beth with his other arm and wrapped it around her like a vise, putting the claws to her throat. "Want to try and take her?" he sneered to Dare. His eyes glowed crazily, and Willyn felt sure he hoped Dare would.

She had to make a decision. If she pursued Beth, Dare would, too, and as things stood, there was a good chance he would be hurt. They outnumbered the Amara, but Scarlett was much stronger than Willyn had anticipated. Maybe even stronger than Anna suspected.

And Ross literally had Beth by the throat. He would slice her open without pause.

As if reading her mind, Scarlett walked forward until she was under one of the weak lights. "It's simple. Walk away now and the girl lives." She smoothed a hand over her red coif as if the stand-off was nothing more than an inconvenience. "Make one more move in her direction and..." she tilted her head to the side.

Ross took his cue and made a slow incision down the side of Beth's neck. She whimpered in response but her body was frozen by terror. With rigid steps, she staggered along with Ross as he retreated into the depths of the tunnel. There was nothing Willyn could do, and Beth seemed to understand that better than anyone.

Willyn watched Scarlett stroll away with Tyr at her side. The dark-skinned man's silence had served as Scarlett's ace in the hole. Maybe they had been supernaturally outgunned or maybe not, but Willyn wasn't going to risk the lives of Dare and her friends without being sure.

One last whimper from Beth and Willyn's eyes shot to her young face. A single tear slid down the girl's cheek.

"Hang on, Beth," Willyn murmured. "I'll find a way. I promise." Emitting the breath that had been aching for release, she continued to stare after losing sight of the Amara. The emptiness was overwhelming. She felt Dare's hands on her shoulders and his unwavering support of the choice she'd just made.

She could only hope it had been the right one.

18

"Come in. I've been expecting you." Ronja waved her hand to convey her wish for Beth to follow as she sauntered down the hallway of the old plantation home. Restoration was in progress, but the house still lacked the opulence Ronja was used to. The luxury she demanded.

She had been surprised. The girl, Beth, appeared much younger than she'd imagined, but then visions often lacked clear detail. No matter. Beth was here to serve a purpose and would be used to that end. Nothing more. Ronja had summoned an eighth woman to the Amara's ranks and intended to use Beth to circumvent the future. A future Ronja had predicted for herself years before.

There were to be seven of them, and just as the sages had been betrayed by their wives, so would the females of the Amara. If there were eight of them, they could withstand the loss of one and retain the magical number needed to restore the demon Bastraal to human form. Only then would he embody the full power he coveted. That they all coveted.

The world would be a deliciously horrid place once her master returned. He'd made Ronja a promise in return for her years of service, that every wish residing in her black heart would be fulfilled, and now, almost a millennia later, the time was drawing near. Ronja tossed her silky hair over a pale shoulder. She would soon be rewarded. Thank the fiends.

"This will be your room," she told Beth. With a sweep of her hand, Ronja lit a long row of candles atop a wooden mantle. Flames flickered in the fireplace below, yet with no other source of light, the bedroom remained dark, corners filled only with the whispering movement of shadows.

Ronja preferred it that way.

"I don't know why I'm here," Beth said in a shaky voice. "There's been a mistake."

Ronja tempered the fury sparking behind her eyes. "I don't make mistakes, and this is the first and last time I will advise you to choose your words carefully." She turned a cool, stern expression on the girl. "I don't respond well to insult."

She held her hand up again to prevent Beth from foolishly spitting out anything else that might stoke her temper. The girl would betray her soon enough, but she had to accept the Amara and her place among them first. Then she would die and life would return to normal. "Did you not experience an unexplainable urge to move here to Savannah? Was it not absolutely undeniable?" Ronja asked.

The girl nodded mutely, yet she still shook in her black leather boots.

"The invitation was mine," Ronja explained. "Spend the night and explore your feelings. I believe you'll find your answers quite easily." As she glided closer to Beth, her silk, pewter dressing robe caressed the hardwood floors behind her. She ran a crimson fingernail down the girl's cheek, the action seductive and threatening at once. "When you wake, you'll have seen the extent of your power, how much greater it can be with the right influences surrounding you. Then, I'll expect your answer."

Ronja left Beth standing alone, to consider her options. She knew which course the girl would take, but everyone's role still had to be played out. Even with her knowledge of the future, Ronja still had to perform. She had manipulated the outcome as much as she dared, and now she had to bend to the whim of providence. Fate was often selfish and indulgent. Just like her.

It could be a demanding little bitch.

~

Dare loved southern, summer nights. He walked onto the wide, stone balcony and let his eyes drift closed, immersing himself in the warm air as it settled on his skin like velvet. The last of the magnolia flowers were clinging to their short existence, so the breeze still carried their sweet, heavy fragrance. The creamy blossoms luminesced under the moonlight, displaying their magic for any who stopped long enough to notice.

He settled his arms on the thick railing and gazed into the woods, longing for the company of a strong-willed yet innocently beguiling witch. A loving, nurturing female who proudly wore a silver cross next the symbol of her coven. There weren't many that fit that description. *Willyn. What spell have you cast on me?*

As if in answer to Dare's unvoiced question, the doors of the next room opened slowly. Mesmerized, he watched her exit to the balcony, apparently unaware of his presence. Willyn took slow steps toward the railing, but she didn't see him. Her face was directed to the sky, her eyes filled with the same moon that lit the magnolias with such wonder.

She wore a simple white nightgown that fluttered around her feet. Though the loose material was modest from the waist down, the bodice was of sparkling lace, form-fitting with capped sleeves. Dare could make out the curve of her breasts, rounded above the virgin-like gown. He had to remind himself to take a breath as he watched her. He was seeing a side of Willyn he'd never been privileged with before. She was ethereal, the embodiment of female. She was...magical.

He swallowed hard. *I didn't know mothers dressed like that.*

Without realizing what he was doing, Dare cleared his throat and reached out for her, the sudden action bringing her head around with a snap. "Oh. I didn't know you were out here." She sighed and looked again to the stars. "I needed to recharge. Dawn is usually my special time of day, but something seemed to be calling me tonight."

Following the lead of his suddenly romantic heart, Dare walked closer and let his hand find its way to her golden hair. He couldn't resist the pale length of it as it shone like a beacon. A guiding light meant for him alone. "Maybe it was me," he said in a voice thick with need.

She laughed, somewhat hesitantly. "Maybe what was you?"

Still thoughtful, he ran his fingers down to her nape and along her neck to her collarbone where he brushed across the swell of her breasts. He heard the sharp intake of breath. Saw her eyes deepen with yearning, and knew she would be his. Soon.

"Maybe it was me calling to you." He offered an easy smile to balance the raw desire flooding his senses and hers. "I was thinking about you. Wishing you were here with me." He brushed her hair back from one side of her angelic face. "And then you were."

"Dare." His whispered name on her lips was full of abandon and of entreaty. He was sure Willyn wanted him as much as he wanted her, but she was still afraid. "There are things I ... feel for you, things I want to do, but I'm so confused." Despite her words, she let her head fall back as he stroked her hair, her skin.

He leaned in to place a kiss on her exposed neck, tasting the sweet saltiness of her flesh as it pulsed beneath his mouth. If there were truly vampires in the world, at this moment he understood their compulsions. He wanted every ounce of the woman standing before him, to take and take until she collapsed beneath him and pleaded for more.

But only when her mind was settled and her conscience clear. He would hold himself back until that time, even if it killed him.

Willyn was a witch of faith. A woman of conviction. She was a perfect diamond among the most precious jewels. And he would damn well treat her as such. "Willyn," he took her hand and led her toward his room. "Come with me."

As if breaking free of a trance, she glanced around. "I shouldn't. I need to stay in my room." She tugged against him. "If Tadd wakes up..."

"He won't," Dare promised her. "If it will make you feel better, we can leave my doors and yours open. We'll hear him if he needs us."

Us. If he needs us. As soon as he said it, Dare knew it was true. He had liked the boy from the beginning for his impetuous nature. Now he was becoming attached on an entirely new level. Tadd was part of Willyn, and therefore received the commitment and love that went part and parcel with a family.

Family. His family. He wanted them both.

And just like that, Dare felt the last link fall into place. This was more than a summer infatuation. He had been reading the signs all along, but had refused to admit the truth. Now the easy acceptance of both Willyn and her child filled him with clarity.

He'd come to the island to find a life mate, a partner with gifts like his own. He'd wanted it all for the wrong reasons. In his quest to become everything his parents had despised, he'd stumbled headlong into the one thing they'd wanted him to be. The one thing his parents had pretended to be but never really were. Neither he nor his parents had ever come close to being as pure and good as the woman standing in front of him.

The joke was on him. He'd always run from that life, those people, preferring to view churches and their congregations as simple-minded and blind. Now he realized he'd been wrong.

Just like his parents had been mistaken to judge an individual by definition instead of who they were as a person.

He'd wanted to prove them wrong by finding a woman who would make him more powerful than he'd ever been on his own. What he'd discovered was so much more. He'd come looking for a witch who would combine her gifts with his, but the word magic held a whole new meaning for him now. He'd never known true enchantment until he'd brushed up against his fearless little Christian.

And wasn't that an expression that require getting used to.

He smiled at the irony and the cosmic humor of it all. "There's no trap here, Willyn. I just want to be with you." He guided her into his room, pushing the doors wide for extra assurance.

"There's nothing we can do in here that we can't do outside," she protested.

Dare hiked a brow in response.

She stood taller, ramrod stiff. "Don't get any wrong ideas, Dare Forster."

Sitting on the edge of his bed, Dare pulled her in so she stood between his spread legs. "I don't expect anything from you other than what you're willing to give freely. No regrets tomorrow, only the memory of what it felt like to explore our future."

She stilled. "Future?"

"I guess I'll be the one to go out on a ledge." He took a deep breath for bravery. "I think you know that I...care for you." Okay, so maybe he was still hedging. "And I believe, even against your better judgment and valiant efforts not to, that you have feelings for me, too." He pulled her down to his lap. "I respect you, for who you are and even what you believe."

Her eyes went wide. "You do?"

"Yeah. Ain't that a kick in the ribs?" When he saw her start to shut down, he rushed to continue. "But we still have a lot to consider. And a lot to talk about."

She lifted one side of her perfect mouth, giving him just a glimpse of the dimples that drove him absolutely insane. "All you want to do is talk?"

Rubbing his palms down her curves to her hips, he cocked his head. "Talk. Sure. But I'm not going to lie. If bringing you in here also results in getting your hands on me," he kissed her deep, stroking his tongue against hers to make sure she understood his passion, "then I'm not going to argue."

Taking his hand, Willyn pressed her lips sweetly against the rough skin of his knuckles. Then she surprised him and eased his palm to her breast. He could feel her battering heart through the silk, and the evidence of her desire for him was all it took. Gently squeezing the warm weight in his hand, he used his thumb to circle her nipple through the lace.

She responded and so did he, hardening fully against the constraint of his jeans. He knew Willyn felt it and was no longer afraid when her hips shifted closer, cradling him. "Okay," she said with an exhaled breath. "As long as we understand one another."

~

As Dare eased Willyn onto the bed, she relished the feeling of being held in his strong arms, cherished, protected, and... cared for. She was still scared of the emotions stirring around inside her but had finally admitted to herself that she was glad he'd come to Savannah. Despite his initial motives.

Her new feelings for Dare would need further inspection, but it was hard to think straight with his hands moving all over her. He was exploring her body as if she were a work of art he could barely contain his excitement for. The heat of his flesh seared straight through the thin fabric of her gown. She could feel his touch yet he was still barred from full access. The clash of chastity and lust was surprisingly erotic. They were both treading lightly, cautiously avoiding the strong attraction between them, knowing it would take complete control if they let it go too far.

She and Dare had been fighting temptation since the day they'd met, both caught up in their own fears and their supposed common sense. But no more. After tonight, she would begin to know the mysterious man who'd terrified her, angered her, and intrigued her from the start. The serious, dark-haired man with the piercing blue eyes. The one currently working his way down her neck.

She would come to know the real man, because on this night, she would finally let him in. Into her life. Into her heart. Where she believed he'd always been destined to live.

Dare's lips stopped to linger on her shoulder, bare now that he'd slipped the lace off to expose her skin. His mouth loved and suckled, sending shooting waves of lust from the contact point all the way to her core. He found his way back to the roundness of her breasts and worshipped her there until she was afraid she would burst. His gentle assault was destroying her resolve, but she wouldn't stop him. She couldn't stop him. Not yet.

Willyn held her breath when Dare hooked his fingers inside her sleeves and brought his eyes up to hers, seeking permission to continue. She answered with only a look, staring into eyes that were deeper and more inviting than ever in the low light of only stars and moon. He held her gaze as he drew the fabric down her arms, guiding them out of the shimmering material.

He stilled then to look at her as he touched. Reverently. Lovingly. "You're perfect," he said, slipping a hand back to her hair and rubbing it between his fingers. "Beautiful."

She'd rarely known him to be at a loss for words, and that in itself was his greatest compliment.

The white lace began its descent again, and Dare kissed

her lightly on her stomach, then the arch of her hip. He was moving ever so slowly south … "Wait." Willyn put her hands over his, but her hesitation was enough to halt his movements. "I'm sorry, I just…I'm not sure I'm ready."

When she started to fumble for an explanation, Dare slid his body back up until they met eye to eye. He put a finger to her lips as she struggled to find words. Then he returned her gown to its original position, the same way he had removed it, except this time his kisses were only for her lips and cheeks.

Again she whispered, "I'm sorry."

"Shh," he hushed her and laid his forehead to hers. "It's fine. I understand." He feathered his fingers over her cleavage as if remembering what he'd found beneath the lace. "I didn't expect to…" he smiled in lieu of stating the obvious. "Besides, you still have too much on your mind, and when the time is right," he tucked her hair behind her ear, "I want your full attention. No doubts. No second-guessing."

She placed both hands on the sides of his too-handsome face. "Thank you." Then she kissed him for all she was worth and left them both panting. "Mmm. I had to get that out of my system."

"Did you get all of it out then?"

She skated her hands over his arms, appreciating the well-honed muscles. She sighed. "Hardly."

Dare laughed. "Good. I'd hate to be suffering all by myself."

The mention of suffering brought the image of a terrified Beth sharply to Willyn's mind. She snuggled closer to Dare, but he'd noticed the change.

"What is it?" he asked, rubbing her arms in a soothing manner. "Beth?"

He already knew her so well. "Yes. I just wish things had gone differently. That I'd gotten to her sooner."

"You did all you could. It was out of your control."

"I know. I know." Lifting her face to his, Willyn nuzzled the underside of his jaw where it curved to his ear. "I really don't want to talk about it."

"What do you want to talk about?"

Willyn glided her hand from his abs and up to the opening of the gray button-up shirt he wore. The tips of her fingers danced lightly over his scar. "Tell me," she said mildly. "Tell me what happened." She felt him tense.

"It's not a pretty story," he looped his arms around her waist, conveying his need to keep her close.

Willyn couldn't imagine how difficult this was for him to talk about, but she needed to know. She wanted to heal Dare in every way, erase the pain that lingered from his past, but to do that, she had to learn the truth. He had to let her know how deeply he'd been cut. "It hurt you," she whispered. "In more ways than one."

With a deep quivering intake of air, Dare launched into the story of how he'd been burned by his drunken father and some of his friends. He told her how his mother had stood by and done nothing. Willyn had had suspicions about the puckered cross on Dare's chest, but having the truth confirmed brought it all into startling reality.

No wonder he hated what Christianity stood for. He'd been exposed to the most warped version of religious fanaticism and had it used against him so cruelly. His parents and those horrible men who'd been there that night were not Christians. They were nothing more than another version of those ridiculous bouncers earlier tonight. Posers. Sad imitations of something they didn't truly comprehend.

Anger and grief battled for control inside Willyn, but her emotional needs weren't what mattered now. Only Dare.

"You know we're not all like that. In fact, very few would condone what was done to you." Willyn kissed his cheek to soften her words.

"Maybe not, but plenty of church-goers have shades

of zealotry in them. Many judge a person harshly for not conforming to their ideals. Their lifestyles." His fingers dug into her hip. It wasn't uncomfortable, but she could sense his stress over the subject.

Well, she would just have to barge through it. "If people judge, it's often because they're afraid. I have to admit, I understand that fear. I was almost swallowed by it the night I found out who I really am. What I am. But I accepted it. I had to." Willyn pushed up on her elbows to look into his troubled eyes. "I know what I am and that I'm not evil, but if I hadn't experienced all of this first hand, I might still be suspicious of all things occult. So many misrepresentations have been thrown about."

Dare nodded but remained silent.

"But don't you see?" she pressed on. "No group or religion can be weighed solely by the acts of a few. I guess, as much as we know this and try to live as good people, we all have our own prejudices." She placed the whole of her palm against his scar, willing the affection she felt to force its way through the damaged skin and straight to Dare's heart.

He gave her a half-hearted smile, so she tried a little levity. "It's like my mother always said, churches aren't country clubs. No one gets to choose who's admitted and who's kept out."

"And there are rotten apples everywhere," he added, cupping her chin as warmth touched his features again. "I'm trying Willyn. I really am. It might take me a while to...forgive."

"But you'll never forget," she said.

"How are you going to tell Tadd about the coven and that they're all witches? That you are as well?" he asked, throwing her off with the abrupt change of subject.

"Since we're being honest, I had planned to wait until I couldn't wait anymore," she admitted. "I would rather he have a better comprehension of everything before we have that particular talk. Hopefully, after the prophecy has been fulfilled.

After the coven wins."

Dare started rubbing her again, a telltale sign that he was about to say something she might not want to hear. "I think you're out of time."

"Why?" her heart lurched.

"Tadd has magic, too. I sensed it when I visited that impish little brain of his." Dare sat up higher on the pillows. "He'll need guidance. The gift emerges at different times for all of us." When Willyn made a sound of dismay, Dare spoke again. "I want to be there for him, too. I want to help you and him." He paused. "Do you ever think of having another child?"

Willyn sat up, stunned by yet another jump forward. "I... well, I always thought it might happen one day, but I never gave it much thought until...um...lately." The admission was a little scary, but honesty was honesty. "You're really good with Tadd. That says a lot to me."

Dare ran a hand through his dark brown hair. "Whew. I can't believe we're talking about this."

"You started it," Willyn teased.

Yeah. I did. I just wanted to make sure you were okay with the idea." He looked more serious suddenly. "And with the fact any children we had would almost certainly have power as well. Strong magic."

"I would love any child of mine no matter what."

"And I want you to know, that's part of why I wanted a partner with special gifts." He held up a hand when she started to question him. "None of that matters anymore. I was foolish and short-sighted. I know now that I would want Tadd with or without his magic, and the same will be true if we have children." He tugged her down and enveloped her in his arms again. "All that matters is that they would be ours."

Willyn wanted to let herself go and revel in the image of a life with Dare. Marriage. Children. She craved it now, more than she could believe possible. "And I need to tell you," she licked her lips, dry from her nervousness. "I still want to raise my children in the faith I was raised in. It's important to me. I want to share that with them, as I have with Tadd."

"I'd be disappointed if you didn't," he said, surprising her. "I'm not asking you to change, Willyn, just to accept me for who I am as I try to do the same." He grunted. "But if I do turn out to be...the one, don't expect me to be going to mass with you."

Willyn tossed him a trouble-maker's grin. "I'm actually Baptist."

He shivered. "That's even scarier."

She hit him playfully on his arm then yelped when he flipped her over, trapping her beneath the length of him. "Since I really can't believe what we've been talking about, I think we should put our lips to better use." His mouth found hers in a sweet, searching kiss, and the flames ignited again.

Melting into his arms, Willyn pressed closer and let him have his way. He was putting his mouth to very good use, and it was hard to argue with that.

19

Willyn was mooning over her coffee and reliving the night she'd spent with Dare. They'd barely slept at all, since every time they'd rubbed against each other, more thorough methods of touching seemed to follow. They'd shamelessly made out like teenagers. All night long. And she wouldn't take back a minute of it.

Even with her severe lack of sleep, she felt completely wired. Ready for anything.

"Willyn." Shauni had entered the kitchen and was standing next to her with a strange look on her face. "Did you know Snowball was expecting?"

Okaaay. She wasn't ready for that. She almost choked on her bagel. "Expecting what? You can't mean she's..."

"Going to have kittens. Yes." A smile played at the edges of Shauni's lips. "Haven't you noticed her bulging belly? I'd say she was due any day now. Guess we can hold off on getting her spayed, huh?"

Willyn was still speechless.

Shauni put a hand on her shoulder. "Don't worry. She'll be fine. What's a few more cats around this place?"

"I can't believe I didn't know." Willyn shook her head. "Every time I see her, she's in my room, curled up sleeping on the bed or loveseat. I guess I haven't actually seen her standing or walking for a while." She softened. "My sweet girl is going to have babies. Tadd is going to be so excited. I can't wait to tell him."

"So you're okay with it?"

"Of course. A little blind-sided maybe, but who doesn't love kittens?" Willyn shot a sideways look to Shauni. "I guess someone's been having a little romance right under our noses. Wonder who the mystery tom is."

Kylie walked into the kitchen then, sporting exercise clothing and a sheen of perspiration across her forehead. "Someone else is having a romance right under our noses?" she asked, pouring herself a glass of OJ. "Besides Willyn, I mean."

Willyn gaped. "What exactly are you implying?"

"Oh. Nothing," Kylie said with a pucker of her lips. "Just that I went by your room last night, but you didn't answer when I knocked. I peeked in, because I was worried about you, and you weren't there."

"I…"

"And your balcony doors were open, so, naturally, I checked outside," Kylie continued.

"Yes, but…"

"Then I noticed Dare's balcony doors, which happen to be right next to yours, were open, too."

Willyn cocked a brow. "What did you do then? Naturally?"

"I made myself scarce, of course. I wasn't about to interrupt the call of the wild." The young blonde smiled wickedly.

"Oh, for heaven's sake." Willyn waved a hand at Kylie, but couldn't evade the two sets of eyes that stared and waited patiently. She held up her hands, looking between Kylie and Shauni. "We were just talking."

"Mm hm." Kylie was smiling broadly now.

Willyn would usually have gone up in flames at this point, but instead she felt a cheeky grin of her own fighting for release. "We did talk," she insisted before adding, "Mostly."

While Kylie erupted with a gleeful shriek, Shauni leaned

onto the island like a master interrogator. "What did you talk about?"

Buttering what was left of her bagel, Willyn shrugged. "All kinds of things. Us. Our differences. We even talked about..." her train of thought diverged as a lightning bolt of insight struck.

"What?" Kylie prompted.

Willyn finished her sentence with astonishment. "Church. We talked about church." She jumped up, scraping her stool across the gray, flagstone floor. With a hand on her chest, she took a deep breath. "I know where the book is."

She hurried out of the kitchen and straight for the library to make use of one of the computers. Shauni and Kylie were hot on her trail. "It makes perfect sense. I don't know why I didn't see it before." By the time she got there, they'd picked up a couple of stragglers who'd been coming down for breakfast and had seen the three of them rushing through the grand hall.

"What's up?" Hayden asked as she and Claudia took up positions with the others, all of them crowding around the monitor as the screen lit up and asked for a password.

Willyn typed hers in and quickly pulled up a search engine. "In my dream, Beatrice told me her daughter would hide the book somewhere 'he cannot go.' I'm sure that *he* was the preacher, but we were off on the place he wouldn't be able to go. It wasn't the island." She glanced up at her friends excitedly. "It's a church."

"Wait," Kylie said. "He was a preacher. He went to church all the time."

Claudia spoke up, her voice reflecting the enthusiasm Willyn was feeling. "I'd be willing to bet the only churches he ever visited were ones he founded. Churches that weren't true houses of God."

"Because he was evil," Shauni said. "He wasn't really a man of the cloth. He wouldn't have been able to enter churches or walk on sacred ground."

"But Beth went to church," Kylie argued. "She's with the Amara now and could be as bad as they are, for all we know." She sent an apologetic look to Willyn. "Sorry. Just sayin'."

"It's okay," Willyn said, fingers flying over the keyboard as she looked for more specific information. "I don't know what to think about Beth anymore. As far as the preacher, if my dreams were true to form, he was more monster than human. He wasn't just a man with special powers like the Amara. I think he was a demon in disguise or something similar. There's no way he could have entered a house of worship."

"So what's next?" Hayden asked. She leaned over the desk to see what Willyn was typing and had to pull her caramel-colored hair out of the way when it fell forward. "What are you searching?"

"I'm looking for churches that have had fires," Willyn answered.

"Oh, like from your dream. Beatrice said the book would be hidden after the fire." Kylie nodded as if she'd figured the whole thing out.

"Surely more than one church has ever burned in Savannah. We'll still have to narrow down the options," Claudia said.

"I've got a feeling I already know where we need to look, but I want to make sure about the fire." Willyn snapped her fingers and pointed to the screen. "And there it is." She read aloud. "On Sunday evening, February 6, 1898, the cathedral caught fire and was nearly destroyed." Skimming her finger over the lines, she stopped when she got to the next paragraph. "The reconstruction was completed two years later in 1900. I think the time is right for what Beatrice was wearing."

Willyn rolled her chair back and stood. "I realize my evidence is pretty flimsy, but I know I'm right. As soon as the idea occurred to me, I just knew." She met each of their stares. "It's no coincidence that Claire's family attends this church, or that I felt compelled to go there, even though I'm not Catholic."

Hayden supplied the last link in Willyn's chain of reasoning. "The same place Beth showed up, though something tells me she's not normally a faith-driven kind of gal."

"Exactly. She felt the pull just like I did. The book is there. It has to be." Willyn was thrilled to be closer to finding the book and possibly completing her portion of the prophecy. Unfortunately, there was one huge boulder blocking the path. One put there by her own conscience. "I'll wait until tonight. When things quiet down." She shook her head and sighed, hardly able to believe what she was about to say.

"Then I'll go break into the church."

~

The full moon had arrived, hovering in the midnight sky like a watchful sentinel. Willyn could only hope the yellow orb and other energies at work tonight saw fit to be on her side. It wasn't every night she committed a crime against a house of worship. All things considered, and from what she felt she knew of her chosen deity, Willyn believed He would understand.

The oak trees downtown were thick with full, summer leaves, so the foliage blotted out most of the sky and cast darkness on the group of soon-to-be-trespassers as they passed beneath. Whenever they crossed a street, though, there was the lingering moon again, monitoring their every move.

Against loud protests from Paige, she and Anna had stayed behind to watch over Tadd. Claudia and Hayden had also remained on the island, along with the Attingers and all of Joe's family. Safety in numbers was more imperative than ever.

When the spires of the cathedral came into sight, Willyn's stomach suddenly seemed full of creepy-crawlies, but she clamped down on her anxiety until it skittered out through her fingers. The grand church was still beautiful and somehow more sacred in the blue shades of night. With the late hour, or actually, the very early hour, the city was peaceful and inactive. The better for slipping unnoticed into a popular tourist attraction.

They eased down the palm tree-dotted sidewalk running from the front of the church to the back, moving in pairs to appear less conspicuous. Willyn was familiar with the building's layout, and Viv would use her telekinesis to move the door's locks, so they went first, followed minutes later by Dare and Lucia, then Kylie and Shauni. They were all dressed in dark hues and comfortable clothing, ready to run or fight as needed.

When the wooden door swung open, the group of six quickly sneaked in with Shauni closing it behind them and re-engaging the locks.

"This way to the main area of the cathedral," Willyn said. "Something is tapping at my memory, making me feel we should start there."

"I could help, you know," Lucia offered. Her special gift was the ability to find things, lost or forgotten, article or human. It had helped her become a renowned relic hunter.

"Thanks, but I have to do this myself."

Lucia shrugged. "I thought that would be the case. Lead on," she added with a smile.

Even Kylie was quiet as they trouped down the hallway to a door that opened into the massive area containing the nave and alter. The architecture here was absolutely stunning with high arched ceilings seeming to reach for heaven itself. Multiple windows showcased stained glass depictions of Biblical scenes or characters, and murals of the apostles were high above. The church was a work of art, reminiscent of the ancient cathedrals found in Europe. The spiritual love and guiding faith was almost palpable here, and Willyn understood her ancestor's choice for a hiding place.

No malevolent beings could enter here.

Maybe there was still hope for Beth, but Willyn cast aside the thought to focus on her current objective. Locating the book was paramount. It was one of the three items needed to defeat the demon Bastraal. She couldn't allow anything or anyone else to distract her from the task at hand.

Walking up the steps to the apse, or circular dome area housing the altar, Willyn let her eyes close. She let herself travel back to the Sunday mornings she'd spent here in worship. She'd always been fascinated by the ornate, white marble altar. Placing her hands on the heavy piece, she let her inner senses listen and feel. Nothing. No resonations of any kind.

"Didn't you say the church was renovated again more recently?" Kylie asked, viewing the large room with a mix of admiration and concern. It was a big, big place with too many nooks and crannies to list. Like Willyn, she was evidently hoping for a supernatural clue of some kind to appear.

"The latest job focused on paint and stain glass replacement. The basic construction should still be the same as it was after the initial rebuild. I would think the St. Germaine witches who hid the book here would put it in a place that would last, a place impervious to fire and water, and one that would never need to be replaced."

"Like the foundation," Dare said. "If the book is well protected and concealed, it will also be difficult to get to."

Willyn wandered over to a corner near a life sized portrayal of the crucifixion. Several times she'd had to corral Tadd from the area beneath. He loved to run his cars all around the stone tiles of the floor, and he always gravitated to the same spot. With renewed zeal, she hurried to the corner and fell to her knees.

Again she placed her palms on the hard floor, but where the marble of the altar had been cold, the tiles here throbbed with energy and heat. A tingling sensation spread up her wrists, her arms and into her torso. Whatever was beneath the floor here didn't just resonate with her. It rumbled and echoed. "Here!" she cried to the others, momentarily forgetting the need for stealth.

When Dare joined her on the floor, she looked to him for support, dreading what would come next. "I hate the thought of damaging anything here, being the cause of desecration." She heard the others close in. "But the book is under these tiles."

"Let me give it a try," Viv said. "I'll feel it out." Holding her hands out, Viv stared at the area Willyn had designated. After a moment she made a sound of annoyance before kneeling down and putting her hands on the floor, flesh to stone. Her face grew red before she exhaled with a grunt and breathed heavily, having exerted herself on what should have been a simple job for her. "Sorry. I don't think it's meant to be."

"It isn't," Willyn said in a somber tone. "I have to give something of myself for this to work. I have to show my faith to one power by turning my back on another."

Dare put his hand on her shoulder. "Material things," he said.

"I know. It just feels so wrong." Willyn looked at the others. "What can I use?"

Shauni opened a compact tool bag that hung across her chest. Though hoping to avoid the destruction of anything in the church, they'd also known to come prepared. Shauni handed Willyn a small but heavy hammer.

"Watch your eyes," Dare said as he stood to stand back with the other women.

Willyn grasped the handle and sent up a quick request for forgiveness before bringing the head of the hammer down in the center of where she'd felt the energy. The large white square cracked in a spider web design and spread to three of the surrounding tiles before the popping noise that accompanied the fracture stopped suddenly.

"It's as if it were made to break that way," Lucia said. She made the sign of the cross over her chest and mumbled something in Spanish. At least Willyn wasn't the only one uncomfortable with the assault on the temple.

They all worked to move the broken pieces away and piled them on a piece of cloth Shauni had extracted from the bag. It didn't take long before a slab of concrete was revealed. It was obviously separated from the surrounding material and cut in a perfect square. Willyn ran her fingers along the seam, found a good grip, and lifted. The lid was heavy, so Dare slipped his hands under and heaved until it skated to the side atop the remaining tiles.

An object lay inside, bundled in brown fabric resembling muslin. Willyn had no doubt about the contents, but she still unwrapped the substantial item until the book was revealed. She gently touched the leather cover only to receive another jolt. It wasn't painful, but potent and enlightening in a way she couldn't describe.

She wrapped the book back up and motioned for Kylie to open the empty satchel she held. No one wanted to carry the valuable tome back to the island without some sort of protection.

Willyn got up from her kneeling position as the others gathered the broken shards to carry away. She consoled herself with the assurance that the cathedral was going to be receiving a rather large and anonymous donation in the days that followed. It was the least she and the coven could do to show appreciation to the church that had unknowingly guarded the book all these years. And it would more than cover the damage to the floor.

The group was walking back down the hall toward the back door when Willyn paused.

"What's wrong?" Viv asked, noticing the abrupt change.

Willyn put a hand to her amulet. The clear stone at its center remained quiet. It wasn't emitting the glorious sound Shauni's had after she'd passed her test. "Something's not right. I'm not done, yet."

"Let's just get out of here, return the book to Anna, and get her take on things." Kylie seemed more nervous now than when they'd originally entered the church. They all did.

Shauni nodded. "Right. We need to hurry."

Now that she wasn't focused on her silent necklace, Willyn picked up on the disturbing vibe coming from somewhere outside the church. It wasn't very near, but it was getting closer. "The Amara." It was all she had to say. In an instant they went from covert operation to emergency evacuation.

Willyn was sure they were all thinking the same thing. They'd come up against the Amara before and would do so again. Many times. The fear festering in each of the witches wasn't for their own safety.

It was for the book.

"We should stay together when we hit the streets this time," Dare said, taking control and tossing out a tactical plan. "Kylie. You and Shauni stay together no matter what and protect the book."

"If things get ugly, I'll arrange for an air mail delivery by bird if I have to," Shauni said. The comment would have sounded crazy coming from anyone else, but she could actually pull it off.

They maneuvered their way out the exit and were moving down the walk before the door had time to close behind them. Viv sent a twisting motion over her shoulder to the locks as they departed, so the church wouldn't be open to intruders. Any *other* intruders.

"They're out there," Lucia said quietly, her accent unable to disguise the nervousness lurking beneath.

"I feel it, too," Willyn said. "It's like they're more hyped up than usual. I've never been able to feel them like this."

Dare pressed Willyn to move quicker by putting his hand on her lower back. "They must know you have the book. Somehow."

A flash of intuition blasted Willyn from down the street on her left as they crossed toward the park. Peering in that direction, she saw a female figure step out of an alcove. Though she couldn't make out the woman's features, she was sure it was Beth standing there, staring at her as if she were sending Willyn a silent message.

Willyn made her decision in an instant. The book had been found, yet she hadn't completed her task. It had to be about Beth. It simply had to be her. The girl must be the missing part of the equation that Willyn needed to solve.

But Dare would never let her go to Beth, not by herself. Sparing a glance for him over her shoulder, Willyn used the only leverage she possessed. Dare understood what was at stake and how crucial the ancient text they'd discovered in the church actually was. She saw her opportunity coming from ahead, a cluster of young people out for a night on the town. Perfect.

"We need to be up there with Kylie," she told Dare, her voice shaking with the deceit she planned. This time, she was the one giving him a little push of encouragement. "Hurry. I'm right behind you. You need to be closer to the book in case anything happens."

Dare seemed momentarily perplexed but quickly did as she requested. He angled himself in front of Willyn, fully expecting her to stay with him. Just as they were about to pass the group of revelers, Willyn veered toward the side street where Beth had been and ran in that direction, sure Dare would notice her absence at any second.

"Willyn!" She heard him call out for her as she rounded the corner but couldn't tell if he'd seen her yet or not. She hated doing this to him, but every mystic particle in her body screamed at her to continue on. This was what she had to do, and only she could be sure of that. Beth would lead her to wherever she had to be to complete her trial. To whomever she had to see. The girl was still up ahead, but she darted into the road and disappeared in the shadows of the hulking trees.

Willyn steeled herself and cast out any remaining fear. Then she followed.

20

Dare realized almost immediately that Willyn had slipped farther away from him than he wanted. Turning to scout the area, he assumed she'd been caught up in the crowd of kids making their way across the square. He waited until they moved on, expecting her to pop out from the mob at any second, but she didn't. Willyn was gone.

A whisper of panic breezed through his stomach. He cast his eyes around the square, turning in a circle and searching until he caught a glimpse of pale golden hair reflecting the moonbeams. She was running away from him and the other witches. *What the hell is she doing?* "Willyn!" he yelled, sure that she heard him. She didn't stop.

With the book found, and Tadd safe on the island, Dare realized there was only one thing left that would make Willyn throw caution aside. Beth. And if he hadn't been sure about the girl before, he could unequivocally state his opinion now. He didn't trust the little schemer. Not at all. And if Willyn was going after her, it meant trouble.

The Amara was close. All the women had felt them. Or had they been sensing Beth? Had she been turned that quickly? He'd bet Ronja would love adding a mare to her collection of miscreants. And something told him Beth would appreciate the increase in her powers with Ronja's evil turbo boost.

With no time to spare, he quickly caught up to the others.

"Willyn's gone. I think she's after Beth," he said, filling them in as briefly as possible. "I'm going after her."

Viv took a step in his direction. "I'll come with you. And Lucia," she added, motioning to the other woman. "We might need her to locate Willyn if she's gotten too far ahead."

"Shauni and I will get the book to Anna. Don't worry." Kylie spoke with the authority of someone well beyond her years, but that was nothing new. The college girl often surprised them in times of crisis.

With words of encouragement and safe-being all around, they went their separate ways. Dare sprinted toward the street he'd seen Willyn take, hearing the pounding feet of Viv and Lucia as they ran to keep up. He was grateful for the glowing moon and the light it cast on the city. It would save them time and make it easier to see their quarry.

"Stay straight on this road," Lucia called from behind.

Dare kept his eyes glued to the dark street, glancing at the historic architecture of homes as he passed, making sure they didn't accidentally miss Beth. There were plenty of courtyards and recessed basement entryways where a person could hide. Soon they were crossing Troupe Square, and on a direct route to Forsythe Park. "I think I know where they're going," he told the others as they slowed to catch their breaths.

"Good," Lucia said between pants, "because I've suddenly lost her signal."

Dare's teeth ground and his brows furrowed. "Damn it. That's not good."

Lucia's worried eyes met his. "She's being blocked by someone."

Dare nodded. "Come on. The old hospital is across the park. I think that's where Beth is taking her."

"Where she's luring her," Viv said, clarifying what they all suspected. Beth was leading Willyn straight into a trap.

With renewed energy, they shot straight across the grass and past the café that resembled an amphitheater. The fountains spurted gaily for passerby, as if it were just another starry night in Savannah. For Dare, it had become hell on earth.

The heat seemed more oppressive and the shadows looked larger, jeering at him, mocking his futile attempt to find Willyn. The limbs of the oaks were crooked arms reaching for his heart to pull it out and toss to a wandering beast. But nothing scared him more than what he feared might happen to the woman he loved.

Why hadn't he told her? Damn his cowardice. What if he didn't get another chance? Running harder, he forced the cynical thoughts from his mind. He would find her. She would be all right.

And he *would* tell her. He had to.

There! He caught sight of her again, though her form was small with distance. She was standing in the vacant parking lot of the dilapidated hospital. Her body language screamed of hesitancy and fright. *Listen to your instincts, Willyn. Wait for me.* Pumping his arms and legs, Dare was too winded from the exertion to shout for her.

He heard Beth's voice as he crossed the street, telling Willyn they shouldn't talk out in the open. *Almost there. Almost.*

He saw Willyn clench her fists and knew she'd made up her mind. She disappeared around the back corner before he could let her know he was coming. When he made it to the back, she was nowhere to be seen. Viv and Lucia caught up with him, both gasping for breath like he was.

"She went in." Dare studied the brick building on the back side where it butted against the older portion of white elegance gone to ruin. "I don't see how they got inside."

"Does it matter?" Viv asked. "If it saves us time, we should go back to the front. Those boarded windows won't be much of a barricade."

"You're right," Dare said. "Let's go." They walked now to

catch their breaths and restore their energy. All of them knew
they would have to be as close to full potential as possible. The
Amara were in there with Beth and Willyn, but neither Dare
nor the witches could tell who or how many.

They were going in blind.

Bounding up the curved staircase on the front side, they
broke through the thin boards with only a few well-placed
blows. One by one they eased through the window, careful not
to cut themselves on the jagged remnants of glass. Paint cans,
tarps, and scaffolding littered the old building, but it looked
as if the remodeling had ceased a while ago. Maybe Beth had
chosen the site for that reason. No one would be around to
interrupt her plans.

A scuffle overhead drew their attention to the ceiling, where
water stains were plentiful. The three of them spread out until
Lucia called out in a hushed voice, "This way."

Swiftly but silently they ascended, with Dare taking the
steps two at a time, until they emerged in another hallway. To
his left, he noticed a strange difference in the level of light. He
made his way to the wide, double entry. There were no doors
hanging, just a gaping hole. The room beyond was large, and
had probably housed rows of beds in the past. Beds with sick or
dying people who would have left traces of their misery behind.

It was the perfect place to work black magic.

Willyn stood in the middle of the infirmary, her back turned
to him as she talked to Beth. Bursting into action, Dare moved
forward only to ram into some type of invisible barrier. "What
the?" He beat his fists uselessly at the undetectable wall.

Willyn turned, her mouth opening in distress as she cried
out to him. He re-doubled his efforts to force his way through
the barrier but did nothing more than hurt his own fists. Viv
and Lucia were beside him, equally at a loss for how to break
through.

"Ah-ah-aaah," a sweetly sinister voice cooed to him before

Scarlett stepped out from behind the wall on the side. "It's no use, darling. You don't have what it takes to beat me." She tossed a dismissive look to Viv and Lucia. "And neither do they." Wearing sleek fawn-colored pants with a ruffled pink shirt, she was the picture of high society. Not a single ruby curl on her head was out of place. Her hair was parted to one side and clamped with glittering barrettes above both ears. "But I'm so glad you're here in time for the performance. We're calling it, 'Death of a Witch.' Act one is just about to start."

Terror pierced Dare's chest with an icy rod. "No! Willyn!" He pounded against air that felt like granite, screaming for Willyn to run until his voice grew hoarse. Viv was on the phone, trying to call Anna. Tears were in her eyes and her voice as she told him she couldn't get a signal.

Heart galloping and muscles tense, Dare looked on helplessly, racking his mind for a solution. He saw Willyn jerk her head at something that caught her attention. Then she looked back at him with love, sadness, and acceptance. The liquid coursing through his veins turned to ice as Dare stared past her into the far reaches of the room. Two hulking shapes rose from the shadows like harbingers of doom. Tyr and Ross. They were headed straight for her.

~

Willyn scanned the room, searching the decaying infirmary for any way to escape. Tyr and Ross were creeping closer, and both were sending out strong waves of hatred and the thirst for violence.

Seeing no obvious solution, Willyn looked at Dare and allowed a thousand regrets to swamp her. How could she have been so reckless? Chasing after Beth had led her right into the hands of the Amara. She wasn't gifted with superhuman strength and speed like Paige, or the ability to control energy like Kylie. As far as being a witch, she was still green, and couldn't best Scarlett's power. And she wouldn't last long in a physical fight with the two men.

She'd failed. If they succeeded in killing her, the chain of events that were supposed to flow from one woman in her coven to the next would be broken. She'd let everyone down, and all because she'd followed her heart and had refused to heed her sisters' warnings about Beth. She'd tried to save the girl, even after she'd displayed a dark and disturbing side of her personality.

Willyn had only wanted to help, and it had ultimately brought her here. Her amulet remained silent, and now the very person she'd tried to save walked in from a side door with a disgusted look on her face. "If you had left me alone, none of this would have happened," Beth said, crossing her arms over her chest and wrinkling her nose as if viewing something repugnant. "I didn't need you, and I thought you'd get the point when I didn't answer your calls."

Willyn swallowed the anger that jumped to the forefront. "I wanted to talk to you about the nightmares you've been causing. Whether you meant to or not, you hurt my child." Willyn breathed deeply, holding onto calm. "I won't tolerate that, but I was trying to give you the benefit of the doubt. I still tried to help you at the club that night." She motioned to Ross. "You did not go with him by choice."

Beth lifted a shoulder and gazed out the windows behind Willyn, seemingly unconcerned. "True. But I was wrong about that. I've learned many things since then." Her eyes landed back on Willyn with a vengeance. "Ronja has taught me so much. She's shown me that I'm not alone. That I'm not bad for being who I am. I'm this way for a reason, and I want to find out more. I want to have more."

"I never said you were a bad person," Willyn said, glancing at Dare from the corner of her eye. He was speaking heatedly with Viv and Lucia, and none of them looked happy. This was not good.

"You would have eventually," Beth said sharply. "People like you always do."

"That's enough taunting, Beth." Scarlett glided over the floor as if she were at a debutant ball instead of plotting murder in a decrepit old building. The air smelled foul, and as the odor expanded, Willyn realized it was coming from Scarlett and the two men. It was the smell of evil, and if the overwhelming stench was any indication, these three were one-hundred percent pure. "Let's get this done. I can't wait to report to Ronja. Even with the book, Anna's coven will be wrecked. With the loss of a witch, the power of the nine will essentially be..." Scarlett ran a long fingernail down Willyn's stomach and laughed, "gutted."

Dare began pounding at air again, and Willyn realized why when she felt arms wrap around her and pick her up to spin her full-circle. The deranged laughter stabbing her ear drum could only belong to Ross. The shifter held her in arms of titanium and shook her roughly while squeezing her hard enough to break ribs. She panicked as her lungs struggled to draw oxygen.

Scarlett laughed as Ross continued his torture, and Tyr stood to the side. The Native American man stood by, expressionless and silently intimidating. Beth circled to a position that would give her a better view of the action.

Then she smirked.

White-hot rage tore loose from somewhere deep inside Willyn. She was bombarded by memories of Beth in her church dress, so lost and nervous. Dare's quick judgment and how his aggression had been hiding a strong yet tender man inside. She thought of the preacher and his unholy followers. The unspeakable torment and death forced on Beatrice so many years in the past.

Tadd. His bloody eyes and terrifying cries.

Power coursed through her body, begging for release and retribution. Paige's introduction to self-defense techniques flashed in her mind, and Willyn re-enacted the motions she'd performed on training day. Ross might be stronger, and the Amara might still bring her down, but she wasn't going until a little bit of their blood ran to mingle with hers.

Ross was holding her close, so she threw her head back, ramming the thick bone of her skull into his face. She heard a satisfying crunch when she hit his nose. Momentarily caught off guard, his arms loosened enough for her to bring her fists up her body, so her forearms could press outward and down. The strength in his hands was no match.

Once free, she immediately stepped out and pivoted to send a sidekick to his gut. Although he made an *oof!* noise, the shifter didn't slow down for long. Tyr was still watching quietly, probably waiting to jump in if his colleagues actually lost control of the situation. Beth stumbled back against the wall, having seen the ferocity pouring out of Willyn.

Ignoring Tyr and Beth, who currently posed no threat, Willyn danced away from the approaching Ross, but kept an eye on Scarlett. The redhead's magic was crippling at the very least. For all Willyn knew, the blow that would end her life might be one spell away if the vile witch chose to get involved.

Sensing his lunge, Willyn took advantage of Ross's momentum and struck out with her right arm. The heel of her hand hit his nose again, causing blood to splatter and Ross to howl. A human howl, full of pain and rage. The unnatural blue of his eyes pulsed as he growled at her, his left eye jumping with a tic. His lack of movement was more terrifying than his assault had been. With arms still raised in a defensive posture, Willyn waited for the shifter's next move.

And that was when Scarlett decided to play.

The scent of cinnamon warned Willyn magic was coming,

and this time it circulated in the air with the additional pungent smell of decay. Whatever Scarlett was churning up was going to be ugly and would put a stop to Willyn's retaliation. Her revolt was over, and she gave one sigh of remorse before the pain wrapped around her like a python. It slithered up from her feet and encircled her body, hobbling her legs and entrapping her arms. She was frozen, unable to run or defend herself.

Ross grinned cruelly as blood from his mangled nose dripped down to stain his teeth. His first punch rattled Willyn's brain and made her left ear buzz. The next slammed into her other cheek and sent her head flying back hard enough to crack her neck. After that, the blows landed all over her body, causing focal points of pain wherever he hit. Ross spaced the areas of his attack apart, so each punch would be felt as sharply as the first.

Suddenly Ross stepped away and the brutal beating finally ceased. Soon after, Scarlett's magic peeled off, unwinding in a reverse manner. Willyn dropped to the floor in a heap. Dust puffed up around her when she landed, but she couldn't bring herself to care. All she felt, all she knew was pain.

Dare had stopped pounding to get in and was instead focused on Ross. He was attempting to drive thoughts into the shifter's head, to control his actions. When Dare's shoulders slumped and he slammed his palms against the transparent barrier, Willyn knew his magic had failed to pierce the obstacle, just as his fists had.

The floor started vibrating, and Willyn mustered the energy to move her head in search of the source. The windows and their white frames with peeling paint were shaking as if an earthquake was building under the earth. It wasn't seismic activity, though. The trembling and shuddering were coming from Viv. She was trying to tear apart the very building if that's what she had to do to get to Willyn.

They were trying, her love and her sisters. They were trying to save her.

A set of brown high heels clicked across the floor and stopped as they entered Willyn's floor-level view. Scarlett spread her arms and gave a great thrust of her chest. The shaking stopped, and Willyn knew the black witch had expanded her shield. None of Dare's or Viv's tricks were working. No one could get to her. Anna could match Scarlett's magic, but she would never get here in time.

Finality and grief covered Willyn like a cold blanket. It was over. She was going to die, and the prophecy would shatter along with her life force.

As if on cue, Ross gathered Willyn to his chest and hoisted her to her feet. The change in position allowed her to feel her injuries more acutely. Her lower lip was split, bruises were forming all over her, and most concerning of all, she could feel heat spreading beneath her ribs. As a healer, she knew exactly what that meant. She was bleeding internally.

Willyn didn't want Dare to see her pain, or her fear. Allowing all the love she felt for him to rise up, she locked her gaze onto his deep, blue eyes and smiled. A singular drop ran down her cheek, blood or tears, she couldn't say, but she held his stare until he lifted his hand and pressed it against the solidified air. The emotion in the gesture caused Willyn to suck in a breath. He would stay as close to her as he could, until the end. He would be there for her.

Stretching out her arm, fingers open and reaching, Willyn sent a silent plea to the man she'd come to love. To trust. *Take care of my boy.*

Dare let his head fall forward, hitting his fists against the barrier one last time before raising his eyes back to hers and nodding. A single tear slid down his face, a reflection of Willyn's sorrow.

Ross jerked her arm back, twisting it painfully as he brought it behind her waist, so he could grasp both of her wrists at the same time. Scarlett looked at Ross and nodded. In response, the shifter held his free arm out for Willyn to see. She watched as his human limb transformed into that of a tiger, the extended claws thick, yellow, and razor-sharp.

The time had come, and she would leave this world in the same way she had lived her life, filled with grace and humble devotion. Since both of her hands were fastened behind her, Willyn couldn't clasp them together at her chest. But she was still able to drop to her knees. A position she knew well. Gazing at Dare and thinking of Tadd, Willyn began to speak. "Our father, who art in Heaven, hallowed be thy name."

Ross jerked on her arms, sending shafts of pain into her shoulders, but she stayed calm and serene, allowing the peace to rush into her heart. "Thy Kingdom come, thy will be done, on earth as it is in Heaven."

Scarlett bent down to laugh in Willyn's face before her refined features curled into a sneer. "That's right, little Christian. Pray to a god that has forsaken you." She slapped Willyn, and looked suddenly furious, as if the prayer had offended her. "You're a witch! Do you think you'll be welcomed? You're going to burn. Burn! Just like your ancestor did before you. Just like your coven will do when Bastraal comes to power."

Scarlett straightened and stomped away, unwilling to look back. She acted like she was trying to regain some of the self-control she'd so quickly lost.

Willyn still looked straight ahead at Dare. She held onto her faith, knowing Scarlett's words were false. The putrid souls of the Amara clan could never know true grace. "Give us this day our daily bread, and forgive us our trespasses, as we forgive those who trespass against us."

Dare kneeled slowly, letting his hands settle on top of his thighs. His eyes never left Willyn's. "Lead us not into temptation." Though his face was etched with sadness, Dare began speaking. Willyn couldn't hear his voice, but she could feel that the rhythm of his speech matched hers. "But deliver us from evil." That his lips formed the same words. "For Thine is the Kingdom, the Power and the Glory."

Dare was reciting the Lord's Prayer. For her. For love.

"For ever and ever." Willyn's spirit lifted and filled with light. "Amen."

Just as Ross's arm began its arc down, claws headed for Willyn's throat, a glorious sound began to fill the room. Ross froze in mid-motion as Scarlett whipped around to glare at Willyn's amulet, the clear stone in the middle rang out, clear and true. If diamonds could sing, this is the sound they would make.

"No! No!" Scarlett exploded with wrath. "It doesn't matter! It's too late! Kill her Ross! Kill her now!"

Along with the sweet sound of Willyn's necklace, a crystal blue light poured into the room, filling every dark corner. Everyone, on both sides of the barrier, looked up to find the source of illumination.

The entire ceiling and several feet of the upper portion of the walls were immersed in light as it began to spread downward, miraculous with its purity. Tiny particles glittered within the cloud of light, but Willyn didn't recognize the source of the beautiful display by sight. She felt in her soul.

Willyn didn't need confirmation, but Scarlett's reaction to the light provided it. "You have no place here!" the redhead screamed toward the luminescent ceiling. "Leave! Get out!" Anxiety danced over the black witch's countenance, and for the first time since Willyn had encountered her, Scarlett looked afraid. In fact, she seemed terrified. She stumbled two steps back and held her arm up defensively. Willyn followed her alarmed stare.

Two bodies were emerging from the light. They appeared to be naked, but were cloaked in a pale shimmer, so their flesh wasn't clearly visible. Except for their faces. A woman with onyx skin hovered next to a male being, one with the palest of blonde hair, almost as white as his face. The man's chest pushed forward in a barely noticeable movement. As she studied the unexpected pair, Willyn realized they were both shifting back and forth, ever so slightly. Then she saw why, and even her faithful heart was surprised.

They were being held aloft by the wings on their backs.

Tyr had finally decided to get into the action, spurred by the arrival of the angels. "Scarlett," he called to the redhead as she cowered in the corner. "Scarlett, hold it. Hold it."

Willyn assumed he was referring to the force field Scarlett had erected, but she only shook her head in response. Movement against the wall caught Willyn's attention. Beth was creeping along the side wall and out the door, like a rat whose hole had been invaded by the cat.

Ross dropped Willyn's arm and changed completely to the tiger, a creature ferocious and able to fight but also able to run fast if the skirmish took a wrong turn. He really was such a coward.

The eyes of the male angel lifted at the corners as he gazed down on Willyn, she felt his smile though it never fully formed. The female, however, held another in her sights. She flung her arm wide until Scarlett screamed and put her hands over her ears as if in pain.

Then it felt like the atmosphere shifted, and both of the bright beings held their hands out to Willyn before fading away and vanishing into the light. The blue wash that had flushed into the room pulled slowly out in pursuit of the angels, like a film played in reverse. The heavenly visitors had disappeared as suddenly as they had come.

But so had Scarlett's wall.

With a bellow of unrestrained rage, Dare barreled into the infirmary and tackled Tyr before the bronze-skinned man could react. He punched and hit until Tyr began to look dazed, then Dare jerked the man's head up and looked into his face. Dare's mind control was almost visible as he drilled it into Tyr's battered brain. The Native American man lay there, unmoving, all four limbs stretched out like his body was staked to the floor.

Dare got up and turned to face the tiger Ross had become. Even in his animal form, Ross took a step back, away from Dare's merciless advance.

The sound of another impact made both men glance toward Scarlett. Whatever the female angel had done to waylay the dark witch's power, it was evidently still in effect. Viv's petite frame was as tense as Dare's as she spread her fingers before curling them into her palms to get an invisible grip. Then she rotated them in a clockwise pattern. Scarlett's upper body followed suit, completely out of control as Viv's powers twisted her torso. When it looked as if Scarlett's spine would snap, Viv pushed her hands forward and threw the redhead into the wall.

"My turn," Lucia called out, her accent thick with anger. She took a running leap into the air and landed a kick into Ross's tiger-hindquarters. He was sent sprawling across the infirmary, stirring dust up as he scraped his claws into the floor in an effort to stop his momentum. The large cat swiveled his head, darting his eyes to both exits, debating which would be the better choice. He had to get past Dare or Lucia, and both were threatening violence with their demeanor.

Willyn knew she and her friends had gained the upper hand, and she would have no issue watching Ross and the others receive the punishment they were due. Unfortunately, she couldn't afford to stay for the last act, despite the change of script. The pooling in her gut was beginning to grow cold. She was still bleeding, and was too weak to heal herself. Maybe the angels had missed that one?

"Dare," she said, or tried to say. Her voice was little more than a faint scrape of vocal chords. But somehow he heard her. Forgetting his lust for revenge, Dare turned from Ross, allowing the tiger to make his escape. He knelt beside Willyn and took her hand, eyes widening when he felt the coolness of her skin.

"We have to go," she mouthed, hoping he understood. He shouted for the other women, and soon Viv and Lucia were beside him, both looking at Willyn with shared concern.

Dare lifted Willyn gently, and pain racked her from head to toe. She let her head fall against his strong shoulder and felt his muscles bunch as he began to run. Then she fell into blackness.

21

Every time the boat slapped back down on the water's choppy surface, Dare cringed and held Willyn tighter, trying to protect her from the jarring race across the ocean. "We should have taken her to the hospital," he said for the third time.

Lucia put a hand on his back. "We're almost there."

Lucia and Viv didn't argue with him, and it would have been a wasted effort if they had. The one time Willyn had opened her eyes, she'd locked them on Dare as she'd begged, "Get me to the island." Despite his fear that she needed medical attention, he'd conceded. Every once in a while, though, he repeated his concern. If they had made the wrong choice by bringing her out this far from the mainland, it was doubtful they could get her to an emergency room in time. "Hurry, Joe," he said, more to himself than anyone.

As Dare had carried Willyn out of the old hospital, Viv had called Joe to pick them up. When Scarlett's magic had evaporated, so had the cell phone blockage. Joe had been there in an instant, and now they were shooting into the night toward the island, Anna's home, where the coven's magic was strongest.

Dare prayed it would be enough.

Yes. He prayed. He was still shocked by how quickly his childhood faith had flooded back in, and was even more surprised that it settled nicely against the pagan segment of his spirit. Neither side antagonized the other or raised any doubt. In fact, he felt stronger, more complete than he had in years. All this time he'd only been hurting himself with the festering hatred that had filled his marrow. No one else.

He looked down at Willyn's skin, paler than the moonbeams shining down on her beautiful face. She'd been the only one to reach him, to force her way through his walls with her stubborn goodness. She was *his* angel. His savior. He couldn't lose her now.

The boat idled to a stop, streaming up next to the dock in silence. The island and all its inhabitants seemed to be holding a collective breath. Willyn's gentle soul had touched many, and the absence of her dimpled smile left a deep, dark void.

With Joe aiding him, Dare somehow kept his balance as he transitioned from boat to land, the woman in his arms feeling lighter by the minute. It felt as if something inside her had flown, and the thought sent adrenaline and sheer panic surging through Dare, lending him heroic strength and stamina. Quinn and Paige were waiting on the beach with a car, but he ran past them, sure he could get Willyn to the house faster if he cut through the woods.

Lights blazed everywhere in the manor, turning the yard yellow and silencing the crickets. Open wide, the double-doors revealed an apparently worried Anna who motioned for Dare to hurry. She stepped aside as he bounded up the stone steps. "In here. Put her on the couch so I can take a look at her," she said in a hushed voice.

Dare had never seen Anna intimidated or frightened, and the tremble in her hands caused each chamber of his heart to give one great squeeze. He moved swiftly, placing Willyn on the green, velvet sofa and putting a pillow under her head with tender care. "I knew we should have taken her to the hospital. I knew it." Dare swallowed the alarm in his voice and looked up at Quinn as he walked over to stand with Anna. Staring up at his childhood friends, Dare begged, "Please tell me what to do. She wanted to come here, so I just thought…"

Anna nodded. "You thought she might know something you didn't." She rubbed her hands over her cheeks. Her lips. "I'm not sure. I'm not a healer, but…"

"What?" Dare stood when she didn't answer right away. "What? Tell me."

"I feel like she should be here, too, but I don't know why." Anna placed a hand on Willyn's wrist, putting two of her fingers against the pulse that struggled to remain. "Tell me, Little Mother. Help us out, would you?" Anna closed her eyes and waited. She crinkled her forehead, took a deep breath, and waited some more. Finally she shook her head. "Nothing. She's beyond my reach." She removed her fingers, and Willyn's small hand fell limp against the velvet.

"What does that mean? What do we do?" Dare heard a distant buzzing. It grew louder and louder inside his mind until his control snapped. He grabbed Anna's shoulders, clenching tight with distress. When she grimaced, Dare let go and slammed his fists into his thighs. He'd rather inflict punishment on himself. "I'm sorry," he rasped out. "But I'm just so scared."

Upstairs, Shauni's young dog, Skid, suddenly set off on a round of barking. The yips were high-pitched and frantic, as if the dog were sounding an alarm. He turned into a black blur as he ran back and forth on the upper walkway outside Tadd's bedroom door, making enough noise to disturb the spirits. Before anyone could think to shush the animal, the heavy wood door opened, and Tadd trudged out sleepily. He spoke quietly to Skid as the animal slowed and sat down, quivering beside his favorite boy.

Tadd edged over to the railing to peer between the posts. His gaze went immediately to Willyn's unconscious form on the couch, and soon he was making more noise than the dog had. "Mom! Mom!" he bolted along the upper hallway and around the corner to the stairs. Dare was afraid the boy might try to jump most of the steps, but he didn't.

Hayden tried to intercept Tadd as Shauni came from the other direction to quiet Skid, who had started barking again as he followed Tadd down. The entire coven was there now, but the determined five year old paid heed to none of them.

Dare stood back when Tadd rushed up to hug Willyn. He was filled with the same dread that showed on the child's face and wouldn't try to stand between them. He couldn't face the reasoning that told him to let the boy hold his mother. He couldn't admit how afraid he was that it might be Tadd's last chance to do so. Dare just wasn't ready to accept that. There had to be a way. He whirled back to Anna. "By the gods, you are the Savannah Coven! There has to be something you can do!"

Anna's cheek shimmered as she slowly shook her head. Tears. Tears from the most talented witch he knew. If she couldn't help Willyn...

Someone else sobbed, but Dare didn't look to see who it was. He didn't care. This wasn't right. It wasn't supposed to happen this way. Was he being punished? Had Scarlett been right when she'd said God would forsake Willyn? Or was he the one being rebuked?

As he fought to contain his own grief, Dare watched Tadd as the boy ran his small hands over Willyn's cheeks. "Mom," the child whispered. "Mom." He put his golden head on her stomach and wrapped his arms around her. As upset as Tadd obviously was, he wasn't crying. In fact, he was calmer than any of the adults in the room. He sat up and stared at Dare with an all-too-mature look on his face. "My mom's hurt."

Dare kneeled to Tadd's level and cleared his throat before speaking. "Yes. She is, but we're going to do..."

"She's hurt in her belly." The little boy patted his own stomach to demonstrate. "Real bad."

"Tadd, I promise you we'll do everything we can to..." Dare felt the air rush from his lungs. Could it be possible? He met the child's serious gaze with his own. "How do you know she's hurt in her belly?"

Tadd shrugged. "Don't know. But she is." He turned back to Willyn and patted her face. "Mom fixes me sometimes if I cry real hard, but she doesn't know I know when she does it. I can feel it. She doesn't think she's 'sposed to help me, so she doesn't do it much. I can tell she always wants to, though." He put his hands on Willyn's stomach, palpating gently, like a tiny doctor in Iron Man pajamas. "She gets sad when I hurt myself. Now I know why."

Afraid to interrupt or distract Tadd, Dare eased away and watched as the child studied his mother. Willyn needed a miracle, and he believed one had just arrived. A miracle of her own creation.

Tadd spread his fingers, covering most of the upper left side of Willyn's abdomen. He closed his eyes and began breathing more rapidly, increasing the rhythm until his pace matched the quick, shallow pattern of his mother. In steady increments he controlled his breaths, slowing them down and making them deeper. Dare listened intently, watching Willyn's chest as it rose and fell. She was slowing down, too.

After several minutes, Tadd exhaled suddenly and slumped over to lie on his mother. Dare jumped forward, terrified he'd hurt himself, but Tadd only turned his head, nuzzled against Willyn, and yawned a great stretching yawn. "I'm sleepy now."

Dare glanced at Willyn to find the slightest blush in her cheeks. Definitely more color than before. As if to help him confirm what he saw, Anna kneeled down and took Willyn's wrist again. She made a sound of relief before a smile bloomed. "Her pulse is stronger and steadier." She hugged Dare and let her worry out in one ragged sob. "She's going to be all right."

Dare hugged her back as the other women gathered close,

each one needing to check for themselves. Easy laughter and murmurs spread like wild fire. No one mentioned the prophecy or the fact that they were still on track with fulfilling it in the coven's favor. All anyone cared about was their sweet sister and that she was going to recover.

It was amidst the smiling faces, hugs, and claps on the back that Willyn fluttered her eyes open. She blinked several times before casting glances at all of them in confusion. Dare rubbed her arm and kissed her forehead. "It's okay. You're safe. Back home."

"Oh. Okay." She let her lids drift down then opened them again as she lifted her hand to stroke Tadd's hair. He was asleep on her stomach, worn out from his role as healer. Dare grinned. The kid had done good. Real good.

Willyn looked at Dare. "How did I get here? I don't remember much. What happened?"

Stroking her blonde hair from her face, Dare gazed into her sky blue eyes and smiled. "Where do I begin?"

~

Willyn woke to the warmth of mid-morning sunlight shining into her bedroom. She remembered speaking with Dare in the early morning hours with the coven gathered around them, but the scene was shrouded in fog. She'd been barely coherent, yet she recalled one thing clearly. Tadd had healed her. Her little boy had magic.

Speaking of which, a familiar weight was lodged against her side, and the cap of blonde hair was a dead giveaway. Whoever had brought her to her room had also nestled her son in with her. The considerate gesture was most likely the act of one person. Dare. Somehow he had morphed from her adversary to her protector, and it seemed his job as body guard extended to her son as well. She found the notion comforting and her eyes grew misty.

Sniffing away the sudden emotion, she tried to sit up, only to find another body snuggled up to her other side. A very-pregnant Snowball was sleeping contentedly with one white arm stretched across her round belly. Again, Willyn asked herself how she could have missed that bulge.

She smiled to herself. A woman recovering from a beating, a child who'd tapped all of his newly-discovered magic, and an expectant cat. They were quite the lazy trio.

Unfortunately, she had to get up to pay a visit to the bathroom, which would break up the cozy picture. As she pushed up with one arm, she noticed Dare sleeping in the corner of the room, his male body overwhelming the delicate chair with cream and white stripes. As if sensing her perusal, he opened his eyes while a languid smile spread across his face. "Hey," he said and yawned.

"Hey, back." Willyn tried to slip out from between her bedmates without disturbing them, but Dare jumped up and waved for her to be still. "I'll take Tadd back to his room now," Dare told her, lifting her sleeping son without waking him. Dare was becoming a real pro. "Besides," he continued, "the girls wanted to see you as soon as you woke up, so I'll go get you something to eat and let them know the way is clear."

"I can come down," she said.

"Nope. Sorry." Dare eased open the door adjoining with Tadd's room and walked backward quietly. "You're to stay in bed. Strict orders."

"From whom?"

He grinned. "Everyone."

He was gone before she could protest further. Stay in bed? Her room, maybe. For now. But she had to get to the restroom.

She was drying her hands when she heard a semi-controlled riot that could only be her coven. They were trying to be quiet so Tadd could sleep, but their attempts only resulted in a low rumble as opposed to outright cocktail party.

"Morning, sleeping beauty," Kylie called out as she crossed the room and claimed a seat on the bed next to Snowball. The cat slept on, undisturbed. The rest of the women entered one by one, each greeting Willyn with a smile or a hug. It was wonderful to be surrounded by such love and support. By a family that accepted her for who she was, every part of her.

Some took seats where they could while others remained standing. In her usual shoulder-width stance, Paige crossed her arms across her chest and gave Willyn a cheeky grin. "So, word on the street is that you got a few well-placed knocks in before Ross and Scarlett regained the upper hand." Pride poured from the soldier with a model's face as she blew white-blonde bangs out of her eyes. "Sounds like you held your own."

"Sure," Willyn said with a wry laugh. "Right up until I didn't." Unwilling to be foolish, she let her exhaustion drive her back to bed, where she slipped under the cool sheets and propped her pillows behind her back like a queen. She deserved a day's rest, so maybe the coven's prescribed isolation was a good idea after all.

Shauni came over and slipped her palm lightly around Willyn's cheek. "You did well, Willyn. You were essentially all alone and did what you had to do to survive and finish your challenge." She winked. "Unbelievable how good it feels to hear that necklace sing, isn't it?"

"And right behind it, the appearance of angels," Willyn said. "Just when I think nothing else can shock me." She shook her head. "Thank goodness for their timing."

"I know someone who said she saw an angel once," Viv said. "She was a scientist, too, but a biologist." Viv sent a smirk toward Shauni. "Which is really more of a soft science."

"So you say," Shauni answered, unperturbed.

"Anyway, she said she was stranded on the side of the road, in a barren stretch of Arizona one night when out of nowhere a middle-aged man appeared who got under her hood and fixed the problem with tools he just happened to have with him." Viv put her hands on her hips. "She didn't mention wings but that she cranked her car and looked through the windshield to thank him. He was gone. Not just from the immediate vicinity but gone, gone. She always believed he had been some sort of divine intervention."

"I can assure you what we saw were angels." Willyn sent a silent thanks to her two rescuers. "Why should we be surprised? Ross can turn into a wolf, and Shauni carries on conversations with turtles. What are a few heavenly messengers in the scope of things?"

Anna cleared her throat. "I guess it goes to show that even an old witch like me can still learn a thing or two." She looked at Dare as he came into the room with a tray. "Make that two old witches."

"Who are you calling old," he replied, setting the tray down over Willyn's lap. "You'll always have a few months on me."

Willyn noted the presence of a daisy in a tiny crystal vase. The man never ceased to astound her. She took a sip of her sweet, creamy coffee, just the way she liked it, then she met Anna's eyes. "What's in the book?"

"The first portion is a historical accounting of what took place the first time Bastraal made an appearance. We knew he wasn't able to take human form, and that the original three sisters banished him, but the things he did before they sent him back." Anna shuddered. "It's beyond comprehension."

"Why haven't we seen anything of him this time?" Hayden asked. "If he can affect this world while still in demon form, why wouldn't he be helping Ronja and the Amara?"

Anna shook her head. "I'm not sure. The answers may be in the book, but I haven't read all of it yet. It's rather lengthy."

"So we may encounter him before this is over," Paige stated in a no-nonsense voice.

"Possibly." Anna didn't expound on what that might mean for them, or the people of Savannah. "Regardless, Ronja is going to come at us harder each time we succeed. She fully expected to defeat us with ease. Now that we've beaten her twice, she'll have to admit we're worthy adversaries."

Lucia sauntered to the window to look out at the sun-washed yard, like she was expecting dark clouds to roll in. "Then she'll treat us as such." The Spanish vixen turned back to Anna. "We'll have to train harder. Learn faster."

"We will. But it should be encouragement that we've done as well as we have." Anna nodded to Shauni and Willyn. "Neither of you had any idea what your fates held in store, but you've come away victorious." She tilted her head toward Dare. "And with extra bonuses."

Willyn smiled at Dare who stood relaxed against the wall, while Shauni fingered her silver bracelet embellished with small, gleaming emeralds, a gift from Michael.

"About that," Paige interjected with a glare for the two women with hearts popping out of their eyes. "I have to say, I don't appreciate the pattern you guys have established," she said with her hands on her hips. "No offense, Dare." She thumped the heel of her boot on the floor. "But as for me?" *Thump. Thump.* "Not happening."

Kylie sighed. "Well, if hooking up with someone is what it takes, I'm not going to argue. You know I love all of you, but this place is weighing *waaaay* too heavily on the estrogen side."

Lucia nodded vigorously. "*Si.*"

"Careful what you wish for," Dare said with a meaningful lift of his brows.

Willyn lifted the daisy to her nose and glanced at him. "Sometimes we don't know what we need, and wishes come true despite our best efforts to stop them."

Dare sidled up next to her and placed a chaste kiss on her cheek. "Truer words," he whispered. Then he backed away and headed for the door. "I've got some things to get done before the day's out, and you need to get some more rest." He pointed to her half-empty plate. "After you eat every bite."

"When will you be back?" Willyn asked, hoping she didn't sound as needy as she felt. She couldn't stand seeing him walk away. Now that she knew what he meant to her, she wanted to spend every minute with him. Every day. Every night. There was so much more for them to explore together.

He looked at her oddly, a strange gleam in his eye. "Tomorrow. I'll see you tomorrow."

"Um…now that you mention it. I've got a few things to do as well." Anna jumped up and followed Dare out. Suddenly all of the others had somewhere they needed to be.

"Where's everybody going?" Willyn stuffed a bite of pancake in her mouth. "I can help with whatever it is. Just let me finish eating."

Hayden and Claudia glanced at each other with apprehension but quickly covered it up. "Tell you what," Claudia said. "I'll keep you company for a while. As long as you promise to stay in bed."

Willyn grunted. "What is this? I'm feeling better. I am."

Claudia ignored her and took up residence on the loveseat. "Just one day. Then you'll be medically cleared."

"I'm the nurse here, you know. And I'm not a weakling."

Claudia lifted one side of her mouth. "Oh, I know you're not. But you've had a rough few weeks. It won't kill you to take one day off, will it? Besides, Tadd is sleeping next door, and you'll want to be close when he wakes up."

"That ruse isn't going to work forever." Willyn thought of her son's healing powers and mused over the implications. She was definitely going to be having that talk with him now. Evidently much sooner than later. "All right. One day, but that's it."

"Deal. I'll bring the book up so you can take a better look at your spoils of war."

Willyn liked the way that sounded. The coven was right. She *had* done well, relying on the techniques she'd learned from Paige, the faith she had in God, and the love she'd found in Dare. The three were a potent combination. "Okay. I'll take my day of leisure." She sipped her coffee and tore back into the pancake. "But tomorrow I'm going downstairs."

Claudia smiled as she flipped through a magazine she'd found. "Tomorrow. You bet."

22

Willyn did stay in her room all day and all that night as well. In fact, she'd fallen back to sleep at some point and was only now opening her eyes because the world seemed to be bouncing erratically. "Mom. Wake up. Mom. Wakie-wakie get-to-shaky." Well, that explained the bouncing.

"Hey, Kiddo." She rolled over to face Tadd. "I see you're feeling better."

"You, too, huh? I helped your belly?"

Filled with energy and elation, Willyn sat up and kissed him on the head. "You did great. I feel stronger than ever." She took a deep breath. "Tadd, do you have any questions about what happened downstairs? About what you did? Maybe you felt something strange?"

"Nah. Anna and Claire kinda' talked to me and said you would, too, but that's not why I want you to get up." He started tugging on her arm. "I want to show you what's downstairs."

"Okay. Just let me find my robe." Willyn was out of bed when a staccato knock sounded on her door. Tadd ran to open it.

"There you are," Claire said to Tadd before smiling at Willyn. "You look a sight better, hon," she told her with a wink. "How are you feeling?"

"Much better," Willyn said, grateful as ever for the older woman's help and motherly attention. "I think I could climb

K2." She twirled to show her happiness. Her challenge was over. She and the people she loved were all safe and well. And she had fallen for a good man. Finding worthwhile love twice in a lifetime truly was a blessing.

"Good. Good." Claire held up a finger. "You wait here now. The girls will be up with breakfast soon."

"But I'm coming down today. I have so much I want to do. I can't stay in bed one more minute."

"No, no. Just wait on the girls, you hear?" Claire tapped Tadd on the shoulder. "You come with me, young man. I still need your help."

"I want my mom to come down and see the…" Tadd started, but Claire shushed him.

"She'll see it soon. We need to make sure it's perfect first." Claire kneeled to whisper in Tadd's ear, making him smile and giggle.

"What are you two up to now?" Willyn asked.

Claire shook her head, her brown eyes glowing. "Wait here. That's an order." She turned her head to the side and looked down the hall. "Here come reinforcements now." She exited with Tadd in tow as Shauni and Hayden bustled in with a black garment bag and a breakfast tray.

"What is going on around here?" Willyn asked, sensing the enthusiasm in her two friends, just as she had in Tadd and Claire.

"You've got a new dress. We all do," Shauni explained.

Willyn cringed. The coven only wore their dresses for rituals or when the next witch was being chosen to pass her test. "I just finished my trial. It can't be time to pick the next of us. What about my safety period?" Shauni had earned a short time of protection from the Amara after her success, so she had assumed the same applied to her.

"We're not choosing," Hayden said as she hung the bag on the closet door. "There's going to be a party." She slid a mischievous look to Shauni then grinned at Willyn. "You definitely deserve one."

Relief swept through Willyn. "Whew. Good to hear. I don't think I'm ready to crank it all up again."

"No worries," Shauni said, and with that, the two women were gone again, instructing Willyn to eat before they left.

"What is it with the witches in this house?" she said to herself. "Do I look like I'm starving?"

After downing everything on her tray, as directed, Willyn jumped into the shower to get ready for whatever big event was happening today. All of her visitors had been vibrating with anticipation, and while none of them would tell her anything concrete, their secretive demeanors told her a surprise of some kind was in the making. The coven had held a celebration after Shauni's success, but everyone was acting differently this time, as if they knew something Willyn didn't.

She had just finished her hair and makeup when a firm knock on the door preceded Dare's arrival. She'd been suspicious before, but the hesitant look on his face was the clincher. Something was definitely up.

He was dressed in black dress pants and a white collared shirt. The only concession to casual was the undone top button and sleeves rolled to his elbows. Willyn drank in the sight of him and realized her previous desire to see him in a tuxedo had just been replaced. Relaxed sophistication fit him perfectly.

It also made her want to loosen a few more buttons.

Dare's eyes left hers and shifted to the garment bag. "Have you seen your dress?"

She tilted her head and smiled at his nervousness. "Not yet." She crossed to him and placed a kiss on his tense lips. "I was just about to take it out. You seem a little edgy. Is everything all right?"

He nodded and swallowed before motioning to the bag. "I hope you like it. Claire and Mrs. Attinger worked on it all day yesterday. Everyone agrees it looks like you."

Hoping to get an answer to the growing mystery, Willyn unzipped the garment bag to reveal an ivory satin dress with an embellished waistline and spaghettis straps. As she pulled it out for further inspection, she noticed the criss-cross design of the straps in back. Long and whispy, the dress was simple in design but elegant. It was beautiful, and she loved it.

It looked like a wedding dress.

Now she was the one swallowing against a dry throat and trying to catch her breath. She laid down the dress as her eyes sought out his. She asked the question burning in her stomach with one whispered word. "Dare?"

He closed in and took her hands, looking at her with a mix of adoration and fear.

Standing in her flowered robe, Willyn couldn't have felt more like a princess. The knight before her was strong and true, brought down by the weapon no armor could shield against. He was in love with her. She could see it on his face and hear it as he spoke.

"Willyn." He took a deep breath. "When I came here to the island, I had a clear goal in mind, one that I'm no longer proud of and have no desire to pursue. I was blinded by hate, controlled by memories of pain and betrayal. For years, they occupied my mind and guided my actions." He held her hands tighter. "But none of that matters any more. I don't care about what I wanted then. All that matters is what I *need*."

Willyn couldn't speak. She could only listen, encased by the sensation of love and honesty flowing from Dare.

"You are a witch with power, and neither of us can change that," he continued. "But that's not why I need you. Your pure heart, determination to fight for those who are in trouble, and the fierce love that you have for your child and friends. These are just a few of the reasons that I love you." He grinned and ran a finger over her cheek. "And those dimples don't hurt either."

Willyn finally found her voice. "Say it again." She pulled him closer, needing to feel the warmth of his touch. "Tell me again." The man she'd done her best to push away was the one thing she now had to have in her life, by her side, every day. Dare's hard-won love was her drug of choice.

One of his arms snaked around her waist to tuck her in tight against him. "I love you, Willyn. So much I can't stand the thought of going one more day without you as mine. Truly mine. Or one more night." He kissed her lightly. "I understand your beliefs. I respect them, and I know how important commitment is to you, for yourself and for your son." He kissed her again. "And I want that, too. I want a life with you. With Tadd. I want you both more than I could have ever imagined."

Willyn smiled with tears in her eyes. "What exactly are you saying, Dare?"

"I've planned a ceremony for us, if you'll have me. I couldn't get a church this quickly, but I thought you might want to be in charge of all of that anyway."

He was beginning to look nervous again, and Willyn couldn't help herself. She twisted the dagger a little more. "What would I need a church for?"

Now he broke out in a sweat. "I want to marry you. Or...you to marry me. We should get married. Be my wife." He started to step away, wiping a hand through his hair. "I know I'm not good enough for you, but I want to be, and isn't that the most important..."

"Yes," she said quickly, holding onto his arm as he retreated. There was no way she was letting him out of this one. "Yes. I want to marry you, or you me." She laughed. "I think that's the best idea I've heard in a long time." She jumped into his arms and kissed him all over his face before settling her head against his chest with a long, happy sigh.

Then she looked up at him curiously. "So if you couldn't get a church, why is everyone tip-toeing around with sneaky grins and whispers?"

Dare looked again at her dress, lying across her bed where she'd left it. "Considering our mixed religions, I thought it might be a good idea to have a handfasting, too."

"A handfasting." The idea fascinated her. "That would be perfect. Here on the island with our friends." She lifted one side of her mouth. "That's what all the fuss is about."

"It is. I fully intend to be with you for the rest of our lives, but honestly, the sooner the better."

She slipped a finger under the edge of his collar. "The sooner to get me in bed, you mean?"

He growled low and dove for her lips again. "Damn straight."

Willyn let him take his fill, enjoying the raw sensuality coursing through him as he ravished her mouth yet carefully kept his hands in the permitted zones. There was something deliciously sexy about holding back, waiting until the right time to discover the secret pleasure two people in love could create.

But when Dare's hand fell to her hip and stroked around to the back of her thigh, she decided they'd been good long enough. She tore her mouth away from his, taking rapid breaths to cool her rushing blood. "What time are we doing this thing?"

"I'm ready when you are." His eyes were locked on her mouth as if he couldn't wait to taste her again. She gave him one more chaste peck then shoved him away. "Will you send up a couple of the girls?" she asked. "I might need a little help." She winked and shooed him with her hands. "I only need about fifteen minutes."

She looked at his dark hair and blues eyes burning with lust against skin that appeared more tan against the white of his shirt. His lips were parted slightly, still wet from their kiss. She blew out a breath and put a hand to her stomach. "Make it ten."

~

The ceremony was beautiful. On the far side of the mansion, away from Willyn's bedroom view, Dare and the others had decorated a portion of Anna's vast gardens. In the center of the area was a large stone fountain, water flowing from three tiers and trickling down with a magical sound. The plants surrounding them were in full glorious bloom, thanks to the early summer sun, and the path leading up to the fountain had been covered with a carpet of white petals.

It was here that Willyn walked with Tadd, both of them moving forward to meet their future and intertwine their lives with another. Both of them coming to stand side by side with Dare, forming their own unit within the larger one of the coven. It was here they joined with him, in the bright, joyous sunlight, and here that they became a family.

Willyn had expected to find Anna at the end of the walkway, presiding over the vows, but she was surprised to find Mr. Attinger instead. The silver-haired man spoke with a baritone voice, casting the circle and asking all of the guests to share their positive energy with Willyn and Dare.

There had been no time to write her vows, but Willyn needed none as promises of love and honor flowed freely from her heart. Dare's words were as true as her own, and even before the cord was wrapped around their wrists, she felt bound to him by fidelity and hope. A link had already formed between them, an eternal union of heart, mind, and soul.

When the circle was dismissed, Tadd cheered along with the others, but all Willyn saw was Dare. Her mate, her lover, her husband. They kissed and sent up another round of applause, and she didn't pull away until she felt a small hand tugging on hers.

"Let's go eat. There's a big cake and everything." Tadd

looked up at Willyn and Dare expectantly. One of his small hands held Willyn's, and the other grasped Dare's. She didn't have to answer, since Dare scooped her son up and started toward the house, guiding her along with his free hand on her waist.

They ate cake. They laughed. They celebrated. And all the while Willyn could barely keep her eyes off of Dare for more than a minute at a time. How things had changed since he'd first come into her life. She had changed, and so had he, both of them meeting each other half way, giving and taking in equal measure. But wasn't what relationships were all about? Compromise. Blending.

And she for one loved the resulting combination.

Willyn was on her second glass of golden champagne when Hayden rushed out of the house after having gone in for some backup hors d'oeuvres. "Willyn! Hey. I hate to interrupt the party, but I knew you'd want to know."

"What is it?" Willyn asked, almost afraid to hear the answer. Hayden looked a bit frantic.

"Snowball is having her kittens."

After years as a nurse, many of them in the emergency department, this medical announcement was enough to make Willyn lose her cool. She was both elated and concerned for her cat. No matter the species, labor was labor. She glanced around until she found her husband at the dessert table talking to Quinn. "Dare, quick! Get Tadd and bring him in." She looked back to Hayden. "Where is she? And will you get Shauni?"

"I'm on it," Hayden said. She started to dash away but skittered to a stop. "She's in the library, under the chair near the middle window."

"How did you find her there?" Willyn asked with a frown.

"I, uh, heard her." Hayden gave her an apologetic look before heading off to find Shauni.

Willyn grimaced. "Heard her?" She glanced to the house.

"My poor baby."

In no time at all Willyn was on the floor in the library, in her gorgeous white wedding gown, kneeling by the chair and reaching under to stroke Snowball so the feline would know who was intruding on her private moment. After assuring her cat, Willyn eased the chair to the side so she could get a better look.

Her sweet Snowball was grooming three tiny kittens in the efficient way of a new momma cat. The last one was almost goop-free, thanks to its first bath. Willyn clutched her hands to her chest and felt her eyes water. Snowball glanced at her briefly before returning her attention to her new babies, and Willyn could have sworn there had been a moment of motherly understanding, as if the cat was saying, "So *this* is what the fuss is all about."

Hushed voices soon filled the room as Shauni, Dare, Tadd and the others all filed in slowly so as not to disturb or agitate the brood. Shauni had a towel-lined box with her, in case Snowball was interested in a better home. Willyn studied Anna's expensive antique rug and gave silent thanks that it was mostly clean. She looked up to find her host smiling at the cats, like everyone else was. "Sorry about the mess," Willyn told her.

"Please. " Anna waved away the apology. "This moment is more than worth it."

As soon as Viv noticed the coloring of the kittens, one white like Snowball and two orange like her tom cat, she got tears in her eyes, too. "Aww. My Kiko's a daddy."

"Yeah," Kylie agreed. "I guess we now know who the culprit was."

Tadd was still in Dare's arms, gazing down in awe. "How did they get out of her stomach?"

"Oh. Well." Willyn was caught unprepared and was still searching for an appropriate way to go about it when Shauni tapped her on the shoulder.

"You need to decide if you want to explain or let him see for himself." She pointed to Snowball, who had lain back down on the carpet and seemed to be breathing heavily. "Looks like we've got another on the way."

Meeting Dare's eyes in panic, Willyn waited until he shrugged and said, "Might as well take the opportunity. If we lived on a farm…"

She nodded. "Fine. But I'm letting you field the questions that will most assuredly be coming later."

Dare grinned wide and ruffled Tadd's hair. "I'll be delicate."

They all turned their heads back to the action when Snowball emitted one sharp *Rowr!* before bending around to begin the work of bathing once again. The other three kittens mewed and tried to lift their heads in the absence of their mother's warmth. With a quick lift and turn, Snowball deposited the latest edition to the pile of its siblings and resumed cleaning.

When the strange blob began to take the shape of a small cat, its coloring and pattern became more visible. White feet were not surprising, but the dark gray and brown stripes over most of its body, except for the white belly and chest, announced to them all that there would be more than one male cat handing out cigars. Or whatever the feline equivalent of that might be.

Claudia jumped up and down then hugged Viv, who was still glowing with pride. "Way to go, Ashbi!"

Kylie laughed then bent down to whisper in Willyn's ear, "Looks like your good girl has been being bad."

Willyn simply shook her head and gazed at her cat. "Snowball," she uttered, as any shocked parental unit would.

"Guess there's no stopping love," Anna said, winking at Willyn. "It's just been in the air around here."

Tadd turned in Dare's arms. "Why did Claudia say that about her cat? Our cat had the kittens. Why did they talk about Kiko and Ashbi?"

Dare groaned, a low sound that confirmed his discomfort.

Luckily, Tadd wiggled to let Dare know he wanted down, then scooted over to join Willyn. He was on his knees yet keeping his distance. "There are four of them." His eyes were wide with wonder. "Two of them look like Snowball."

"Yep," Willyn answered, letting her son take it all in. She had to admit, she was glad she hadn't gotten her cat to the vet in time. The birth was a wondrous thing to share with her child, and he would adore the kittens.

Tadd twisted his mouth in concentration. "The other two don't look like Snowball." He continued to stare, little wheels a-churning.

"Nope." Willyn cast her eyes over Tadd's blonde head to look at Dare. That one only lifted his hands in surrender. No help at all.

Tadd looked at the kittens. Then he looked at Viv and Claudia. Then he looked back at the cats. Again to Viv and Claudia. Back to the kittens.

With a wrinkle between his brows, he sat on his haunches and put his hands on his knees before finally saying in a wonder-filled voice, "Ohhhh."

23

A summer sunset was lighting up the horizon, and the party was still going strong. After the crowd had vacated the library and left Snowball to get to know her family, they'd all gathered back outside to eat, drink, be merry, and forget about prophecies and demons. At least for a little while.

Willyn was sitting on a bench, watching her sisters laugh as Lucia tried to teach them a dance requiring quick feet and loose hips. Paige had grumbled at first but had turned out to be a natural. Anna and Quinn were gesturing to some of the pink roses in bloom, probably remembering their mother who had planted the bushes as her contribution to the lovely gardens. Joe and his wife, Claire, were slow dancing to a tune only they could hear, clearly still crazy about each other after years of marriage.

Willyn smiled. She could visualize the happy times ahead for her and Dare. The strength and wisdom he would be able to give Tadd. The talks about baseball and all those numbers she could never understand. And she could just imagine how protective he would be of a daughter. Willyn's head swam as she pictured a little dark-haired girl with her light blue eyes. Tadd would make a wonderful big brother.

"Considering the sappy look on your face, I have a feeling I'd better get to work." Dare strode over to sit beside her, wrapping an arm around her waist before allowing it to slip higher, his finger teasing the underside of her breast. "What are you thinking about?"

She settled against him, the heat of his thigh against hers sending a bolt of wanting straight to the core of her womanhood. She was *soooo* happy they were married. "Rainbows and puppy-dog tails," she said with a smile. "I thought the sappy look was a dead giveaway."

His fingers circled in a light, feathery pattern that made Willyn catch her breath. Then he leaned in to kiss the sensitive area just in front of her ear, letting the warmth of his mouth linger. "I'd like to put a few different ideas in your head, if you're interested."

Willyn clenched her muscles, trying to gain control of her body as it responded to his sweet assault. "With your magic?" she asked in a breathy voice.

Dare let his other palm drop to her leg while his mouth did wonderful things to her ear. "No." He squeezed her thigh. "With my hands."

Willyn searched the courtyard until she spotted Tadd tossing a ball to Skid as the dog bounced and barked joyfully. Joe Jr. was standing nearby laughing and encouraging the duo. As if sensing her stare, Joe Jr. lifted his eyes to Willyn. After a quick assessment of her and Dare, the young black man gave her a wink and nodded at Tadd, indicating he would keep an eye on the boy.

Normally, Willyn would have been embarrassed about being so obviously in lust, but given that it was her handfasting night, she had more pressing matters to worry about.

Like she and Dare getting to one of their bedrooms as fast as possible.

She rose from the bench, pulling Dare along with her, and did her best to maintain a steady, unhurried pace as she led him toward the nearest door. If anyone else noticed their sudden departure, they wisely kept it to themselves. They entered the massive house, which was unusually quiet and filled only with the sound of their footsteps, whispers, and hushed laughter as they ran up the stairs and around the upper hallway, not stopping until they were safely inside Dare's room with the door securely locked.

Willyn twirled into the room, coming to a stop with what felt like a neon glow shooting from every pore. "Am I Mrs. Forster, now?" she asked, laying the flat of her palms landed on the starched, white shirt he wore. She loved the way the firmness of his chest felt beneath the material. "Or does that only come with a legal piece of paper?"

"We still have a few more steps to make it legal, but the only title I care about," Dare slipped his hands around her waist as he lowered his head to hers, dark hair falling forward across his brow, "is *wife*."

He skimmed his lips slowly back and forth across hers, offering a hint of what was to come. The gentle friction made her want to pull him in tight, to feel the slick heat of his tongue on hers. She wanted to join with him in every way possible, feeling his heart melt into hers as their bodies did the same.

But first, there was one more thing she needed to take care of.

She pulled away. "Dare. When we first met, you made me so angry. The way you looked at me made me feel judged and misunderstood." She laughed lightly. "Now I think you know me better than anyone, and you've brought strength and passion into my life. Things I didn't even realize I needed." She stroked his chiseled jaw. "Now let me give something to you. Let me give you peace."

She spread his shirt and pressed her fingers to his chest. "Let me take away the last reminder of what you went through." She held his eyes with her own, channeling every ounce of love she felt for him into his very essence. "Let me heal you."

Dare released a shuddering breath before closing his eyes.

When he opened them, Willyn could see his acceptance before he spoke the words. "Yes. I'll let you take the scar. I don't need it anymore. But Willyn, you must know." He pulled her close and kissed her deeply. "You've already healed me."

With a laugh in her heart and tears in her eyes, Willyn pushed a surge of white energy into his skin. The scar had been born of evil and therefore didn't stand a chance against the power of love. It vanished like ash in the wind, leaving no trace of its existence. Like it had never been there at all.

Dare put his hand over hers where it still rested on his chest. "Thank you." His thumb teased the skin of her wrist. "You're my wife now, Willyn." He held her in place with his eyes, the blue of them darkened by desire. "You're all mine."

She felt the heat of her blood rush through her veins. His words made her head light and her heart pound. The silken touch of her dress was suddenly unbearable, since her skin had somehow become over-sensitized. Her body ached and stung everywhere. Each breath she drew was quivering with need.

Willyn absolutely loved the gorgeous wedding gown, but she had to get out of it. Right now. The only thing she wanted covering her skin was Dare. His hands, his lips, his mouth. She heard someone groan and realized it was her.

Dare's hands were already busy with her back zipper, so she returned the favor by unbuttoning his shirt. They clashed together in a frenzy of searching hands and mouths, unable to get at each other quickly enough. Willyn struggled with a button then stopped to draw a ragged breath. "Forget this," she said, before grasping each side of the open shirt and pulling with all her might. Tiny, gleaming buttons shot in every direction, pinging off walls and furniture.

Dare stilled and gave a her look of surprise. "Damn," he said, breathing as heavily as she was. "I didn't think I could get any more turned on." He shook his shirt off his arms then picked Willyn right up out of her loosened dress. "But I was wrong."

In only her panties and strappy heels, Willyn clung to his bare shoulders as he carried her to the bed. They were connected at the mouth, unable or unwilling to stop devouring each other as they lay down together and fought over who would get Dare's belt undone first.

He won, but then he grabbed her wrists and pinned her hands to the side, gently pressing them against the sheets. He seemed to be distracted by how much of her skin he was finally able to see and touch, drawing back to stare then running his hands over all of her curves as if memorizing the layout.

He gave her a naughty grin. "All mine."

Two could play that game. Willyn slid her hand over flat, hard abs and into Dare's undone pants. He moaned when she found purchase. Licking her lips and smiling, she whispered, "All mine," before letting her lazy caress and lowered lids tell him just how much she approved of his offering.

His eyes closed for a quick, breathless moment, then he was tearing out of his clothes. Soon she was the only one wearing anything, but Dare planned to remedy that as well. He curled his fingers under her panties and dragged them down her legs, easing them over her white, high-heeled shoes that were still in place. She started to reach down to unstrap them when he intercepted her.

"Leave them," he said, slipping one of her fingers in and out of his mouth and making her almost go insane. "I think they're sexy."

Willyn fell back against the pile of pillows with absolutely no desire or energy to argue with him. She had never worn shoes to bed before, and had certainly never done other-bed-activities in them, but oddly enough, a deep, scintillating thrill shot through her at the idea. She could feel his eyes on her as he ran them from her sparkly shoes all the way up to her parted lips and knew she'd married a man who would always keep things interesting.

Her life had taken a very sharp and unexpected turn, but sometimes that was the best way to come across the most amazing and unforgettable experiences. Dare was definitely both of those things, and she was grateful she'd found him.

A small lamp was burning in the corner, casting soft amber light over the room and their bodies as he lowered himself to her and gently maneuvered himself between her thighs. He kissed her once, pressing his lips to hers in the timeless way that communicated the deepest of emotions. Here was her husband, true and passionate, filling her up with a wondrous mix of desire and tenderness. Hot, primal lust that was somehow still love-making at its finest.

Willyn sighed against his mouth. This moment was perfection.

Dare lifted himself up and braced on one elbow while his other hand came up to brush the hair from her face. "I love you, Willyn Brousseau Forster." Then he entered her.

Her breath hitched in her chest as intense pleasure clutched her from within. Correction, she thought as he filled her. Perfection has been improved upon.

As one they began to move, pulling and straining in an attempt to absorb and feel as much of each other as possible. Her soft golden skin pressed against the darker tone of his. Muscles flexed in his arms and chest as he took her. As he ravaged her.

And that's exactly what it was. She was his wife. He loved her, he was careful with her, but the intensity in his expression when he pinned her arms over her head made all manner of butterflies take flight in her stomach. He was her dark prince. And she was being thoroughly ravaged.

The sweet, growing tension between Willyn's legs was enough to make her curl her fingernails into her palms and cry out. Dare growled in response and moved inside her in a way that made her very grateful she'd found a bad boy turned good. He seemed to know tricks she'd never even heard of. How to stroke her in places that made her come completely undone.

"Yes. Yes." She heard the words and once again realized, after the fact, that they were escaping her own lips as she met him stroke for stroke, trapping him and holding him for a second longer when she wanted to. She arched against him and whispered his name, the sound bringing his eyes to hers.

When their gazes met, it was like a detonation. Waves of coiled pressure traveled from somewhere deep inside her and washed out to engulf her in a mind-numbing climax. She would swear she was floating, but couldn't bring herself to care. All she felt was one surge after another of the most amazing release she'd ever known.

Somewhere in the distance she heard Dare give one great cry before he stilled. He hovered over her then dropped, trying to keep the bulk of his weight from crushing her. When his arms gave out he slid to her side but held on tight with one arm around her waist.

It was a few minutes before either of them could remember how to speak. Or find enough breath to do so.

"Wow," Willyn finally managed, sliding a hand over to pat his biceps.

Dare made a sound that might have been a laugh or a grunt, so she tilted her head to look at him. "You all right?" she asked, staring at him as he lay there with one arm fallen across his eyes like a man in pain.

He used his free hand to pat her on the thigh just as she had him. "Wow," he said before taking a long, deep breath and letting it out with a huff. "I think that summarizes it."

Laughing and rolling over to curl into his side, Willyn began to stroke his stomach, fascinated by the hard ridges there. She had lots of good territory yet to explore. "I thought they were called six-packs. You seem to have eight."

He did laugh this time then grabbed her hand as it started to inch lower. "Careful. You might get more than you bargained for."

Willyn rolled on top of him and straddled his hips. "Oh, I've already gotten that." She kissed him. "And I find that I quite like the surprise of it."

"Really," he said in a low, sensuous voice as he rubbed both hands up and down her back, massaging in a way that shouldn't feel nearly as sexual as it did. Every tiny part of her had been transformed into an erogenous zone. As long as Dare was involved.

She threw her head back to allow him access when his hands eased around to her front and stroked up over her waist, stomach, and...

A knock sounded sharp and fast on the bedroom door, and the voice that followed it was like a tub of ice-cold water on the fire she and Dare were re-kindling. "Mom. Are you in there? I want to watch a movie, but it's PG-13, and Ms. Claire said you had to say if it was okay." Another impatient knock.

With a grunt, Dare fell back onto the mattress. "I guess he slipped away from Joe Jr."

Willyn offered him an apologetic smile. "I guess so. That's not surprising." She rubbed his shoulders with regret. "Welcome to my world."

Rising up to give her a peck on the lips, he hoisted her up and off to the side in one swift motion. "Don't you mean our world?" He was already pulling on his pants and looking for his shirt. "Why don't I take this one? Since I failed miserably at the whole kitten thing." He gave her a wink. "I can make a judgment call and bring us up some rations after the movie crisis has been averted."

Willyn sat up with the sheet wrapped around her and glanced nervously at the door when the knocking started anew. "Are you sure? You don't have to."

He stopped her with a finger to her lips. "What if I want to?" He kissed her soundly, promising her without words that they were far from finished with what they'd started. He stroked her cheek and smiled with a devilish glint in his eye. "Don't go anywhere. It won't take long, and I expect to find you still wrapped up in that sheet when I return." He pointed at her feet. "And still wearing those shoes."

She lay back on the pillows and shrugged impishly. "As you wish."

Dare finished tucking in his shirt and slipped into his shoes, foregoing socks for expediency, then he was opening the door and corralling Tadd so he couldn't peek into the room. Before shutting the door again, Dare peeked around it to say, "Don't move. I'll be right back, Sweetheart."

As the voices of her husband and child faded, Willyn lifted her arms above her and enjoyed a nice, long stretch then blew out a sigh of joy and contentment. Her heart was so full it was practically leaking bliss. Thinking of Dare and all that she planned to do with him before the night was over, she looked down at the white shoes she still wore. *Sweetheart*, he'd said. Willyn laughed out loud.

She loved it when he called her that.

Suza Kates writes both paranormal romance and romantic suspense. She lives in Savannah, Georgia with her family and five ridiculously spoiled cats.

For more on Suza and her books visit

www.suzakates.com

CPSIA information can be obtained at www.ICGtesting.com
Printed in the USA
LVOW040647210912

299607LV00001B/22/P